LOVE IS NOT ENOUGH

When they settled on the sofa after dinner, he pulled her gently into his arms. Then he pulled her onto his lap and escalated his assault on her senses. Nuzzling her neck, he inhaled her sweet scent.

The muscles of his chest flexed beneath her fingers. That was not enough. She slipped her hands beneath his sweater, caressing the smooth skin.

His hand cupped her breast, fondling the soft globe. Then it slid beneath the fabric of her neckline. His thumb stroked the already rigid nipple.

She managed to catch her breath long enough to whisper his name. "Do you remember those ladies at the museum?"

He raised his head, frowning. "What?"

She cleared her throat. "The ladies we saw at the museum, do you remember what they said?"

"I'm not sure."

"They said for me to enjoy it while I can. I've decided to follow their suggestion."

He took a deep breath. "Are you saying what I think you're saying?"

She sighed. "I'm saying that if you'd like to spend the night, we don't need to make up the guest room."

BOOK YOUR PLACE ON OUR WEBSITE AND MAKE THE ARABESQUE ROMANCE CONNECTION!

We've created a customized website just for our very special Arabesque readers, where you can get the inside scoop on everything that's going on with Arabesque romance novels.

When you come online, you'll have the exciting opportunity to:

- View covers of upcoming books

- Learn about our future publishing schedule (listed by publication month and author)

- Find out when your favorite authors will be visiting a city near you

- Search for and order backlist books

- Check out author bios and background information

- Send e-mail to your favorite authors

- Join us in weekly chats with authors, readers and other guests

- Get writing guidelines

- AND MUCH MORE!

Visit our website at
http://www.arabesquebooks.com

Love Is Not Enough

MARILYN TYNER

BET Publications, LLC
http://www.bet.com
http://www.arabesquebooks.com

ARABESQUE BOOKS are published by

BET Publications, LLC
c/o BET BOOKS
One BET Plaza
1900 W Place NE
Washington, DC 20018-1211

All Kensington Titles, Imprints, and Distributed Lines are available at special quantity discounts for bulk purchases for sales promotions, premiums, fund-raising, and educational or institutional use. Special book excerpts or customized printings can also be created to fit specific needs. For details, write or phone the office of the Kensington special sales manager: Kensington Publishing Corp., 850 Third Avenue, New York, NY 10022, attn: Special Sales Department, Phone: 1-800-221-2647.

First Printing: December 2003
10 9 8 7 6 5 4 3 2 1

Printed in the United States of America

ACKNOWLEDGMENTS

I usually use this page to thank the people who have helped with the research for a specific novel. This particular book did not require such research.

I decided to use this space to express a very special thanks to all of my readers. To those of you whom I've met or who have written to tell me how much you enjoy my novels, knowing that you appreciate my work makes my efforts worthwhile.

CHAPTER 1

Kendall Chase closed her eyes and let the sweet music wash over her, calming her mind and soothing her spirit. It was just what she needed after her early morning conversation with her mother, not that their conversation was any different than usual.

Putting distance between them by moving to Maryland from Pennsylvania had been the best decision of Kendall's life. Now, five years later, she finally realized that the deep need to please her mother was a lost cause. Her mother would never be happy with her.

She took a deep breath and opened her eyes when the music ended. The elderly lady in the pew in front of her caught her attention.

According to some of the other members of the church, Mabel Jenkins was at least eighty years old. Her only son had died while in his twenties, and she had outlived her husband.

When the service ended, Kendall made her way

to her elderly friend, greeting her with a hug. "How are you today, Miss Mabel?"

"I'm just fine, sugar. How are you? You still working yourself too hard with those parties?"

Kendall shook her head. "I'm fine. I haven't had any parties in two weeks, so I'm not working too hard."

"Can I still count on you for dinner?"

"Of course. How could I turn down one of your meals?" She looked around. "Whenever you're ready we can go."

They worked their way to the door with Miss Mabel greeting more friends along the way. As they neared the exit, Kendall suggested, "Why don't I pull the car closer? I'll come back in and get you."

"All right, dear."

A short time later, they arrived at Mabel Jenkins's small Cape Cod house where she lived alone. Most of her friends had passed away. Some of those who were left had moved away to live with their children. Others were either in assisted-living apartments or nursing homes. Miss Mabel was determined to stay in her own home. She managed quite well with very little help from her friends.

Kendall waited while Miss Mabel unlocked the door. Then she followed her into the living room.

"Sit down, dear. I think I'll turn up the air conditioner before I light that oven."

"Is there anything I can do to help?"

"No, dear, the meal is already cooked. I just have to reheat it."

Forty-five minutes later they sat down to eat. As

they ate, Mabel talked about the repairs she was having done to her house.

"I'm a little upset about the way things are going."

"What's wrong?"

She sighed. "It's taking longer than he told me and the work isn't what I expected. It seems like people just don't take pride in their work anymore."

For the first time since she met the elderly lady, Kendall saw a hint of sadness in her expression. In spite of her losses, Mabel Jenkins had never allowed life to get her down.

"Didn't you have a contract?"

Mabel's expression changed to disgust. "For all the good that is. He insisted the extra cost couldn't be avoided and that he was having trouble keeping reliable workers."

What could Kendall say? Aside from hiring a lawyer, which her friend could hardly afford, Mabel had little recourse.

"If there's anything I can do to help . . ."

Mabel shook her head. "Don't worry about it, dear. I'll manage." She determinedly moved on to other topics. There was no sense upsetting her young friend with her problems.

Kendall was unable to erase Mabel's dilemma from her mind. She called her friend a week later to check on her, carefully avoiding the subject of the repairs. It was up to Mabel to bring up that unpleasant subject.

There was no mention of repairs during their conversation until Kendall heard the doorbell ring in the background. "I'm sorry, dear. I have to go. That must be Ben Whitaker."

"Ben Whitaker?"

"Yes, the contractor."

Kendall bit back the first response that came to her mind. "Oh, okay. I won't keep you. I'll talk to you later." She hung up the phone. At least the contractor was showing up for work again. Maybe he would finally finish the job this time.

By the following Saturday, Mabel Jenkins's problems had been pushed to the back of Kendall's mind. She was running late for her appointment.

Kendall hated being late. Lateness might not be a big deal to some people. She was not one of those people. There had been too many circumstances in her life that she had been unable to control.

She and Valerie had been sure that there would be enough time for her to see the house before Kendall's appointment with Evelyn Norton. There would have been if the home owner's real-estate agent had informed her client that a prospective buyer was coming.

Aside from not being prepared for visitors, the woman had been understandably cautious about letting two strangers into her home. Kendall and Valerie had waited while the home owner called her agent before allowing them entrance.

To add to that unforeseen delay, Kendall was coping with the mass exodus of people getting a jump on the Fourth of July weekend. Normally, she would not have scheduled a meeting on a Friday evening.

Her client was among the travelers who would be leaving town the following day. Eager to get started on her party plans, she wanted to meet with Kendall before going away.

Kendall forced herself to ease up on the accelerator as she steered toward the exit ramp. All she needed was to have an accident on top of everything else.

Finally, she pulled up to the curb in front of a large colonial house on the outskirts of Baltimore. She glanced at her watch. She was twenty minutes late. Not a good beginning for making an impression on a new customer.

She had met Evelyn Norton at a party she'd arranged for a member of her church. Evelyn had called a week earlier to discuss hiring Kendall to plan a surprise birthday party for her husband. The purpose of today's meeting was to decide on the basic plans.

Kendall's first statement when Evelyn opened the door was an apology. "I'm sorry. I've been house-hunting, and my agent and I ran into a problem getting into the property. On top of that, traffic was unusually heavy."

Evelyn smiled and held up her hand. "It's no problem, Kendall." As she led the way through the living room, Evelyn explained, "I put a deposit on the place for the party some time ago. Then I started thinking about hiring a caterer and a DJ and the decorations and all the trappings. I felt overwhelmed. When I saw what you did for Joan, I thought you might be able to help."

"I've given it some thought since you called and I've come up with a few ideas."

The two women adjourned to the dining room. Evelyn studied the plans as she listened to Kendall's presentation. Afterward, she nodded.

"It sounds good, Kendall."

"Thanks. I'll write up an estimate. We can meet again next Saturday, if that's all right with you."

"That's fine."

As Kendall rose to leave, Evelyn recalled her apology. "You mentioned that you're house-hunting. Have you had any luck?" she asked, walking her to the door.

"Not yet."

"Are you looking for any particular style?"

Kendall shrugged. "I like the detail in a lot of the old houses, but I don't want to be aggravated by the upkeep that's usually involved with them."

Evelyn's eyes lit up. "I might have just the answer for you. The company I work for specializes in historic renovations."

"You work for a building contractor?"

"Yes, why?"

Kendall shrugged. "Nothing. I've just heard a few horror stories about contractors."

"I admit there are some unscrupulous contractors out there. I assure you, Ben isn't one of them."

"Ben?"

"Ben Whitaker. Do you know him?"

"No, I don't think so."

"Anyway, Ben sometimes buys old houses, renovates them, and resells them. He just finished one, or at least it's almost finished." She hesitated before opening the door. "Let me get his card."

Kendall digested the information while Evelyn was gone. She was almost positive Ben Whitaker was the name Mabel Jenkins had mentioned.

There was no point in pursuing her suspicions with Evelyn. Evelyn had already made it clear that she considered him to be completely trustworthy. Since he was her employer, it was understandable that she would defend him.

Evelyn returned a few minutes later and handed Kendall a business card. "It just occurred to me that you might not want to contact him directly, but you can give the information to your agent."

"Thanks, Evelyn. If you have any other questions or anything else comes up, give me a call. Otherwise, I'll see you next week."

On Saturday morning Kendall drove to her favorite craft store to price the items she would need for the favors and decorations for Evelyn's party. She could have settled for one of the items she had seen at another store, but nothing was exactly what she had in mind.

Many of the other items needed for the party, such as vases and table linens, were part of her inventory. Early in her professional party-planning career, she had started collecting her own supplies to avoid the expense of rentals. Some caterers supplied the linens, but other options were sometimes necessary for smaller dinner parties. Her experience had taught her that the clients often lacked sufficient linens for the number of guests they invited.

By the time she put the key into the door of her apartment, Kendall was hungry and tired. After she placed the Chinese take-out cartons on the dining room table, her next stop was the bedroom. She undressed, donned a comfortable robe, and returned to spread her notes on the table.

Between bites of food, she finalized her plans for the decorations. Then she typed up the estimate and a contract. When her vision began to blur from exhaustion, she set the work aside and called it a day.

On Tuesday morning, Kendall's party planning took a back seat to her more lucrative career as an event planner for a large corporation. Later that morning, she approached the vice president's office with a stack of envelopes in her arms.

"Hi, Joy, I think Mr. O'Brien's expecting me. Is he in?"

The secretary nodded. "Morning, Kendall." She glanced at the phone on her desk. "He just got off the line. Go right in."

John O'Brien looked up from his desk as she entered. "Good morning, Kendall, have a seat." He leaned forward, his forearms resting on his desk.

Kendall placed a folder on the desk and opened it, removing a large envelope. "These are your documents for the meeting in Atlanta. I have the other packets here. If you'd like, I'll deliver them to the other employees."

He scanned the contents of the envelope. "That'll be fine." Turning his attention back to Kendall, he asked, "How are the plans coming for the meeting in November?"

"Fine. I had to find another caterer, but everything's in order now. You might want to remind the prospective attendees that we'll need a commitment from them." She leafed through the folder she had brought with her in anticipation of his question.

"I may be getting a little ahead of myself," she added. "We still have plenty of time before I'll need a final count."

He nodded. "It's probably not a bad idea to send a memo to the other offices, though."

They discussed the arrangements for another half an hour. Kendall rose from her chair. "I guess that's it for now." She indicated the folder. "I'll get these itineraries to the other employees."

After hand-delivering all but one of the stack of envelopes, Kendall returned to her desk. A few minutes later, she was approached by Francine Turner.

"Hi. Barry said you were looking for me," Francine explained.

Kendall handed her the remaining envelope. "Those are your documents for the trip. I'm reminding everyone to call the airline the day before the flight to make sure there haven't been any changes."

Francine scanned the documents. "Let's just hope they don't change to an earlier departure time."

"At least there won't be a problem if you arrive later than planned. The registration and reception won't start until afternoon."

"Thanks, Kendall." She returned the papers to the envelope. "I hear you've been working hard on the November conference. I guess you're looking forward to resting this weekend."

"Actually, I have a dinner party on Saturday."

Francine shook her head. "Well, at least you can relax on Sunday. I don't know how you do it. Between your job here and your party planning, when do you have any time for yourself?"

"The party planning is part of my time for myself. I enjoy it. Besides, the party planning fees have helped with the down payment for my house."

"How's the house-hunting going?"

"Don't ask. I've been driving poor Valerie Hamilton crazy." Kendall had introduced the two women after meeting Valerie at church, and the three women had become friends.

Francine chuckled. "She can handle it. I'm sure you're not the worst client she's had."

Francine turned to leave. "I'd better get back to work. Good luck with the house-hunting."

Two weeks after their first meeting, Kendall met with Evelyn Norton again to finalize their plans. Their meeting was drawing to a close when the doorbell rang. Evelyn excused herself to answer it. She did not return alone.

The man who accompanied her was probably six-foot-two or three. The slightly graying hair at his temples hinted that he was in his middle to late thirties.

"Kendall Chase, this is Ben Whitaker. Ben promised to help Jim enlarge our family room."

Since he was the owner of his company, Kendall expected that Ben would be content to sit behind a desk and delegate the labor to his employees. The muscular build revealed by his casual jeans and knit shirt suggested he took a more hands-on approach.

Ben smiled and held out his hand. "It's nice to meet you."

Kendall hesitated a second before responding. His hand seemed unusually warm as it engulfed hers. The warmth spread up her arm, and remained even after he released his grasp. She rose from her seat, signaling an end to her meeting with Evelyn.

"I have everything I need now. I'll be in touch before the party. I'll let you get on with your family room plans."

Evelyn glanced at Ben and back to Kendall. "I'll walk you to the door. I'll be right back, Ben."

He nodded. "I'll go on to the family room. Jim gave me an idea of what he has in mind."

He frowned as the two women walked away. Then he shrugged. *Maybe her unfriendly attitude is my imagination. Or maybe she's one of those people who looks down on men whose jobs don't require a suit and tie. It wouldn't be the first time I've run into that.*

Kendall regretted that unfriendly attitude the next day when she chatted with Mabel Jenkins after church. "I met Ben Whitaker yesterday. If I hadn't been meeting him for the first time, I might have given him a piece of my mind."

Mabel frowned. "I don't understand."

"You remember telling me about the problems you had with your repairs and him overcharging you?"

Mabel's eyes widened. "Oh, no, honey. Mr. Whitaker wasn't the one who gave me such a hard time. He's the one who fixed everything."

Kendall shook her head. "Now I don't understand."

"I was telling my tale of woe at the senior center. One of the other ladies told me about Mr. Whitaker. He did some work for her son. I told her I couldn't afford to hire another contractor. She insisted I should call him anyway."

"What happened?"

"He was just wonderful. He did the work in just

a few days and what he charged wasn't even half of what the other man charged."

"That's great, Miss Mabel, but what about the other contractor? Hadn't you already paid him?"

"That's the best part. I don't know how he did it, but Mr. Whitaker got back most of the money I paid the other man."

"That's wonderful. I'm really glad it worked out for you."

Kendall recalled her initial reaction to Ben Whitaker. She was thankful that she'd learned the truth before meeting him again. She might not have been able to restrain herself from voicing her misguided opinion.

The following Saturday afternoon, Kendall packed up her minivan and drove to the banquet hall. For the next two hours, she and Evelyn worked steadily. Finally, the decorations and table favors were in place.

They stood near the door admiring their handiwork. "What do you think?"

"It looks great. I love the table favors and centerpieces. You put a lot of work into those."

"I couldn't find exactly what I wanted already made." Kendall shrugged. "Actually, they went pretty fast after the first few. Besides, it's not like I had to make two hundred of them."

"I especially like the little test-tube flower-holder place cards. They're perfect for a science teacher who's as wrapped up in his work as my husband is."

Kendall glanced at her watch. "The caterer is scheduled to arrive in about an hour." She turned toward Evelyn. "If you want to leave, I can manage the rest."

"If you're sure, I probably should get back home before Jim gets suspicious."

After her client departed, Kendall sat down at one of the tables with the stack of napkins to be folded. The caterer arrived just as she finished draping the serving tables for the food and dishes.

Kendall had freshened up and changed her clothes in the ladies' room when the guests began arriving. Half an hour later, Evelyn entered with what seemed to be a genuinely surprised Jim. His wife had told him that they were attending a party for one of their friends. Since his actual birthday was the previous Wednesday, he had not suspected a thing.

The evening appeared to be a huge success. The usual toasts and speeches began as dessert was being served. Kendall's attention was totally captured by Ben as he approached the podium.

"I first met Jim about ten years ago through his wife, Evelyn, my secretary. It wasn't until five years ago that I came to really appreciate him. Don't ever let anyone tell you that men don't value friendships. He was there for me at one of the most difficult times of my life." He raised his glass. "Here's to many more years, Jim. I wish you all the best."

After he finished his speech, he approached Jim. When he smiled, Kendall's breath caught in her throat. This smile was nothing like the one she had seen at their first meeting. The difference was like comparing a candle to a hundred-watt lightbulb. More than Ben's words, it revealed his high regard for Jim's friendship. She could only imagine the effect it could have when turned on a woman in a romantic encounter.

Ben Whitaker was not a man one would easily forget. Aside from the smile, there was an indefinable aura that seemed to emanate from him. Some might describe it as arrogance.

She frowned. No, not arrogance, just highly developed self-confidence. Maybe it had not been developed. Maybe he had been born with it. What surprised her even more than the unusual aura was that he seemed totally unaware of his powerful presence.

Kendall shook her head. She forced her attention away from the strangely unsettling vision. A few minutes later, she almost jumped when she heard a familiar baritone voice behind her.

"Excuse me, I told Jim's mother I'd see if there's any more chocolate cake."

Kendall turned to face him. Even at five-foot-six and wearing heels, she had to look up quite a distance to meet his gaze. Why hadn't she noticed that detail at their previous meeting? She immediately wished she had simply answered without facing him. She cleared her throat.

"I think there's more in the kitchen. I'll check with the caterer."

Ben's gaze followed her. After meeting her at Evelyn's house, he'd guessed that she was somehow responsible for the party. His attention had been drawn to her several times that evening.

The unfriendly attitude he had noticed at Evelyn's house was no longer in evidence. Maybe she felt her professional duty called for a more cordial demeanor.

This evening had given him the opportunity to observe her more closely. She was not a petite woman. He chided himself for thinking that the grace she exhibited was unusual for a woman her size. She was not exceptionally tall; he judged her to be about five-six or seven.

Her dark brown hair was parted at the temple and brushed back behind her ears, ending just below the nape of her neck. His closer observation had revealed a smooth complexion that reminded him of that old-fashioned description cafe au lait.

The eyes that had looked up at him were a soft brown the color of milk chocolate, accented by thick black lashes.

She returned a few minutes later, followed by a waiter with slices of cake on a tray. Her lips curved upward in what he supposed was her notion of a smile. Even that was an improvement over the stone-faced expression he had encountered at their previous meeting.

"Is there anything else I can get you?" she asked as the waiter placed the tray on the table.

"No, thanks."

At that moment, Evelyn approached them. "Janice said she'd sent you to get another slice of cake. You remember Kendall, don't you, Ben?"

"Of course."

"I'm not sure I told you before. Kendall is responsible for the success of this party."

"You're the caterer?"

Kendall shook her head. "No, I hired the caterer."

"Kendall's a professional party planner," Evelyn added.

Ben frowned. "A party planner? This is what you

do for a living—planning parties and weddings?"
This was the woman who looked down on a mere
building contractor?

Evelyn opened her mouth to explain that party
planning was only a sideline. She looked askance
at Kendall, who quickly spoke up. It was evident
that, for whatever reason, she wanted him to believe that party planning was her only income.

"Actually, I don't do weddings. I do celebrations
like this, even smaller dinner parties. You'd be surprised how many people like to entertain, but don't
want the hassle of planning and arranging the details."

Ben raised an eyebrow. "Parties like this I can
understand, but people actually pay you to arrange
their dinner parties?"

She nodded.

He shrugged. "Oh, well, to each his own." He
lifted a plate from the tray and glanced at Evelyn.
"I'd better take this to your mother-in-law."

Kendall watched him walk away. Evelyn watched
Kendall. A moment later, Kendall turned her attention back to Evelyn.

"Is there something else you wanted, Evelyn?"

"Only to thank you for a great party." She glanced
at her husband. "I'd better get back to the table."

As she returned to her table, Evelyn reflected
on the exchange she had just witnessed between
Kendall and Ben. She had told herself that the antagonism she'd sensed in Kendall when she originally introduced them was her imagination.

This atmosphere was not the same, though. This
was not antagonism. It was more like a strange tension, even a wariness.

Evelyn's eyes widened. She shook her head, searching her memory. She had seen that reaction between two of her friends who had eventually succumbed to the attraction they had fought for months. Was it possible that this was a similar situation?

She knew nothing of Kendall's background, and little of Ben's personal life. Being very familiar with his work schedule, she was reasonably certain that he was not currently involved in a serious relationship and had had little or no romance in his life since his wife's death.

Maybe that situation was about to change. She hoped so. A little romance would be good for him.

Evelyn was not alone in her opinion that Ben had been too long without female companionship. His mother, Rosa, had held her tongue with a great deal of effort. Holding her tongue had not included refraining from introducing him to a number of eligible females in the past few years.

When the family gathered at his home for a cookout the week after Evelyn's party, she took advantage of yet another opportunity. She arrived with a guest, the daughter of an old friend.

"Ben, this is Marita Jefferson. You remember her mother, Delia, the friend of mine who moved to Raleigh?"

Ben nodded and extended his hand in greeting. "Yes, I remember Mrs. Jefferson. It's nice to meet you, Marita."

"Marita's new to the area. She moved here from California about a month ago."

Marita glanced at Rosa. "Mom told me to be sure to look up her friend. I hope you don't mind my barging in today."

He shook his head. "Not a problem. I'm used to my mother bringing unexpected guests." He gave his mother a pointed stare. He was well aware of her attempts at matchmaking.

Marita looked from one to the other. Having been on the receiving end of a few matchmaking attempts by her own mother, she recognized the situation.

He led the way to the back porch. "Make yourself at home. Mom, would you get Marita a drink? There are sodas in the cooler and iced tea in the fridge. I'd better get back to the grill."

The day passed pleasantly, in spite of Rosa's matchmaking. Marita was an intelligent, beautiful woman. What would it hurt to invite her out to dinner?

A smile lit Rosa's face when she overheard his invitation. Her smile faded when she reminded herself that he had dated some of the other young women, too. Nothing had ever come of those dates. She sighed.

CHAPTER 2

Two weeks later, Ben made one of his regular visits to his mother. After his father died eight years earlier, he'd started making daily visits to check on her.

Rosa had finally convinced him that these visits were unnecessary, suggesting that he and his sister, Laura, were being overprotective. After a while, he compromised by decreasing his regular visits to once a week. He still held to this ritual.

They talked for a while with no mention of Marita. Then Rosa could contain her curiosity no longer.

"I talked to Delia the other day."

Ben smiled and shook his head. "That's nice, Mom."

"Have you seen Marita since the cookout?"

"Yes, we had dinner a couple of times."

It had become clear to Ben almost immediately that Marita was not interested in a long-term relationship, at least not with him. He supposed she had only agreed to go out with him to placate both of their mothers. He was actually relieved since there had been no real spark of interest on his part.

Rosa waited for more information. She sighed when none was forthcoming.

"I know what you want to hear, Mom, but it's not going to happen."

"I guess you think I'm just a meddling old woman."

Ben chuckled. "First of all, you're not exactly old. Secondly, I can handle your meddling. It could be worse."

"I'm just concerned about you. I worry that you're still grieving after all these years."

He shook his head. "Believe me, I'm not still grieving, Mom. Marita's not the first woman I've dated since Christine's death. I just haven't met the right woman."

He frowned when a vision of Kendall immediately came to mind. It was not the first time in the past few weeks that he had been haunted by velvety chocolate-brown eyes. They were beautiful eyes. They were sad eyes. Maybe that was why they haunted him.

It seemed to Ben that after that conversation with his mother, Kendall was almost constantly on his mind. Of all the women he had met in his life, what made her so intriguing? Maybe he was just curious as to what caused that disturbing expression in her eyes.

In the past five years, he had determinedly avoided any romantic entanglements. His experience with Christine had left him feeling drained— and guilty. He never wanted to go through that again.

Avoiding serious relationships had been easy. There had been no strong attraction to any of the women he dated. That had suited him just fine. His life was ordered and peaceful. His work was fulfilling.

Meeting Kendall had changed all that. He was no longer content with his life. She made him long for something more. He wanted, needed to know if the physical attraction was a mere hint of deeper feelings as yet undiscovered. There was only one way to answer that question.

That evening after dinner, he called her. She answered on the third ring.

"Hello, Kendall, it's Ben." There was no response. "Ben Whitaker. We met through Evelyn Norton."

"Oh, yes, I remember. How are you?"

"I'm fine. I'm calling to ask you to have dinner with me on Saturday."

"Dinner? If you're planning a party, it might be better to do it here."

Ben shook his head. Maybe she really was a snob about dating a man who went to work in jeans and a T-shirt.

"It's not about a job. I'm talking about a date."

"Oh." She hesitated. He was actually calling her for a date?

"Kendall, if the answer is no, I can take it."

"No, I mean yes. I'll have dinner with you."

"Good, I'll pick you up at seven."

They said their good-byes and hung up. Kendall stared at the telephone. She had been unable to get him out of her mind since Evelyn's party. She had squashed the vague hopes that he might be interested in her. One call had revived those hopes.

*   *   *

Kendall scrutinized her reflection in the mirror. The plum-colored silk three-piece dress with its loose jacket, matching tank, and slightly flared skirt was one of her favorite outfits. When the doorbell rang, she slipped her feet into pale-gray slingback pumps and took a deep breath.

"Here we go again," she murmured to herself.

She had almost convinced herself that her reactions to him were a figment of her imagination until she opened the door. Her memories had not done him justice.

"Hi, Ben. Come on in. I'll get my bag." She turned toward the bedroom.

He smiled as she walked away. He was sure that she was totally unaware of the grace of her movements.

When she returned with her clutch bag, he opened the door. "All set?"

A few minutes later, they were settled in his car. "I was afraid that you might be busy with parties this weekend. Do you arrange them during the week, too?"

She decided that she might as well confess. "No, my regular job keeps me busy during the week."

He glanced at her. "Your regular job?"

She nodded. "The private parties are only a sideline. I'm an events planner for a corporation."

He felt a twinge of guilt at his initial reaction to what he assumed was her full-time career. He had been mistaken about her reaction to his job. Otherwise, she would have refused to go out with him.

"Evelyn didn't mention that when she introduced us."

She shrugged. "I guess she didn't think it was important."

"Working all week and arranging parties on the weekend, it's a wonder you have time for a social life at all."

Kendall made no reply. If he only knew. Her work was not the reason her social life was practically nonexistent.

After they were settled in the restaurant and had placed their orders, Kendall asked some questions of her own. He talked about his mother and sister, but said nothing about a wife. She was curious, but something in his attitude made her reluctant to probe.

Ben noticed that she told him very little about her own family. He learned that she was an only child whose father had died when she was eight years old. Her widowed mother had never remarried.

For the remainder of the evening, the conversation was mostly limited to their jobs. "How did you get into the party planning as a sideline?"

"It actually started as a result of planning events for my company. I was responsible for arranging a retirement party for one of the executives. Another executive's wife asked me to help plan an anniversary party for her parents. That was the beginning."

"You don't advertise?"

"No, every job I've had came as a result of someone who attended another party or a recommendation from a friend. If I did this full time, I'd have to advertise. As it is, I have more than enough work to keep me busy."

"I saw what you did for Jim's party. It looked like there's a lot of work involved."

She shrugged. "It depends on the number of guests and the type of party. Smaller dinner parties are fairly simple." She tilted her head to the side. "What about you? I understand the construction, but how did you get into historical restorations?"

"I like old houses. I studied period houses when I was hired to do a few jobs, and soon people were referring me to friends and acquaintances."

Most of the conversation for the remainder of evening centered on their jobs. Ben told her about some of his more extensive renovations and restorations. Kendall explained some of the details involved in planning conferences and training sessions.

When Ben walked her to her door, Kendall had no idea if she could expect to hear from him again. He had appeared to be enjoying the evening. On the other hand, it would not be the first time that her first date was her last.

He waited while she unlocked the door, and followed her into the small foyer. "I had a good time tonight, Kendall. I'm glad you agreed to join me."

"I enjoyed myself, too, Ben."

"Good. Maybe we can do it again next week if you're not busy."

She hesitated. She should be finished with her meeting by Saturday evening. "I don't have any parties on Saturday. I have a small luncheon on Sunday, but that shouldn't interfere. I'd love to have dinner with you."

He smiled. "I'll pick you up a little earlier, say six o'clock. Is that okay?"

"That's fine."

* * *

On the following Friday evening, Kendall opened her door to Valerie's husband, Gary. "Hi, Kendall, thanks for helping me. I rented a hall that has its own caterer. Then I started thinking that maybe I'm in over my head with the DJ and the decorations. I should have just arranged to have it at a restaurant."

"I seem to be hearing a lot of that lately. It's no problem, Gary. What's the point in knowing a party planner if she can't help plan a surprise party for your wife?"

He followed her into the living room. "That's part of the problem, keeping it a surprise."

Other than the buffet menu that he had selected, Gary had difficulty deciding anything else. He finally gave up.

"You know what? You do this all the time and you know Valerie. Why don't I just leave it up to you?"

"Are you sure?"

He nodded. "I'm sure."

"I have some ideas. It's good that you've taken care of the caterer since we don't have much time. Why don't you come by tomorrow? I'll try to contact a DJ and come up with some ideas for the decorations."

Gary called the next day to tell her he was unable to get there before four-thirty or five. The luncheon scheduled for the next day eliminated the possibility of rescheduling the meeting. If she dressed for her date before her meeting with Gary, she would still be ready on time.

She was dressed when Gary arrived shortly after

five o'clock. It was close to six when their meeting ended. Kendall walked him to the door.

"You saved my life, Kendall. I can't thank you enough."

"You know I was glad to help, Gary."

"Let me know if there's anything else you need." He leaned over and kissed her cheek. "I'll see you next week."

As Ben approached Kendall's apartment complex, he saw a man leaving. The stranger smiled at her. Then he leaned over and kissed her cheek before heading toward a car parked nearby.

Ben stopped the car. He frowned and then took a deep breath. Memories flooded his mind. It was like déjà vu. He could not do this again. He drove away. He only traveled a few blocks before he stopped again. Even after what he had just seen, he could not simply leave her waiting. He picked up his cell phone and dialed her number.

"Hi, Kendall. This is the first chance I've had to call. I ran into a problem at one of the sites. I'm afraid I'm going to have to cancel dinner. I'm sorry."

Well, Kendall, are you really surprised? "That's okay, Ben. I understand."

"I'll be in touch."

Sure you will. She said good-bye and hung up the telephone without waiting for his reply. She sighed. *You knew it was too good to be true.* She went to her bedroom and undressed.

*   *   *

Remnants of disappointment remained with Kendall through the following week. She set them aside on Saturday, determined not to spoil her friend's birthday party. She arrived at the banquet hall late that afternoon. Francine met her there to help set up the decorations before the other guests arrived.

Gary had told his wife that they were attending a party for one of his business associates. He had taken Valerie out the previous evening, ostensibly as the only celebration he planned for her birthday. His ruse worked.

When she had recovered from her initial shock, Valerie hugged Kendall. "I can't believe you two actually kept this from me." She glanced at Gary. "Of course, he told me he could never have pulled it off it hadn't been for you."

"I was glad to help. You know that."

There was no need to mention the hard work that had been involved in the last-minute arrangements for the festivities. She watched Gary and Valerie greet their guests. The smiles on their faces made it all worthwhile.

On the Saturday after Labor Day, Kendall was awakened by the insistent ringing of the telephone. She had had parties every weekend for the past month. Expecting business to be slow during the summer, she'd soon learned that not everyone migrated to the beach for the weekend. She welcomed the money, but she had been looking forward to finally having a weekend to sleep in.

She burrowed deeper into the covers in an at-

tempt to block out the sound of the telephone.
When the answering machine clicked on, Valerie's
familiar voice penetrated through the fabric.

"I know you're there, Kendall. Pick up the phone.
It's important. I found a house for you."

Reluctantly, Kendall lifted the phone from its
base and, after some fumbling, placed it to her ear.
"What's this about a house?"

"I found a house that might interest you. I think
it's just what you're looking for. I thought you
might like to go and take a look at it today, before
someone else snatches it up."

"Spoken like a true salesperson."

Valerie laughed. "Hey, girlfriend, you're the one
who told me to keep my eyes open and let you
know if anything interesting turned up. I haven't
seen it yet, but it sounds like it might be what
you're looking for. It's three bedrooms, two baths,
and a semi-finished basement. I should warn you,
though, the price is a little higher than you wanted.
If you like it, we can always make an offer."

"What time do you want to go?"

"Can you be ready by ten o'clock?"

Kendall looked at the clock. It was eight forty-
five.

"I guess I can manage to get myself in gear and
be ready by then. Do you want me to come to your
office?"

"No, I'll pick you up. See you in a little while."

Kendall replaced the phone and dragged herself out of bed. While the coffee was brewing and
her eggs were boiling, she took a shower. Half an
hour and two cups of coffee later, she felt more
like herself.

*   *   *

When Valerie rang her bell at ten minutes before ten, Kendall was dressed and unloading the dishwasher. Leaving that task, she went and opened the door to her friend.

"Hi, are you ready to go?"

Kendall nodded. "Let me get my purse."

The two women arrived at the property less than half an hour later. The house was a modest-sized English Tudor-style with a one-car attached garage. The stone path leading to the front door and the fence surrounding the small yard were a perfect complement to the structure.

"What do you think?" Valerie asked as they exited her car.

"I like the outside, but I'll reserve my final judgment until I've seen inside."

"It should be in good shape. I understand it was recently completely renovated."

Kendall nodded as they walked through the rooms. She loved the stained woodwork, moldings, and deep windowsills throughout the house. The medium-sized whirlpool tub in the master bathroom and the modern kitchen were the only departures from what would be expected in a period house.

That was fine with Kendall. She imagined the pleasure the tub would afford after one of her really hectic weeks. She was of the opinion that showers were great when she was in a hurry, but for relaxation nothing compared to a luxurious bubble bath.

The built-in bookshelves in the smallest bedroom were a big plus. It would be a perfect room for her home office. Half of the basement was fin-

ished, and separated from the area that held the
furnace and water heater. The finished half would
be a great place to store the items she kept in stock
for parties.

When they completed their inspection, they returned to the living room. "Well, what do you think
now?"

"Okay, Valerie, you did a good job. I like it. It has
everything I need. I'm glad he left the pocket doors
between the living room and the dining room intact."

Valerie smiled. "You mean the parlor?"

"Right, the parlor. It does seem to be the best of
both worlds. It has the old-fashioned style I like
without having to worry about repairs."

She surveyed her surroundings again. Then she
sighed. "The price isn't bad, but I really don't want
to go over my budget. I don't think my prequalifi-
cation for the mortgage will cover the difference,
either."

"That's not necessarily a problem. We can always apply for an increase."

"Do you think there's a chance that the owner
will come down a little?"

"We can only try. The owner is a contractor who
renovated it himself, so maybe he'll be willing to
come down on the price."

Kendall remembered Evelyn's earlier statement.
"Evelyn Norton told me that her boss was selling a
house he had renovated. You wouldn't happen to
know the owner's name, would you?"

"Not offhand. It may or may not be the same
contractor. I've seen a few old houses purchased
by contractors with the sole purpose of renovating

and reselling. This is the first one that's come on the market since you started looking."

As they walked to the car, Valerie suggested, "How about lunch? You don't have a party this evening, do you?"

"No, this is a free weekend for a change. Lunch sounds fine."

On Tuesday afternoon, Kendall received a call from Valerie. "I have great news. Your offer was accepted."

"That is great news. I've been trying to prepare myself for the disappointment of having the offer rejected. As much as I hated paying rent, I'm glad I waited and didn't settle for a condo."

"There's more good news. Since it's unoccupied, we can probably get an early settlement date."

"When will you know?"

"I'll set a tentative date. After you sign the sale agreement we can finalize it. Is there any chance you can stop by after work? If not, I can bring the papers to the house this evening."

"I can come to the office. I should be there between five-thirty and six."

"Good, I'll see you then."

As Valerie led Kendall to her office that evening, they were met by one of Valerie's coworkers. "Valerie, there's a Mr. Logan on the phone. He said he spoke to you this afternoon."

"Thanks. This is Kendall Chase, Darren. She came by to sign some agreement papers," she explained.

"Would you tell Mr. Logan I'll call him back in a few minutes?"

"I'll tell him, but I'm not your secretary, you know." Before she could answer, he turned and stalked away without even acknowledging the introduction.

Kendall raised an eyebrow. "He's not exactly pleasant for a salesman."

Valerie shook her head. "Only when he's making a sale. Or when he sees someone else's sale fall through."

They proceeded to Valerie's office. When they were seated, Valerie took a sheaf of papers from a folder on her desk.

"I hope you were serious about wanting a settlement date as early as possible."

"When is it? Tomorrow?"

Valerie laughed. "It's not that bad. How about in three weeks. The actual date is the ninth, a Saturday. I've already cleared it with the seller. Is that date okay for you?"

Kendall flipped through her day planner. "The ninth is fine. I don't have anything scheduled that day."

"Great, I'll give you a call with the exact time."

Kendall picked up the papers and began reading. The seller's name seemed to jump out. "It *is* his house," she murmured.

Valerie knit her brows. "Whose house?"

"Ben Whitaker. You remember I told you that Evelyn mentioned her boss was selling a house he had renovated." She left out the information about their dinner date.

"If I'd known that, I might have been able to get you a better deal."

Kendall shook her head. Considering Ben's abrupt cancellation of their date, if he'd known she was the buyer it might have had the opposite effect.

"You did fine, Valerie. I'm more than satisfied."

She signed the papers and handed them back to her friend. Valerie placed them in her briefcase, but made no move to leave.

"What's the matter? Is there something you haven't told me? I can't believe there's a problem with the house since you just let me sign the sales agreement."

"No, no, it has nothing to do with the house. I have a favor to ask."

Kendall frowned. "What kind of favor?"

Valerie hesitated before mumbling, "A blind date?"

"No way, girlfriend."

"Please, Kendall. A friend of Gary's is in town. We planned to attend a play and this is the last week. Gary doesn't want to desert his friend, so he asked me to see if I could get one of my friends to join us."

"And you immediately thought of me. Why don't you pick on Francine or one of your other friends?"

"Because you're my best friend."

"Uh-huh. Considering past experiences, that's even more reason for you to pick on someone else." She'd had enough bad luck with the most recent date she'd arranged on her own.

"Come on, Kendall. Didn't I just find you the house of your dreams?"

Kendall raised an eyebrow. "I'm not sure that's worth the agony of another blind date. Besides, how does Gary know he'll be able to get tickets?"

"He called this morning and reserved the tickets. It's just dinner and a play. How bad can that be?"

"I have a feeling I'm going to find out."

"Then you'll go?"

"Okay, Valerie. I'll go, but after this you can cross me off your list for blind dates. I don't care how many favors you think you've done for me. No more blind dates."

Valerie sighed. "Okay. No more blind dates."

Gary's friend, Allen Wilson, was a forty-one-year-old divorced attorney. Kendall thought she noticed a look of disappointment when they were introduced, but she dismissed it. She was determined not to assume the worst.

Forty-five minutes later, seated at the restaurant, she was beginning to think the evening might not be as bad as she feared. She was soon to change that opinion. After they finished their entrees, the waiter came to take orders for dessert.

"I think I'll have the cheesecake," Kendall said.

"Do you think that's wise?" Allen asked, surveying her generous curves.

Kendall took a deep breath. She would never have considered making a remark about his slight paunch.

When her eyes met his, her hand itched to wipe the smirk off his face. Determined to remain pleasant, she ignored his implication.

Her smile never reached her eyes. "I think it's a very good choice. I understand the cheesecake here is delicious."

"That's not what I meant."

Kendall's mock smile disappeared abruptly. "I didn't think so, but I decided any other insinuation would be very personal and extremely rude."

Valerie coughed and hid her smile behind her napkin. "I'll have the cheesecake, too."

After Gary added his order, the waiter quickly departed. Gary immediately turned the discussion to the play they planned to see that evening.

The rest of the evening passed pleasantly enough. The play prevented further conversation until intermission. Valerie was quick to take care of that problem. She started discussing the play as soon as the curtain went down. The discussion continued during the trip home.

When they arrived at Kendall's apartment, Allen opened his car door. Guessing he planned to walk her to her door, Kendall quickly opened the car door on her side.

"That's all right, Allen, don't bother."

He closed the door and sat back, folding his arms across his chest. "If you insist."

Gary spoke up. "Wait, Kendall, I'll walk with you. It's late. You can't be too careful these days."

When they reached the door of her apartment, Kendall put the key in the lock and turned toward Gary. "Thanks, but this wasn't really necessary."

"Yes, it was." He hesitated, frowning. "I'm sorry about this evening. My only excuse is that I haven't seen Allen in years. I'd forgotten that he's not only tactless, but a bit of a jerk."

Kendall shook her head. "You don't have to apologize for him, Gary. I enjoyed dinner and the play was great."

"Well, at least it wasn't a total loss. I guess I'd better get back before Valerie reads Allen the riot act."

As she prepared for bed, Kendall reflected on the evening's fiasco. She supposed it could have been worse. She had enjoyed dinner and the play. The evening would also serve the purpose of preventing Valerie from attempting to arrange any more blind dates for her.

CHAPTER 3

When Kendall returned from church on Sunday, she checked her telephone messages. The first two were unremarkable. One was from Valerie, apologizing again for the date the previous evening. The other was from a prospective client. It was the third message that made her entire body tense. The voice on the tape was all too familiar.

"Hi, K.C. It's Scott. I guess I'm the last person you expected to hear from, but I need to see you. It's important. Please give me a call. My number is—"

She pushed the button erasing the message without hearing the telephone number. *What made him think I would ever speak to him, let alone meet with him? How did he get my telephone number?*

It didn't matter. He could call ten times a day. She'd simply continue to erase the messages. She tried to ignore the little voice in her head that wondered if he also knew her address. She took a deep breath. That was okay, too. She would soon be moving.

For five years she had tried to forget him completely. After a few years, the fear originally associated with him had been replaced by anger and disgust. She had finally given up and accepted the fact that no matter how hard she tried to erase all memories of him, he would always be lurking there in the dark recesses of her mind. After what he'd done, how could she forget?

Pushing thoughts of Scott Holmes aside, she went upstairs to change clothes. Soon Kendall's mind was occupied with party plans. She called the prospective client who had left the message. After arranging to meet with the woman on Tuesday, she set to work finalizing plans for an anniversary party the following Saturday.

Her concentration was abruptly interrupted by a vision of Ben. *Forget it, Kendall. Haven't you learned your lesson?* It had only taken one date for him to regain his senses. His rejection and the disastrous date with Allen had brought her back to reality. They served as a reminder of the shallowness of men.

She chided herself for that generalization. *You're being unfair, Kendall. Not all men are turned off by full-figured women. There are plenty of men in love with women your size and larger. Even the blind dates you've had weren't all jerks like Allen. At least, they weren't as tactless. They just made it clear that they weren't interested in a relationship, like Ben.*

She shook her head. Speculating on Ben Whitaker's reasons for canceling their date was a waste of time. She was unaware that Ben was entertaining questions of his own, which meant that putting her speculations to rest would not be as easy as she hoped.

Evelyn looked up as Ben walked in. "Morning, Boss. I thought you planned to be at the construction site today."

"I stopped there first. I have a few things to do here and then I'll head back to check on the work."

He headed toward his office, and then turned back toward her. "It may be a little early, but do you have any thoughts about the Christmas party this year? The new building should be finished by then. I thought we might have it there. Since we won't actually be moving until January, the open space would be perfect."

She shook her head. "I've been so busy I hadn't thought about it. With the new projects you've taken on, I have my hands full trying to keep track of everyone. I'm not sure I'll have time to arrange it. I'm sorry."

She tilted her head to the side. "I have a suggestion, though. I could give Kendall a call and see if she can fit it into her schedule."

He had never called again after canceling their second date. Pangs of guilt assailed him at the mention of her name. Why should he assume or expect that he was the only man she was dating? It was not as if they had been seeing each other on a regular basis.

Now Evelyn was suggesting he hire her to plan a party. Did he have the nerve to make such a request? He told himself that this was different. This was business. Besides, he would have to see her again anyway at the closing.

"I guess it wouldn't hurt to find out what it would cost. She's buying the house I just renovated. Maybe I'll mention it to her at the closing on Saturday."

Evelyn smiled. "So she did contact you."

He knit his brow. "What do you mean?"

"She told me she was house-hunting and I mentioned your house to her."

He shook his head. "She didn't contact me. I got a call from the real-estate agent. I guess it's just a coincidence."

"I hope it's not too late for her to do the party. I suspect December is a busy month for her."

He nodded and proceeded to his office.

Evelyn's smile widened. So Kendall was buying his house and he would see her again at settlement. An old saying flitted through her mind. *There's no such thing as a coincidence.*

She had forgotten about her annual task of planning the Christmas party until Ben mentioned it. His question had brought Kendall to mind immediately. While she would never have made an overt attempt at matchmaking, her suggestion was perfectly sensible.

She was more than Ben's secretary. She was his friend. His wife's illness and death had been devastating. She had watched his struggle helplessly.

Aside from the spark of interest she had seen in his eyes when she introduced him to Kendall, she recalled the feeling of tension between them at the party. If her intuition was on the mark, the Christmas party might just be the little push he needed.

Ben had also heard the saying that coincidences did not exist. What were the chances that the woman buying his house would be the same woman he had left waiting with very little reason for canceling their date? The same woman who had been on his mind since their first meeting, even more so since their date.

Guilt did not explain his preoccupation. Neither did his curiosity about that sad expression in her eyes explain his preoccupation. He had met other women with hurt expressions. He had felt a certain sympathy for them, but nothing more.

His ruminations were interrupted by Evelyn's voice on the intercom. "Bob's on the line. Do you want to take it or should I tell him you'll call back?"

"I'll take it." He picked up the receiver and his attention returned to work.

On Saturday morning Kendall was met by Valerie when she entered the real-estate office. "Morning, Kendall. Excited?"

Kendall took a deep breath. "Excited, nervous, and a little scared. For as long as I've wanted this, I guess that sounds a little strange."

Valerie laid a hand on her shoulder. "Not at all. It's a big step, whether it's your first house or not. I think most buyers feel those same emotions."

As Ben approached the real-estate office, a vaguely familiar man entered ahead of him. The light of recognition dawned as he opened the door. He was the same man Ben had seen leaving Kendall's apartment. What was he doing here? His eyes narrowed when he entered to see the man hugging another woman.

Kendall sat nonchalantly in a nearby chair. She looked toward the door as the woman spoke.

"Mr. Whitaker?" Valerie asked, walking toward him.

Ben nodded.

"I'm Valerie Hamilton, Kendall's agent. I believe you two have met?"

Kendall answered. "Yes, he was at a party that I arranged for his secretary."

So she wanted to pretend that their date had never happened. He could hardly blame her.

Valerie linked her arm through the stranger's. "This is my husband, Gary."

With a great deal of effort, Ben remained aloof. Was Kendall having an affair with a married man?

The two men shook hands. "So you're familiar with Kendall's talents. She saved my life last month. I got in over my head trying to plan a surprise party for Valerie's birthday."

She'd helped him plan a birthday party for his wife. Was it possible that was the reason he was at her apartment? Ben looked at Kendall and then back at the couple. Either she was a first-class actress, or he had jumped to what could be an embarrassing conclusion.

Gary kissed his wife's cheek. "I'd better get going, babe."

"Okay, honey, I'll see you on Tuesday."

After Gary left, Valerie picked up the folder on her desk. She glanced at her watch just as the door opened again. "There you are, Bill. Shall we get started?" She led the way to a small conference room in the back of the office.

When they were settled, Kendall concentrated on signing the papers that were set in front of her. She avoided looking at the man across the table.

Ben felt no such need for avoidance. He took every opportunity to examine this woman who was bent on ignoring him. He mentally shrugged. How could he blame her for ignoring him?

When the paperwork was completed, Kendall took a deep breath. "I feel like I've just signed my life away."

"Is this your first house?" he asked.

Kendall nodded. His attitude indicated his intention to pretend their date had never happened. That was fine with her. She had been trying to put that date, and him, out of her mind for weeks.

"It gets a little easier. You get used to the paperwork."

Kendall's eyes widened. "I don't plan for this to be an annual event. I expect to be in this house for a long time."

"Good, I guess that's something every seller likes to hear."

Okay, so we're going to play this like two strangers involved in a purely business transaction. Fine.

"I suppose that's even truer in your case. You must have put a lot of work into the house."

"It was a lot of work," he admitted, "but it's what I enjoy doing. I love bringing old houses back to life. I like to think that the people who buy them will appreciate them and love them as much as I do."

She continued to play along with his charade. "I already love the house." She glanced at Valerie. "I told Valerie it's like having the best of both worlds for me, an old house without the worry of costly repairs and maintenance."

He nodded. "That's the whole idea."

Bill gathered up the papers and handed the keys to Kendall. "It's all yours."

Kendall raised an eyebrow. "You mean mine and the bank's." She shrugged. "Oh, well, it's no worse than paying rent. I just have to keep reminding myself that the house will really be mine eventually. The other advantage is that I'll be able to do whatever I want with the house, things I could never have done in an apartment."

She rose from her chair. "We should get going, Valerie. I still have a lot of packing to do if I'm going to move in this week."

Ben followed them to the door. He stopped Kendall when they were outside.

"I'd like to discuss a project with you, Kendall. Do you have a moment?"

Kendall looked at Valerie.

"I'm in no hurry. I'll wait for you in the car."

Kendall turned her attention back to Ben. "What kind of project?"

"Evelyn usually plans the company Christmas party. She suggested I might be able to hire you to arrange it since she won't have time to do it this year. Can we set up an appointment to discuss the details?"

Her first reaction was disbelief that he had the nerve to ask her a favor. *Okay, Kendall, it's not a favor. This is business.*

"Sure, we can discuss it. We can meet next Saturday, say five o'clock. It may not seem like it, but Christmas isn't far away. There may be a problem getting a place at this late date. A lot of the banquet halls are booked six months to a year ahead of time."

"The place won't be a problem."

She raised an eyebrow. *So much for the easy way out of this arrangement.*

"I'll explain on Saturday."

He reached inside his jacket pocket and pulled out a business card and a pen. After scrawling a number on the back of the card, he gave it to her.

"My home number is on the back. If you can't do it this week, with moving and all, give me a call."

"Fine, I'll see you Saturday, then." She turned and started walking across the parking lot.

Valerie watched them through the rearview mirror of her car. Her friend was not the focus of her attention. She watched Ben as he stood at the entrance. His gaze never left Kendall until she was inside the car.

A few minutes after leaving the parking lot, Valerie glanced toward her passenger. "I see why you were so disgusted with my feeble attempts at matchmaking. You seem to be managing quite well on your own."

"It's nothing like that, Valerie. I told you, I met him at Evelyn Norton's party." As far as Kendall was concerned, their one date was best forgotten and definitely not worth mentioning.

"Uh-huh. So what was that little conversation a few minutes ago?"

"Evelyn suggested he hire me to plan the Christmas party for his company."

"Oh, so you will be seeing him again. And you'll probably be working closely with him to plan the party since he's the one hiring you."

Kendall shook her head. "Valerie . . ."

"You can 'Valerie' all you want to, girlfriend. What I saw in his eyes when he looked at you was more than just 'Help me plan my Christmas party.' "

Kendall rolled her eyes, but she made no further comment. She was tempted to tell her friend about the broken date. That should make it clear to Valerie that whatever she thought she saw was her imagination. It was also likely to arouse Valerie's anger and sympathy. The last thing she wanted was sympathy.

By Wednesday, Kendall had moved into her new home. With Valerie's help, she had repainted the living room and dining room. The movers had completed their job on Tuesday. The only task left was to unpack the many boxes that she and the movers had transported.

On Saturday afternoon, Kendall looked around at the number of boxes still waiting to be unpacked. She considered calling Ben and rescheduling their meeting. She shook her head.

Even though he had assured her that the place for the party was not a problem, she had to find a caterer and a DJ. She needed to meet with him to determine the cost, and any other specific requests that he had in mind. She could back out of the job altogether if she ran into problems.

She had unpacked her new desk, or at least the pieces of wood that would form her new desk, when the doorbell rang. She glanced at her watch. If that was Ben, he was half an hour early. She descended the stairs. Peeking through the blinds in the dining room, she glimpsed Ben standing patiently on the doorstep.

She returned to the foyer and opened the door. "Come on in," she said, stepping back to allow him to enter.

She gestured toward the boxes stacked in the foyer. "Excuse the mess. I'm still in the process of unpacking," she explained, closing the door behind him.

He glanced down at the screwdriver in her hand. "We don't have to do this today. It can wait until you've had a little more time to settle in."

She followed the direction of his gaze and raised the tool. "That's okay. I was in the process of assembling my new desk, not my favorite activity." She dropped her hand to her side once again. "It can wait."

He looked at his watch. "Since I'm early, why don't I give you a hand?"

She shook her head. "You don't have to do that. I'll manage."

"I don't mind. Where's the desk?"

She hesitated. Why was he being so helpful? It was on the tip of her tongue to tell him that she wanted no favors from him. That would be petty. Maybe this was an attempt to appease his conscience.

She might as well benefit from his guilt. He was a professional carpenter. Putting together a desk would be a piece of cake for him. She turned toward the stairs.

"It's up here."

He followed her to the small room with the built-in bookcases. He spied the paper lying in the midst of the parts scattered on the floor.

Bending over, he lifted the paper and began reading the instructions. A moment later, he started separating the pieces into some order, according to the directions. Then he leaned back on his heels, perusing the paper again.

He seemed oblivious to her presence. She was very much aware of him. Her gaze strayed first to where his slacks were now stretched taut across muscular thighs. Lost in her own fantasy, she almost jumped when he spoke.

"This looks simple enough," he said, looking up at her. "Let me have the screwdriver."

She looked from his outstretched hand to the tool as if she were seeing it for the first time. Warmth diffused her neck and face.

His fingers brushed against hers during the exchange. The warmth in her cheeks increased by a few degrees. She silently berated herself. It had been a long time since anything had made her blush.

Get a grip, Kendall. He's made his opinion of you clear. It's ridiculous for you to let him affect you like this.

His attention was fixed on his task, allowing her time to regain her composure. She dropped to her knees across from him.

"What can I do to help?"

They worked easily as a team fitting the pieces together. Less than an hour later, Kendall had her new desk in place.

"Thanks for your help. I hate putting furniture together. Unfortunately, these days it's becoming more and more difficult to find furniture already assembled." She started toward the door. "We'd better get started on the plans for your party." She led the way down the stairs and to the dining room.

"I see you've been hard at work." he said, surveying the rooms. He nodded. "I like it."

"Thanks, it wasn't as hard as I expected."

The walls had been painted in a color wash of varying shades of gold, providing the perfect backdrop for the cozy furnishings. Throw pillows in solid colors of beige and sage green, accompanied by others in a muted paisley print of dark gold, sage green, beige, and brick red, complemented the brick-red sofa. The oversized beige chair with its matching ottoman was covered in the same paisley print as the throw pillows.

Most of the floor was covered by a beige rug with a wide border of sparsely scattered flowers of dark red and gold and a narrower sage-green edging. Beige marble and dark oak surrounded the fireplace which was topped by an oak mantle.

"Have a seat. Can I get you something to drink? I have sodas, or I can make some coffee."

He shook his head. "No, thanks, I'm fine."

She sat down across from him. "What did you mean when you said the place for the party isn't a problem?"

"I have an office building that's being renovated. The renovations should be completed by December, but the company won't actually be moving until January."

She frowned. "You plan to have the party there?"

He nodded. "It'll be carpeted, but we can rent a dance floor, can't we? Once it's decorated, I think it'll work."

"Renting a dance floor shouldn't be a problem."

She made notes for the specifics as to the menu and the amount he wanted to spend. She had planned enough parties to estimate the expenses for the favors and decorations.

"Does this mean you'll take the job?"

"That's up to you. We haven't discussed my fee yet." She glanced over her notes. "I'll give you a figure after I've determined the expenses for decorations and my time. I'll also have more information after I've talked to a caterer and a DJ."

"When do think you'll have the figures final-ized?"

She shrugged. "Depending on how hard it is to find a caterer and a DJ, I should have a figure by next week."

"Good. While we're at it, I'd like for you to plan the children's party, too. I always do a separate party for them."

She looked down at the notepad. "I don't do children's parties."

"Oh, I see." He refrained from asking more questions. No other words were necessary for her message to be clear. The subject was not open to further discussion. Once again, the shutters had closed against her personal life.

"If you'd rather hire someone who'll do both jobs, that's fine."

He shook his head. "No, I still want you to do the adult party. Evelyn or some of the other employees can probably take care of the other. I can probably rope my mother into helping, too."

"In that case, I'll get back in touch with you after I've found a caterer and a DJ. If I have a problem with either, I'll let you know.

"Thanks again for your help with the desk," she said as she walked him to the door. "I'll give you a call later this week."

"Are you sure you'll have time to do that before next week?"

"Unless all of the caterers I usually hire are booked, it won't be a problem."

He surveyed the boxes. "Is there anything else I can help with before I leave?"

She scanned the room and shook her head. "Thanks for the offer, but I can manage. The desk was the biggest job. The rest is just a matter of un-packing and putting everything in its place."

He opened the door. "I guess I'd better let you get back to work then."

She watched him walk to his car. The sigh that escaped her lips had nothing to do with the tiring job of moving. *Let it go, Kendall. You should be used to disappointment by now.*

Kendall had repositioned her new desk and was setting up her computer when Valerie called that evening. "Hi, Valerie, I'm glad you called. I meant to call you this afternoon to invite you and Gary to dinner tomorrow."

"Gary's out of town. His father had bypass surgery on Thursday, so he won't be back for a few days."

"I'm sorry to hear that. How is he?"

"I talked to Gary a little while ago. His father's doing great."

"That's good. So, what about you? Do you have any plans for tomorrow?"

"Not a thing. I'd love to come for a visit, but are you sure about dinner? You don't have to bother to cook. We can just order take-out. Better yet, I can pick up something on my way over."

"I've been eating sandwiches, soup, and take-out all week. I'm going to cook my first real meal in my new house."

"Then why don't I bring dessert?"

"Okay, if you insist."

CHAPTER 4

Valerie arrived a few minutes after three o'clock on Sunday. She placed a small cake box on the foyer table before removing her coat.

Kendall took her coat and hung it in the closet. "I called Francine to invite her. I think she may be out of town." Leading the way to the living room, she added, "Let me put this in the kitchen. I'll be right back."

Valerie was seated on the sofa when she returned. "This is the first time I've seen this room completed." She viewed their handiwork.

"We did a pretty good job with the paint, didn't we?"

"Yes, we did. I love it, Valerie. I don't think I could have done it without your help."

Valerie faced her. "How's the unpacking coming? I don't mind helping while I'm here."

Kendall shook her head. "I didn't invite you here to work this time. There's not much left to do. I finished setting up the computer yesterday, after putting my desk together."

Valerie frowned. "Why didn't you call me? I know how frustrating and aggravating it can be assembling furniture."

"Ben helped me. Actually, he did most of the work." She immediately wished she had kept that piece of information to herself.

Valerie raised an eyebrow. "Hmm, Ben helped? That's interesting."

Kendall rolled her eyes. "He came to discuss the party. I was in the middle of assembling the desk and he offered to help." She fixed her friend with a stare. "That's all there was to it, Valerie."

"Okay, if you say so." She looked around the room. "Do I get to see the rest of the house?"

Kendall stood up. "I still have some work to do upstairs, but you can have a look. Maybe you'll have some suggestions for me."

She led the way up the stairs, stopping first at the room she had designated as her office. Even with the off-white walls, the built-in bookcases and dark oak woodwork gave the room a cozy feeling.

In addition to the desk, there was a high-back desk chair and a tall oak file cabinet. Two small windows were covered with wood-grained mini-blinds topped with plaid valances in aubergine, gold, claret, teal, and beige. A small upholstered chair in the same plaid sat next to a medium-sized drop-leaf table.

"I haven't decided what else to do with this room. It's functional as it is. That was my main concern."

They moved on to the bedroom, where Kendall

had concentrated her decorating efforts. The fruit-wood four-poster bed was set against the palest sage-green wall and covered with a woven tapestry comforter and shams. The pale taupe background of the comforter was bordered by a floral print of peach, melon, turquoise, and green. The same floral print was echoed in the valance above the ivory drapes at the large window to the left of the bed.

The other walls were ivory-colored, providing a neutral backdrop for the sage-green chair and ottoman near the window. Next to the chair, a round table was covered with a matching tapestry cloth.

Matching nightstands on either side of the bed and a dresser between the door to the bathroom and the door to the closet completed the furniture. Ivory area rugs dotted the hardwood floor.

"This is great, Kendall. You did all of this yourself?"

Kendall nodded. "Including the painting. Eventually, I might change some things. I've thought about a border, but I haven't made up my mind. I love the crown molding and I'm afraid a border might be too much." She shrugged. "I'll live with it for a while. It's comfortable and relaxing. That was the most important consideration."

"You're right. The colors work well together."

A few minutes later, they returned to the living room. After they were settled, Valerie voiced a question that had been on her mind earlier.

She tilted her head to one side. "So, are you going to plan Ben's party?"

"I'm not sure yet. I have to work out the figures." She shrugged. "It'll depend on whether he's willing to pay my fee." She paused. "There may not be a party if I can't get a caterer and a DJ."

"What about the hall or banquet room?"

"He already has a place." She explained about the office building. "I haven't seen it yet. He insists it'll work."

Valerie bit her tongue. Maybe her observations at the settlement were a figment of her imagination. Time would tell. After the latest fiasco, she had promised her friend that she would make no more attempts at matchmaking.

Valerie could not help being curious about Kendall's past. Kendall had never discussed her ex-husband or the reason her marriage had ended. Valerie had drawn the line at prying into her friend's personal life. Friendship only went so far.

On Monday, Kendall began the preliminary work for Ben's party. She had called two caterers, neither of whom was available. She finally succeeded on Thursday. Unfortunately, the caterer was one of those who did not provide linens. After convincing him to reserve the date, she called Ben and arranged a meeting for Saturday.

When Kendall hung up the phone, her thoughts naturally turned to her most recent encounters with Ben. As much as possible, she had avoided looking at him in hopes of ignoring the effect that he had on her. It would serve her well to remember that he had no interest in a personal relationship. He had merely hired her to do a job.

When she opened the door to him on Saturday, she took one look at him and all of her good intentions went out the window. It was useless to try to ignore feelings that she could not control. Controlling her actions was a different matter. She had a great deal of experience with that. She ushered him through the living room to the dining room.

When they were seated in the dining room, Kendall handed him a sheet of paper. "Those are the figures. I've broken it down and included my fee. The caterer's fee could change if the number of people increases. The only other difference in the price would depend on whether you want real or artificial poinsettias."

He scanned the figures. "What about other decorations?"

"They're included in my fee." She raised an eyebrow. "That is, if you trust me to make the decisions about the decorations and favors."

"I think I can leave that to you. I saw what you did for Evelyn's party."

When they had completed their business a few minutes later, Kendall rose from her chair. "I don't want to be impolite, but if you don't have any other questions, I have to get ready for a dinner party this evening."

He stood up. "No problem."

She followed him to the door, where he paused. "When would you like to see the room?"

She knit her brows. "The room?"

"The new office, the room we'll be using for the party."

She rubbed her forehead, shaking her head. "So much has been happening, I'd forgotten. I was so concerned about the caterer and the DJ, the place itself completely slipped my mind."

"I'm sorry. I should have mentioned it earlier, before you estimated your decorating budget."

She shrugged. "Seeing the room doesn't matter much in terms of my budget. I based my figures on starting with a bare room. Seeing the actual room will give me a better feel for what I have planned, though. It'll also give me a better idea as to the number of poinsettias we'll need."

"Are you free Monday evening?"

"Monday evening is good. If you give me the address, I'll meet you there."

"I have a better idea. It might be easier for me to pick you up here and drive you there. Is six-thirty all right?"

"Six-thirty is fine."

Kendall would have been shocked to know that Ben experienced the same attraction she was fighting. Desire rose to the surface once again when she greeted him on Monday. The loose-fitting teal-blue dress enhanced her lush curves rather than hiding them. He tamped down the yearnings, reminding himself that this was a business meeting. That reminder might be a moot point. He might have aready ruined any chance of acting on those yearnings.

"Hi, are you ready to go?" he said.

"Let me get my coat and bag."

Ben's fingers first grazed her ear and then her neck as he helped her on with her coat. That simple touch was all it took to accelerate her pulse. In the three years that she had been married to Scott, he had never stirred such an instant response.

Ben waited while she set the alarm. Then he ushered her to his car. Kendall settled back in the luxury sedan as he backed out of the driveway.

* * *

Ben's office building had once been a large hardware supply store. A newer and bigger lumber and hardware store had forced it out of business.

Ben had gutted it, and was in the process of renovating the interior. A full kitchen had been installed with space for several small tables.

In addition to the conference rooms and offices, there was a large open area that would be partitioned into cubicles after the party. Once the painting was finished and carpeting installed, the space would serve well for the party he planned.

Kendall surveyed the room. "Will there be window coverings?"

He nodded. "Vertical blinds will be installed before the party when the rest of the work is completed."

"Do you have a floor plan? The room is basically a big square, but the measurements will be important." She gestured toward the wall behind them. "When I plan the layout for the tables, it'll be helpful to be able to see the placement of the doors to the rest rooms and the kitchen."

He reached inside his jacket and pulled out a folded sheet of paper. "Will this do?" he asked, handing it to her.

His gaze never left her as she walked around the room. She seemed to have forgotten that he was there as she concentrated on the rough plan forming in her mind.

She refolded the paper and faced him. "This is fine. I can estimate where to place the tables to allow for an increase in the numbers if necessary."

Kendall was silent during the drive to her house. A picture was forming in her mind of how to transform the empty room into a banquet hall that the guests would never recognize as an empty office building. By the time they pulled up in her driveway, the picture was complete.

Two days after inspecting the place for Ben's Christmas party, Kendall flew to Atlanta for a conference. When she returned late on Friday, there was another message from Scott.

"K.C., it's Scott. I really need to talk to you. Call me. My number is—"

Again, Kendall immediately deleted the message without hearing the number. Why did he keep calling? After receiving no response to his first message, he should have taken the hint and given up. She clenched her jaws. Scott never gave up easily—except where work was concerned.

That call lingered in the back of her mind as she unpacked. She could think of only one person who might have given him her new telephone number—her mother. She reached for a pair of shoes from her suitcase and stopped with her hand in midair. If her mother had given him her new telephone number, he probably had her new address, too.

She reached for another item from her suitcase, and jerked when the telephone rang again. She finished her task and went downstairs. After retrieving another message from Scott, she deleted it and then turned off the ringer.

There were no more calls that evening. She lay awake for hours, considering her options.

She could call her mother. If she was responsible for giving Scott Kendall's number, maybe her mother could persuade him to stop calling. *Forget it, Kendall. You know she'll side with Scott.* She sighed.

She could call Scott and threaten to call the police if he called again. Or she could actually call the police and file a complaint.

None of those options satisfied her. Maybe he would finally get the message and stop calling without any further action on her part.

As usual, Kendall was not far from his mind when Ben visited his mother on the Saturday following their trip to his office building. Not only was he convinced that an affair with Gary was a figment of his imagination, he doubted that she was involved in any romantic entanglement. His instincts told him that deceit was not part of her character. If she was involved with another man, she would never have agreed to a date with him.

He rang his mother's doorbell, and waited for a few minutes before letting himself in with his key. He had barely closed the door behind him when his mother exited the kitchen down the hall.

"Hi, honey," she said walking toward him. "I thought I heard the doorbell. I was in the garage, unloading groceries."

He leaned over and placed a kiss on her cheek. Then the two of them started back toward the kitchen. He followed her to the garage.

"I'll get the rest of the bags, Mom."

They chatted while he helped her put away the groceries. "Are you staying for dinner?" she asked.

He grinned. "If you insist."

She turned to face him, smiling and nodding. "Right."

During dinner, she brought him up to date on his nieces' latest escapades. "I made the mistake of asking them what they wanted for Christmas. They've already given me their lists."

He raised an eyebrow. "Has Laura seen the list?"

"Of course not. They were very careful to slip it to me when she wasn't around." She smiled. "They also told me I could share it with you."

He shook his head. "I'm surprised they didn't have a separate list for me."

She chuckled. "You haven't seen the list." She took a sip of water. "Speaking of Christmas, has Evelyn started planning your company party? I told her about a month ago to let me know if there's anything I can do to help."

"Actually, Evelyn's not planning the party this year, at least not the adult party. She has her hands full with the new jobs and planning the move in January."

She frowned. "What are you going to do?"

"I hired a professional party planner. As a matter of fact, she's buying the house I just renovated."

"A professional party planner? Now why would you spend money to pay someone to plan a party? I could probably do it for you."

He shook his head. "It can be a lot of work, Mom. We have to rent tables and chairs and hire a caterer and a DJ. Then there's the job of buying or making decorations. Besides, I've already met with her and her fee's not expensive. Evelyn hired her to plan Jim's birthday party."

"You say she doesn't charge much, but she does this for a living?"

"Party planning is only a sideline. Kendall's an events planner for the Meredith Corporation."

"I see."

He smiled. "I do have a job for you. Kendall won't be arranging the children's party."

"You want me to plan that?" She nodded. "Sure, I'll enjoy it."

"Good, I thought you would."

Rosa had sensed a slightly defensive attitude toward the party planner when she made her earlier comment. "What's this Kendall like?"

He rubbed his chin. "She seems rather shy for someone who plans parties."

It was more than shyness. Whenever her image arose in his mind, he envisioned that hint of sorrow in her eyes. He had seen her smile maybe once or twice in the entire time he had known her. Even then, it was not a real smile.

Rosa guarded herself against getting her hopes up. She glanced at him and took another sip of water. He seemed lost in thought. She stood up.

"If you're finished, I'll take your plate."

"That's okay, I'll do it. It's the least I can do."

He started loading the dishwasher. "Who's having Thanksgiving dinner this year?"

Rosa rolled her eyes. "Sometimes I think you don't listen to a word I say. I told you two weeks ago that I'll be cooking dinner this year."

"Anything you want me to do, or bring?"

"No, thanks. Laura asked the same question. You two work every day. I'm retired, remember? I have much more time to cook a Thanksgiving dinner."

He turned on the dishwasher. "If you change your mind, let me know." He glanced at his watch. "At the risk of being accused of eating and run-

ning, I'd better get going. I have some plans I
need to go over before tomorrow."

"All right, honey." She walked him to the door.
She held her tongue when he reminded her to set
the alarm.

On Friday Ben received a call from Kendall. "I'm
sorry to bother you, Ben. I have a problem in the
house. I thought about calling the gas company, but
I don't smell gas. I'll feel foolish if it's something
minor."

"The gas company? What's wrong?"

"The furnace isn't working. The circuit breaker
won't hold. Everytime I push it, it clicks off again.
Is there something you can tell me to do that I
haven't thought about?"

A possibility occurred to him. "I probably need
to come and take a look."

"I don't want to put you to that trouble."

"It's no trouble, Kendall. If there's something
wrong with the furnace, I should know about it. I
can come by this evening."

"I have a meeting with a client this evening.
Tomorrow morning or early afternoon would be
better if that's not a problem."

"Tomorrow's fine. Say about noon or twelve-
thirty?"

Kendall stepped out of the tub late Saturday
morning, and had barely donned her robe when
the telephone rang. A few minutes later, she played
back the message and breathed a sigh of relief

when she heard her mother's voice. She was in no mood to talk to her mother, but she dialed the number anyway.

"Hi, Mom, I was in the tub when you called. What's up?"

"I called to ask you if you're planning to come home for Thanksgiving."

It was on the tip of Kendall's tongue to tell her mother that she was already at home. "No, I can't make it for Thanksgiving."

"You haven't been home in two years, Kendall."

"I realize that, Mom. You know I just moved a month ago. I'm still getting settled in."

"Yes, I know you moved recently. In fact, that was the other thing I wanted to ask you about. Did Scott get in touch with you?"

Kendall took a deep breath. That answered the question that had been on her mind. "He called. Why did you give him my number?"

"He asked for it. He said it was important that he talk to you."

"I'm not interested in anything Scott has to say."

"What harm would it do to talk to him, Kendall?"

"Mom, I'm not going to have this discussion with you. I have to go now. I'm going out and I'm in the middle of getting dressed." She hated lying to her mother, but it was the only way to get her off the phone quickly.

"I'm sorry. Forgive me for interfering with your busy social life."

Kendall's spine stiffened. If it had come from someone else, she might have seen some humor in those words. Coming from her mother, the words and tone were no surprise.

"Good-bye, Mom." She hung up the phone without waiting for her mother's response.

Kendall tried to put her mother's confession out of her mind as she finished dressing. She had already guessed the truth. Having it confirmed should not make any difference.

The doorbell rang just as she finished making her bed. She made the mistake of assuming Ben had arrived early. Her eyes widened when she opened the door to find Scott standing on her porch.

"Hi, K.C. Why didn't you call me?"

Her mother's telephone call should have served as a warning. "What are you doing here, Scott?"

He made a move to enter. She tried to close the door. He grabbed the side of the door and slid his foot into the opening.

"I just want to talk, K.C. I came to apologize."

Kendall said a prayer of thanks when she spied Ben a few feet behind Scott. "I think you'd better leave, Scott."

"Why won't at least hear me out?" He turned abruptly when Ben spoke.

"The lady asked you to leave."

Scott frowned. He looked at Kendall, and then turned back toward Ben. "Who are you?"

"I'm a friend, not that it's any of your business."

Ben moved forward, subtlely edging Scott away from the door. Staring down at him from the advantage of five inches, Ben looked Scott in the eye.

"I repeat, the lady asked you to leave."

Scott clenched his jaw. "Fine, I'll leave." He turned and stomped down the stairs.

Kendall took a deep breath. She stepped aside to let Ben enter.

"Are you okay, Kendall?"

"I'm fine. I tried it again today, but it's still not working."

His question had nothing to do with the furnace problem. She obviously had no intention of discussing her visitor. Ben followed her to the basement.

Instead of going to the furnace, he went to the back of the room and opened the box with the circuit breakers. He shook his head. It was as he suspected. He and Barney would have a talk on Monday. How many times did Ben have to tell him that a furnace should always be on its own separate line and circuit breaker?

"What's the problem?" she asked.

"My electrician was supposed to set up a separate circuit breaker for the furnace. I'll have someone here shortly to fix it."

"It doesn't have to be done today."

"We're in for some pretty chilly weather. I think it's best to fix it as soon as possible unless you have to go out."

"No, I'm not going anywhere."

He took his cell phone from his jacket pocket. "Hi, Joe, it's Ben. We have a problem. Can you come and install a circuit breaker today?" He paused, and then gave him the address. "How soon can you get here?" He nodded. "Okay, thanks."

"I'm glad it wasn't just something I overlooked. I was feeling pretty stupid."

He shook his head. "You were right to call me. I'm sorry about this. It shouldn't have happened. It could have been a disaster if you hadn't noticed the problem until the middle of the night when the temperature was about twenty degrees."

"I don't even want to think about that possibility."

"Joe won't be able to get here for about an hour."

She started up the stairs. "Have you had lunch? I can make you a sandwich or I have some leftover chili."

"You don't have to do that."

"I know I don't have to. You didn't have to come out here so quickly to fix the furnace either." She shrugged. "Besides, I'm hungry myself. It's no big deal."

"You mentioned leftover chili. Is it homemade?"

"Yes. It's not really hot, though."

"You don't like spicy food?"

"Maybe just a little spicy."

"Thanks, I'll take you up on your offer."

Fifteen minutes later, they sat down to lunch. Ben took a spoonful of the chili and nodded. "It's very good."

"Thanks."

They ate in silence for a few minutes before Ben succumbed to curiosity. "Who was that man who was here when I arrived?"

Kendall was not surprised at the question. She took a deep breath and folded her hands on top of the table.

"He's my ex-husband."

"How long have you been divorced?"

"Almost five years. Long enough that he should be out of my life for good."

"I guess he doesn't see it that way." Ben reached across the table and laid his hand on top of hers. "If I'm asking too many questions, just say so."

She focused her attention on her bowl and shook her head. "I don't mind."

Was her ex-husband the source of the sadness in her eyes? During her exchange with Scott, Ben had noticed a new expression, fear. That bothered him more than the sadness.

Although she said she had no objection to his questions, Ben sensed that he had reached the limit for now. He removed his hand from hers and took a sip of water.

In the past few minutes she had given him an important, if incomplete, piece of information. Her words, and expressions, told him more than he had learned in an entire evening on their first date.

His conscience prodded him to explain about breaking their second date. He ignored it. He was not ready to broach that subject, and the discussion that was likely to follow.

Kendall wrinkled her forehead. He seemed genuinely concerned. Surprising for someone who had broken their date without even a follow-up call to explain.

They finished eating a few minutes before Joe arrived. Ben introduced him to Kendall. He then led Joe to the basement while Kendall finished clearing the table. She was relaxing in the living room when they returned.

"I'm going to shove off, Ben."

"Okay, Joe. Thanks."

Kendall added her thanks and rose from the sofa. Joe held up his hand. "Don't bother. I'll let myself out."

After Joe left, Ben turned to Kendall. "You're all set. The separate circuit breaker should take care of the problem."

She walked him to the door. "Thanks, Ben."

"If you have any other problems, don't hesitate to call me."

A moment later, he was gone. Kendall walked slowly back to the living room. He had no idea how glad she was that he had arrived a few minutes after Scott. Would that make Scott think twice about returning? She would just have to be more careful.

CHAPTER 5

Scott's persistent calling and her confrontation with him led to more sleepless nights for Kendall. She was unaware of the toll it had taken until Valerie commented on her appearance when she saw her on Thanksgiving.

"Are you all right, Kendall?"

Kendall bristled. She had never told her friend about her calls from Scott. She had never told her, or anyone else, the reason her marriage had ended.

"What do you mean?"

"You look exhausted. Don't you think it might be wise to cut down on the weekend parties?"

"I'll be okay. I don't have anything planned until Ben's party on the eleventh."

"What about the rest of December?"

"I have a luncheon for twenty-two on the eighteenth. Then I'm free until the end of January."

Valerie shook her head. "And what about all the planning for your regular job?"

Kendall shrugged. "That's easier than the others. I don't have to worry about expense constraints. I just make the basic arrangements and hire whoever I need to handle them."

Later that afternoon, the two women were alone in the kitchen when Valerie shared a disturbing bit of information. "I almost forgot to tell you. Guess who Francine is dating."

"Who?"

"Darren."

Kendall frowned. "The sleaze from your office?"

Valerie's eyes widened. "I'm surprised at you. You only met him once." She tilted her head to the side. "You're right. He is a sleaze, but what made you come to that conclusion?"

"It doesn't take much for me to recognize a sleaze. I was married to one."

"You've never talked about your husband before."

"I didn't want to bore you with details of the worst decision of my life." She sighed. "Even though we're good friends, I was embarrassed at being such a fool."

Valerie shook her head. "You can't be serious about being embarrassed. Girlfriend, I guess we've all been there at one time or another when it comes to men."

Kendall nodded. "Which brings us back to Francine and Darren. How did she meet him?"

"That's the sad part. I introduced them. We met at my office to go to the movies while you were in Atlanta." She raised an eyebrow. "I have to say that he was much more pleasant than he was when *you* met him."

Kendall made no comment about that observation. For a man like Darren, the fact that Francine was tall, slim, and pretty would be enough to account for the difference in his reaction.

"By the way, if you thought he was unpleasant before, that was nothing," Valerie said. "He's really unhappy with me now."

"Why?"

Valerie sighed. "He screwed up the Sterling sale and Mr. Briggs turned it over to me."

Kendall drew in her breath. "What happened?"

"When she signed the agreement, the owner didn't realize that Mueller was planning to level the mansion to build his golf course and condos."

"So how did you get the sale?"

"The client called one day when Darren was out. She was really upset because she had just learned about Mueller's intentions. She's not exactly poor, but she was afraid that Mueller would sue if she backed out. With what he could claim as a loss from canceling his project, the suit could cost her millions. She couldn't afford that kind of loss.

"She went on and on about how the property had been in her family for generations. I think she was actually in tears."

"What did you tell her?"

"I suggested she call Sheila Donovan at the Historical Society." She shook her head. "When she talked about the age of the mansion, I was surprised that she had never considered that they might be interested."

Valerie took a deep breath. "Anyway, Sheila went through some letters and journals that Mrs. Ferguson had saved. It appears that the mansion may have been a stop on the Underground Railroad. Sheila contacted some of the local African American organizations and they went to work researching the property's history.

"Now there's an injunction against any changes being made to the mansion until the investigation is completed. If the mansion is declared a historic landmark, it means that Mueller could still do whatever he wants with most of the land. But he couldn't do anything that would interfere with the mansion itself and the portion of the land inside of the fence."

"And he won't go for that?"

She shook her head. "I talked to him. He insists the mansion is in the way for what he has planned. Talk about someone being fit to be tied."

"I still don't understand how you got involved."

"The owner, Mrs. Ferguson, told her children what had happened and that Darren had been the one to urge her to sign the agreement. If the Historical Society comes through, it could put Mueller out of the picture. We'll be back to square one trying to find a buyer. Briggs knew that Mrs. Ferguson wouldn't be likely to sign another contract when the time runs out on this one. At least, not if Darren is handling the deal."

"Do you think you'll be able to find a buyer for just the land?"

She shrugged. "Who knows? Having the mansion on the property might be a plus for someone."

Kendall shook her head. "Good luck. I hope the commission is worth the aggravation."

"I'm used to Darren. Besides, if I make this sale it'll more than make up for his attitude."

* * *

The first Saturday in December, Kendall had her final meeting with Ben to go over his party plans. When he arrived, she ushered him into the living room.

"Would you like a drink?"

He shook his head. "No, thanks, I'm fine."

"Have a seat. I'll get the decorations."

She returned a few minutes later carrying a cardboard box. When she appeared in the doorway, he stood up and came forward, taking the box from her.

"Where do you want me to put it?"

"Just set it on the coffee table."

After he had examined the items, she carefully returned them to the carton. "Has the number of guests changed?"

He shook his head. "It should be the same as the original number I gave you."

"Then we should be set. I'll need to get into the building early in the afternoon. I've arranged for the rental company to come at one-thirty with the tables, chairs, and dance floor."

He frowned. "You won't have to stay there all day, will you?"

"I hope not. After I get the tables and chairs in place, I should have a few hours before I have to come back with the tablecloths, napkins, and decorations." She bit her lip. "Is that a problem? If you give me a key, you won't have to be there."

He waved away her suggestion. "No, no, that's not a problem. In fact, I had talked to Jim about helping to set up the table and chairs."

"You don't have to do that. You hired me to arrange the party."

"That's right, I hired you to arrange the party.

That meant the decorations and hiring the caterer and the DJ. If the party was at a regular banquet room, you wouldn't have to worry about moving furniture."

She shrugged. "I guess you have a point."

"I have one more question." He rubbed his chin. "It's really more of a request than a question."

"What is it?"

"I'd like for you to join the party. I'm sure the caterer will have his own people to oversee the food service. Once everything is set up, you'll be able to sit back and enjoy your hard work."

"That's an unusual request."

"I just don't see any reason for you to be on duty all evening. You'll have put in a lot of hard work before the party starts. I think you should be able to enjoy the results of your hard work."

Kendall did not answer immediately. Why was he so concerned about her joining the party? Was this an attempt to appease his conscience? If so, it was a little late for that. Why hadn't he simply explained and apologized?

"Kendall?"

She refocused her attention on his request. "Sure, if that's what you want. I had planned to change clothes after I get everything set up anyway."

The telephone rang as she rose to walk him to the door. Forgetting her newly acquired habit of screening her calls, she answered it.

Without even a "hello," Jackie launched into her tirade as soon as she heard Kendall's voice. "Why are you so mean-spirited and narrow-minded? I don't think Scott's asking a lot, just a few minutes of your time. For you to have him thrown out of your house was completely uncalled for."

"Mom, I told you before, I'm not going to have this discussion with you."

"Fine, we'll talk about it when you come for Christmas."

"I won't be there for Christmas."

"I can't believe you're refusing to come home for Christmas."

"I don't know why you're so surprised."

Jackie grunted. "You're right, I shouldn't be surprised. You haven't been home for two years."

"You said that before."

"Well, it bears repeating. You seem determined to cut me out of your life. The way you've been treating me, your father's probably turning over in his grave."

That was the final straw. "I have to go. Good-bye, Mother."

She hung up the telephone and took a deep breath. She had been temporarily oblivious to Ben's presence. She turned abruptly to face him when he cleared his throat.

"I couldn't help overhearing. Don't you think you were a little harsh?"

She raised an eyebrow. "I beg your pardon?"

"Wasn't that your mother?"

"Yes."

"You cut her off rather abruptly. After all, she is your mother."

Kendall was in no mood to be rebuked. "That's right, she's my mother. That is, she gave birth to me. You know nothing about our relationship." She put her hand on her hip. "You think I'm being harsh? I think you're being presumptuous to give me advice about our relationship." She raised an eyebrow. "Furthermore, it's really none . . ." She stopped short.

He finished her sentence. "None of my business?" He took a deep breath. "You're right." He made no further comment. Neither did he apologize for his accusation.

They stared at each other for a moment. Finally, they each came to the conclusion that any further words were likely to lead to a more heated discussion.

She looked away from him and continued toward the door. After a brief glance in her direction, he sighed and left.

Ben sat in his car for a few minutes, reflecting. He had expected that she would be close to her mother considering that there were only the two of them. She had no brothers or sisters and her mother was widowed. That was one of the reasons he was so upset by her attitude. He could not imagine refusing to spend the holiday with his family.

Thinking of his family reminded him that his mother was expecting him for dinner. He backed out of the driveway.

Rosa was attuned to her son's moods. Today he was pensive, not exactly worried, more confused. She held her questions until after dinner when they were enjoying their final cups of coffee.

"What's the problem, son?"

He sipped his coffee. "What makes you think there's a problem?"

"I'm your mother, remember? I know when something's bothering you." She shrugged. "You're an adult. If you don't want to discuss it, that's fine."

He sighed. "It's no big deal. I'm just a little disappointed."

"In what?"

"Not what, who."

She nodded slowly. "I see."

He held up his hand. "I know, I know. We've had this conversation before. What can I tell you? I thought I had overcome that tendency."

"In that case, this person must mean a lot to you. Who is she?"

He rested his forearms on the table. "What makes you think it's a 'she'?" He held up his hand again when he saw the expression on her face. "Never mind. It's Kendall."

"The young lady who's arranging the Christmas party?"

He nodded. "I had a meeting with her today. I overheard a conversation she had with her mother on the phone. I didn't like the way Kendall talked to her."

Rosa raised and eyebrow. "You didn't like the way she talked to her mother?" She closed her eyes and shook her head. "Tell me you didn't tell her that."

"Not exactly. I suggested that she was a little harsh."

"And?"

He shrugged. "And she told me to mind my own business."

She nodded. "I hate to be the one to tell you this, son. She was right." Rosa put her hand on his arm. "Ben, you have no idea what she may have been through with her mother. It's possible that she has good reason to be harsh."

His mother's words conjured up a picture of sad brown eyes. He had assumed that her ex-husband was responsible for that expression. Maybe his mother had hit upon the real source. It was a possibility he had overlooked.

Rosa patted his hand. "Son, if you care about

Kendall, you should at least give her the benefit of the doubt."

The afternoon of the party, Kendall packed up the items for her return trip to the hall. She hung her garment bag on the hook inside the car and headed back to make the final preparations for the party.

Jim and Ben had been on hand earlier to set up the tables and chairs. When the florist delivered the poinsettias, they had followed directions for their placement.

She let herself into the building with the key Ben had given her. All of the tables were covered and the centerpieces arranged when Ben arrived. She glanced toward the doorway. Her eyes widened.

Kendall's peace of mind could have done without the sight of Ben Whitaker in a tuxedo. She was having enough problems coping with his physical appeal. She might have been able to overcome that attraction if she had not seen the gentle, compassionate side of him.

She liked him. In spite of his abrupt cancellation of their second date, she liked him. In spite of his disapproval of her relationship with her mother, she liked him.

She should never have agreed to plan his party. He would have gone out of her life and she would have eventually put him out of her mind.

Instead, in the back of her mind, there had been a glimmer of hope, until their last disagreement. His reaction to her conversation with her mother had effectively killed that hope, although it had done little to lessen his appeal.

"I see you've almost finished. I had planned to arrive early enough to lend a hand." He looked around the room. "It looks great."

"When the tree and candles are lit, it'll be even better."

He nodded. "What can I do to help?"

She hesitated. His attitude threw her completely off balance. She had attributed his friendliness that morning to Jim's presence. At the least, she had expected him to be cool and detached when they were alone again. She had even expected some sign that he regretted his request that she join the party. Was he simply resigned to living with his earlier decision?

She pushed those thoughts aside and lifted a stack of prefolded napkins from a box on the floor. "You can help me put these in place. The only thing left after that is to put the favors on the tables."

He shed his jacket and draped it over the back of a chair. Kendall had trouble concentrating on her task. Her gaze drifted periodically to his figure as he made the rounds of the tables. The shirt did not conceal the flexing muscles in his arms and shoulders when he moved. She unconsciously let out a sigh.

By six o'clock their work was complete and the caterer had arrived. Kendall was explaining the setup when the DJ arrived.

Half an hour later, she left to get her garment bag from the car. When she returned, she excused herself to get dressed. "I won't be long."

Her gown was a simple A-line style of dark red

velvet. She did not recall the square-cut neckline revealing this much cleavage when she tried it on in the store. The garnet earrings and pendant set in gold had been a gift to herself to celebrate the final decree of her divorce. They had been a bargain, but she could never have afforded even this small luxury if she had stayed married to that parasite.

The matching pumps and gold-and-red beaded bag provided the final touch. After applying her makeup, she combed her hair. The side-parted tresses were styled into soft curves feathered against her cheeks. She checked her reflection in the mirror, took a deep breath, and left the ladies' room.

A few guests had arrived when she returned to the main room. Ben's eyes widened when he saw her. The dark red velvet lent a luster to her skin. A smile lit his face. He came toward her with his hand outstretched.

She put her hand in his. She was uncertain if it was the warmth of his hand or the look in his eyes that caused the heat to rise in her cheeks. The heat rose a few degrees when he lowered his gaze, pausing at the tempting cleavage, before taking in the rest of the vision in front of him. His next words dispelled the thought that he regretted including her in the general festivities.

"You look beautiful," he murmured. "Come with me. I want you to meet my family."

After he performed the introductions, Rosa commented, "The decorations are beautiful, Kendall."

"Thank you."

Her son's reaction to this young woman had not been lost on Rosa. There was a gleam in his eyes that she had never seen before, not even when he was married.

She now understood why he was so upset over Kendall's treatment of her mother. Family ties had always been at the center of her son's life. A relationship with a woman who showed little concern for her mother could cause quite a bit of discord.

Soon the room began filling up. Still holding Kendall's hand, Ben led his family to a table near the dance floor. He pulled out a chair and gestured for Kendall to have a seat.

She hesitated. "I really should be overseeing the arrangements."

Ben looked at the caterer, whose staff had finished arranging the food and was standing behind or near the tables. "It looks to me as if the caterer has everything under control."

Rosa seconded his statement. "You've done a wonderful job, Kendall. Sit back and enjoy your hard work. I'm sure if a problem arises, the caterer will come and get you."

Kendall gave in and took her seat. She expected Ben to follow his own suggestion. Instead, he looked across the room at the people coming in the door.

"I'll be back in a few minutes."

Rosa watched Kendall, whose gaze never left Ben. Whatever put that gleam in her son's eyes was not one-sided. Whether it was strong enough to overcome any problems remained to be seen.

Ben crossed the room and met the guests as they entered, taking time to shake hands and greet each one. He was taken aback when Sam Farley entered with Tina Carson, who was on Ben's clerical staff.

"Hi, Tina." He recovered quickly from his surprise and held out his hand. "Hi, Sam, it's been a while."

Tina glanced from one man to the other. "I didn't know you knew Ben."

Ben enlightened her. "Sam and I worked together years ago."

"Oh," she said. The tension she sensed between the two men must be her imagination. Why would Sam agree to accompany her if there was bad blood between them? She set those thoughts aside.

"The decorations are beautiful," she said.

"Yes, they are. I'll pass your compliment on to Kendall." He stepped aside. "Enjoy yourselves."

"Thanks, I'm sure we will."

Ben rubbed his chin as they walked away. Sam Farley was the last person he'd expected to see at his company party. A few minutes later, he rejoined his family.

Rosa raised an eyebrow. "Was that Sam Farley I saw come in?"

Ben nodded.

"What's he doing here?"

"He's Tina Carson's date."

Rosa's reaction was not lost on Kendall. "Who's Sam Farley?"

"He was my partner when I first started the business."

Rosa satisfied the curiosity that Kendall was too polite to express. "Ben has always made it a practice to do repairs for low-income elderly people for little more than the cost of materials. Sam didn't like that. It wasn't costing him anything, but he hinted that Ben was subsidizing the repairs with company funds. They dissolved the partnership and Ben went on his own."

"Mom, you're boring Kendall."

If she had not known about Mabel Jenkins, Kendall might have considered Rosa's comments to be nothing more than a mother's exaggerated pride. Mabel was evidently only one of many who had been helped by Ben Whitaker.

Kendall shook her head. "She's not boring me. What's Sam doing now?"

Rosa shrugged and looked at her son.

"He's still a building contractor. I've heard rumors that his company's in financial trouble. You never know how much truth there is to rumors, though." He patted Kendall's hand and then looked at his mother. "Enough talk about Sam Farley. We're here to celebrate, not relive history."

Later that evening, the guests were enjoying dessert when Ben excused himself and crossed the dance floor. Borrowing the DJ's microphone, he gently tapped it.

"I hope you're all enjoying the evening. I just want to take a few minutes of your time to thank you. A few of you have been with me since I started this company fourteen years ago. Others have only worked for me for a few years, but I'm grateful to all of you. Your hard work and support are responsible for the success of this company."

He smiled. "There's someone that we all have to thank for the success of this evening." He gestured toward the table he had left a few minutes earlier. "A few of you have commented on the decorations. Kendall, would you stand up?"

She would have preferred to slide under the table. Heat diffused her face as she rose from her seat.

"This is Kendall Chase. She's responsible for the decorations and for planning this entire evening."

This statement was greeted with spontaneous applause. Kendall could only take a few seconds of this attention. Then she nodded and took her seat.

Ben continued. "Thank you again. I hope you have a joyful and peaceful holiday."

He handed the microphone back to the DJ and started to return to his seat. He stopped when Evelyn approached him. She took his arm and urged him back toward the DJ's station. She took the microphone from the DJ.

"As one of those people who's worked for you since the beginning, I've been elected to make an announcement."

She motioned to another employee nearby. He handed her a gift-wrapped box and returned to his seat.

"This is from all of your employees. A lot of people these days don't enjoy what they do. If one of those who enjoys his work happens to be your boss, you feel the effects of that enjoyment, too. We've all come to appreciate you for your integrity and fairness. It may sound strange to some people when I say that working for you has been a pleasure." She handed him the box. "Thank you for your support and generosity."

Accompanied by an outburst of applause, Ben accepted the package and the microphone. He took a deep breath. "I don't know what to say except to thank you again. Enjoy the evening."

Evelyn's speech revealed to Kendall another facet of Ben's personality. In spite of her differences with him, she was not surprised that his employees thought so highly of him.

What did surprise her was his reaction. This man who exuded self-confidence was obviously embarrassed by the praise that had been showered on him.

He hugged Evelyn and the two of them returned to their seats, turning the festivities over to the DJ. As he took his seat, Ben looked at his mother's smiling face.

"Did you know about this?"

"Evelyn hinted that the employees wanted to do something special for you. She didn't say what they had in mind."

Kendall turned toward Ben. She tilted her head to the side. "After you insisted that I stand to be recognized, I think it was only fair that you have the tables turned on you."

He had never been comfortable being the center of attention. Rosa took pity on him, effectively changing the subject by asking Kendall about her regular job.

The group chatted for a while before Laura and Craig excused themselves to join the dancers. A few minutes later, the music changed to a slow love song.

Ben smiled. He had looked forward to this opportunity for days. It was one of the reasons he had suggested that Kendall be prepared to join the festivities. He rose from his seat and moved to stand a few inches behind her. Placing his hands on the back of her chair, he suggested, "Shall we join them?"

He pulled her chair out and she stood up. Then she placed her hand in his outstretched palm. She took a deep breath and followed him to an empty spot on the dance floor.

Still holding her hand, he encircled her waist with his other arm. He glanced down. The view afforded him from that vantage point was even more tempting than when he was seated beside her. He pulled her closer.

Kendall's free hand rested on his shoulder. The rapid thumping of her heart was only the beginning. Even through the fabric, her breasts tingled from brushing against his chest as they moved in time to the music.

One dance was not enough for Ben. The DJ must have read his mind. The next number was another ballad, and Ben made no move to leave the dance floor. Instead, he let go of Kendall's hand and slipped his other arm around her, his palm resting at the curve just below her waist.

Kendall automatically raised her free hand to rest it on his other shoulder. She looked up into his face and swallowed hard. She had observed that expression on the faces of other people enough times to recognize desire. She had never before seen that particular expression directed at her.

The remainder of the evening passed much too quickly to suit Ben. When the guests started leaving, he excused himself to take care of his financial responsibilities. When Kendall moved to stand up, he placed his hand on her arm.

"I'll take care of it."

All of the guests had soon departed, including Ben's family. He and Kendall waited while the caterer and DJ packed up. Then he turned to Kendall.

"You're not planning to pack up everything to-night, are you?"

She shook her head. "If you don't mind my keeping the key you gave me, I'll do it tomorrow. The rental company is coming to pick up the tables and chairs at one-thirty. I don't really have much to collect."

She had insisted that the centerpieces and decorations belonged to him since their cost had been included in her fee. The centerpieces and some of the poinsettias had been given away as door prizes.

"I'll pick you up and come with you."

She opened her mouth and closed it again when he raised an eyebrow. "Thanks. If I get here an hour or so before the rental company, I'll be packed up before they arrive."

A few minutes later, Ben retrieved their coats. Once again, his hand brushed her neck as he helped her on with her coat. Her skin was so soft. If this exposed area was an indication of the silkiness of the skin that lay beneath the fabric, he wanted more than an accidental touch.

He walked with her to her car and waited until she was settled behind the wheel. "I'm parked over there. Wait for me and I'll follow you home."

Ben pulled into Kendall's driveway as she opened the garage door. She drove into the garage, exited her car, and waited for him.

He took her hand in his. "Thank you for making the party a big success."

"You're welcome. I'm glad everyone enjoyed themselves."

He leaned over and kissed her cheek. "I'll see you tomorrow."

She nodded and watched him return to his car. Then she closed the door.

He got behind the wheel of his car and waited until the lights went on in a room upstairs. Then he started the car and backed out of the driveway.

After the rental company had departed the next day, Ben suggested they stop for dinner before returning to her house. "There's a little restaurant on the route to your house. I thought that might be a good place to stop. It's informal and we don't have to worry about reservations."

"That sounds fine."

When they were settled in the restaurant, Kendall focused her attention on the menu. That did not keep the questions from running through her mind.

What was she doing here? His attitude and parting kiss the previous night had baffled her. Now she was totally confused. She told herself not to read too much into his last-minute invitation. It was late afternoon and neither of them had eaten since breakfast.

"Have you been here before?"

She shook her head.

"Then I suggest the pot roast. It's very good, just like homemade."

"How can I refuse that recommendation?"

When Ben took her home, he helped carry her boxes into the house and stow them away. Then she walked him to the door.

Instead of opening the door, he turned to face her. "How about having dinner with me on Saturday?"

She hesitated. Why was he doing this again? "I can't. I have a luncheon on Saturday."

Was she really busy or was she reluctant to trust another invitation from him? It was his own fault. Maybe he had waited too long to clear the air. He should have apologized weeks ago. He had no real excuse for putting it off. The time had never seemed quite right. His comment on her relationship with her mother certainly had not helped his cause.

"I see. Maybe another time."

He hid his disappointment. He was determined to overcome the hurdles. He wanted to get to know her better. He had sensed a sweet, generous spirit in her that contradicted her harsh response to her mother. He had to know which woman was the real Kendall. Or was it as his mother suggested? Was her harshness merely a defense to protect that sweet generous spirit?

CHAPTER 6

Kendall arrived home a little after four-thirty on Saturday. By six o'clock, she had changed her clothes and was relaxing in the living room when the doorbell rang. After checking through the peephole, she opened the door to Ben.

"I thought we had canceled dinner," she said, stepping aside to let him enter.

He shook his head. "Not exactly," he reminded her, holding up a large paper bag. "We canceled plans to go out." He shrugged. "You have to eat, though."

She stared at him. Some people might take a look at her and disagree with his statement.

Ben misunderstood her expression. "I hope you don't mind my coming by unannounced. Maybe I should have called first." He sighed and shrugged. "I thought after working all week and again today, you might not feel like cooking."

"It's all right. I don't mind your not calling first."

He raised an eyebrow. "You haven't eaten dinner, have you?"

"No, I haven't. I hadn't really thought about dinner."

"I hope you like Chinese."

"Some of it, yes."

"Good. I brought a few dishes. At least one of them must be something you like."

As she led the way to the dining room, his gaze automatically followed the movement of her hips in the soft velour robe. He would never tire of watching her graceful moves. More than that, he liked the feel of her in his arms.

While he unpacked the cartons, she set the table. They sat down to eat a few minutes later.

"How was the luncheon?"

"The luncheon went well. I'm glad I have a break until well after the holidays."

They talked as they ate. They had almost finished their meal when Ben asked, "Do you have any special plans for Christmas?"

She focused her attention on her plate. "You already know that I won't be going to Philadelphia. I'm having dinner with Francine and her family."

He reached across the table and lifted her chin, looking her in the eye. "Speaking of Philadelphia, I owe you an apology. I've been thinking about what I said to you. My comment on your conversation with your mother was out of line. You were right. It was none of my business. I certainly had no right to pass judgment. Will you forgive me?"

She stared at him. She could hardly believe her ears. "I may have overreacted myself. Of course I accept your apology."

He smiled. "Good."

"Since we seem to be clearing the air, I have to ask you a question."

He should have expected that she would want other answers. His smile faded when the question came.

"Why did you cancel our second date? I remember that you said something had come up. It just seemed awfully sudden and you never really explained."

He took a deep breath. He could put it off no longer. "You're right. I should have explained before now. I owe you an apology for that, too. The truth is that I saw a man leaving your apartment as I drove up. I saw him kiss you."

She frowned. "A man leaving my apartment and kissing me?" She shook her head.

"I'm embarrassed to say that I jumped to the conclusion that you were already involved with someone and I didn't want to get tangled up in that kind of situation." He cleared his throat. "I met the man later. He's your real-estate agent's husband."

"Gary?" She wrinkled her forehead. Then her eyes widened. "You thought I was having an affair with Gary?" She shook her head again. "He asked me to help him plan Valerie's surprise party. He was so grateful, I guess he kissed me on the cheek as he was leaving. I don't even remember."

"When I saw the three of you together I realized that I must have been mistaken. I guess it's my day for apologies. Will you accept another one?"

He held his breath, hoping that an apology would suffice, at least for the moment. He was not ready to explain the underlying reason for his assumption and action.

She nodded. "Of course, I was just curious."

She was still curious. Why was he so concerned about the possibility that she was involved with another man? Why would he jump to that conclusion just seeing Gary kiss her on the cheek? Whatever the underlying causes for his error, it was obvious that he was not willing to explain further.

He smiled. "Thank you. A lot of women might not be so quick to forgive."

She shook her head. "I'm sure we've all been guilty of jumping to conclusions at one time or another. It's not important now." She suddenly recognized the truth of her last statement. For him to admit such an mistake indicated that her forgiveness was important to him. What had happened before this moment no longer mattered.

When they had finished eating, Ben helped clear the table. He glanced at the clock. "I should be going. You're probably exhausted and too polite to say so."

She walked him to the door and turned off the alarm. She turned to face him, unconsciously licking her lips. He chose to take her action as an invitation. He stepped closer and took her in his arms. His intention unmistakable, he hesitated a few seconds to give her just long enough to protest if she objected.

He lowered his head slowly until his mouth settled on hers. His tongue outlined her lips, coaxing them apart. His tongue explored the sweet interior.

He pulled her closer, lightly crushing her soft breasts against his chest. With one hand splayed across her back, the other settled first on the curve just below her waist and then moved lower, gently squeezing her cheeks.

Kendall's arms encircled his waist. Lightheaded, her heart racing, she clung to him. Her tongue played tag with his before darting forward to begin her own exploration. The warm pressure of his hand penetrated the fabric of her robe and spread through her body.

Their kiss ended abruptly when the doorbell rang. The unexpected noise broke the spell. Frowning, she looked up into his eyes.

"You're not expecting company, are you?"

"No." She moved closer to the door, turned on the porch light, and peeked out. Her eyes widened and then narrowed. She clenched her jaw and opened the door.

"What are you doing here again, Scott?"

"I just want to talk."

"How many times do I have to tell you, we have nothing to talk about. You'd better leave."

"Just hear me out."

Ben moved closer, making himself visible to the unwelcome visitor. "The lady asked you to leave."

Scott stepped back a few inches. He glanced at Kendall, taking note of her robe.

"What's he doing here? Are you living with him?"

Kendall took a deep breath.

Ben answered for her. "I think you'd better leave. I'm getting tired of repeating myself. It's really none of your business what I'm doing here."

"It is my business. She's my wife."

"Ex-wife," Kendall said through clenched teeth.

"We're still married in the sight of God," he insisted.

That was too much for Kendall. She reached up and slapped him with all of the frustration and anger that had festered for years.

It took him a few seconds to recover. Then he took a step forward. He stopped abruptly when Ben also moved forward.

Kendall's eyebrow shot up. "You have the nerve to bring God into this? God had nothing to do with our marriage. Your greed and laziness and my gullibility and stupidity are responsible for our marriage. And you're responsible for it ending."

"For your information, I came to ask you to forgive me."

"Okay, you've asked. Now you can leave."

"You call yourself a Christian. Aren't Christians supposed to be forgiving?"

"Whether or not I forgive you is between God and me. Forgiveness is one thing; putting up with having any contact with you is another."

He opened his mouth to respond.

She held up her hand. "Don't say another word, Scott. We both know that you don't really want my forgiveness. Get out of here. If you ever call me again or come here, I will call the police." Without another word, she slammed the door.

She turned off the porch light and returned to the living room. With her arms folded tightly across her chest, she sank down onto the sofa. She focused on the cold fireplace, willing the trembling to stop.

Ben lingered at the door for a few minutes. Thanks to the streetlight, he saw Scott get into a silver-colored coupe and drive away. He then joined Kendall in the living room and took a seat beside her. When he gently pried her arms apart, her entire body trembled. He moved closer and took her in his arms.

The warmth of his body slowly banished the

chill that had settled in her chest. She took a deep breath.

"I don't usually lose control like that."

"Under the circumstances, maybe it's something you should have done a long time ago."

She looked up into his eyes. She was not accustomed to the desire she had seen in his eyes more than once. She was even less accustomed to the tenderness she saw there now.

The fear Ben glimpsed in her expression aroused his anger and frustration. Anger at Scott for being responsible for the fear in those gentle brown eyes. Frustration that there was little he could do to ease that fear.

"I won't ask you if you're all right. You'd feel obliged to lie and tell me you're fine."

She laid her head against his chest. Her voice was little more than a whisper. "I'll be all right. It was just so unexpected having him show up again."

He hesitated a moment. "At the risk of being accused of meddling, I have to ask. Have you considered getting a restraining order?"

She sighed. "I have one. That's why I told him I'd call the police if he contacted me again."

Although he had suggested it, Ben was aware that having a restraining order was sometimes useless. "Maybe I should stay here tonight."

She raised her head and met his steady gaze. "Stay here?"

"You do have a guest room, don't you?"

"Yes, but that's not necessary, Ben."

"I know. Indulge me?"

She could not believe that Scott would actually try to break into the house. Even so, the prospect of his returning that evening was unsettling. She nodded.

"I'll go make up the guest room." She stood up and started toward the stairs.

He followed her. "I'll help. It's the least I can do since I'm an uninvited guest."

Together they made up the bed in the guest room. "I'll get some towels. There's an extra toothbrush, toothpaste, and soap in the bathroom next door." She ran her hand through her hair. "I guess that's it."

"I'll manage." He took her hand in his, leaned over, and kissed her cheek. "Get a good night's sleep."

She nodded. "I will."

The next morning, Kendall awoke feeling surprisingly well-rested. When she heard the shower running in the guest bathroom, she knew why. Just knowing that Ben was in the house had eased the tension caused by Scott's visit.

She got out of bed, slipped into her robe, and made her way downstairs. She had just poured herself a mug of coffee when Ben appeared in the doorway.

"Good morning." He sniffed. "Coffee smells good."

She poured another mug as he came toward her. She handed it to him and gestured to the containers on the counter. "Help yourself to sugar and cream. What would you like to eat? I have eggs, no bacon or sausage, though. I could make an omelet, if you like. I have some blueberry muffins, English muffins, and bread for toast."

A short time later they sat down to a breakfast of scrambled eggs, English muffins, orange juice, and coffee. "Was the bed comfortable? I've been meaning to try it out myself."

"The bed was fine. There was just one thing missing." He rubbed his chin.

"A razor? I have some disposable ones. I didn't think about it last night."

"I can understand that. I'm just glad you had an extra toothbrush."

She smiled.

"I was beginning to wonder if I'd ever see that," he said.

She knit her brows. "What?"

"A smile, a real one."

She bit her lip and looked down at her empty plate. "I didn't realize they were that scarce."

"I haven't known you very long. Maybe they're not as rare as I thought." He took a sip of coffee. "By the way, you still owe me a dinner."

"We had dinner last night."

He shook his head. "That didn't count," he insisted. "Since Christmas is out of the question, what about New Year's Eve? Do you have other plans?"

She frowned. "I don't really like going out on New Year's Eve. There are too many crazy drivers on the streets."

He tilted his head to the side. "I have a solution for that."

"What's that?"

He hesitated. Finally, he decided to go for it. All she could do was refuse. "We'll have dinner at my house. I'll pick you up in the afternoon."

"I still have to get home that evening."

He shrugged. "Not really."

She raised an eyebrow.

"I have a guest room, too. I'll bring you home the next day." He reached across the table and took her hand in his. "I know we didn't get off to a very good start. I'd like a chance to remedy that. I'd like for us to spend some time together, to get to know each other better. Since you don't want to go out, this is a perfect solution." He smiled. "I don't know anyone I'd rather spend New Year's Eve with."

She lowered her gaze to their clasped hands. She looked up into his eyes. When she met his gaze, she encountered an expression that was more than a desire to become better acquainted. What she saw was simply desire, if desire could ever be considered simple.

After the kiss they had shared the previous evening, the look in his eyes came as no surprise. Now she had to decide if she was ready for what might be involved in getting to know each other better.

Ben waited patiently. Patience was important. After what he had seen, he guessed that she had been through a rough time with Scott. His instincts also told him that she was not a woman who would settle for a casual fling. That was fine. A casual fling held no appeal for him.

She took a deep breath. "It seems that you've thought of everything."

He shrugged. "Is that a yes?"

"Yes."

He smiled. "Great. I'll even cook dinner. What would you like?"

She smiled. "Surprise me." She gently pulled her hand from his grasp and stood up. "Would you like more coffee?"

He nodded. "Thanks."

She refilled both of their mugs and rejoined him at the table. They chatted for a while longer until Ben glanced at his watch.

"I should be going."

She walked him to the door and turned off the alarm. Then she turned and looked up at him. "Thank you."

"You're welcome." He took her hand in his. "Will you promise me one thing? If Scott shows up again, call me. I don't care what time it is."

She hesitated. "I don't think he'll come here again."

Ben's gaze never wavered. "You didn't answer my question."

She bit her lip. "All right, Ben, I promise."

He nodded and opened the door. Before leaving, he leaned down and kissed her cheek. "I'll call you later."

Kendall watched from the doorway until he backed his car out of the driveway. Then she closed the door, reset the alarm, and went into the living room. She sat down on the sofa and leaned back with her eyes closed.

What was she getting into? No man had ever made her feel this way. Ben had voiced her own thoughts. She wanted to know more about him. *Be honest, Kendall. You want more than that. You saw the desire in his eyes. He probably saw the same in yours.*

She had allowed herself to be conned by Scott. In her own defense, she had been young and naive. She had also been brainwashed into thinking that she should be grateful to any man who gave her a second glance.

She was older and wiser now. She would never again settle for whatever crumbs a man threw her.

She wanted the whole cake. She was willing to compromise, though. It didn't have to be on a silver platter; china would be just fine.

Less than a week later, on Christmas Eve, Kendall visited Mabel Jenkins. Concerned that the elderly woman would be alone for the holiday, she had asked her about her plans. Mabel had assured her that she would be spending the day with their minister and his family.

Mabel opened the door and led the way to the living room. "Have a seat, sugar. I baked some cookies this afternoon. Would you like some hot chocolate to go with them?"

"Please don't go to any trouble."

"It's no trouble at all. I was going to fix a snack for myself anyway."

"Is there anything I can do to help?"

"No, thank you, honey. I'll just be a few minutes."

When she returned, there was a gift bag on the coffee table. She set the tray beside it and took a seat next to Kendall on the sofa.

Kendall gently pushed the bag toward her. "This is for you."

Mabel pursed her lips. "You shouldn't have done this."

Kendall smiled. "Yes, I should have. Open it."

"In a minute," she said, walking over to a cabinet that was laden with gift-wrapped packages. She returned with a long shallow box and handed it to Kendall.

"This is for you."

Kendall opened her mouth and closed it again. "What was that you said a minute ago?"

Mabel shrugged. "You've helped me a lot, Kendall. I know you're busy, but you find time to visit me and I haven't forgotten the times you've taken me shopping." She picked up the bag Kendall had indicated earlier. "Now open your gift."

While Kendall unwrapped her box, Mabel poked through the tissue and pulled out a small box. Her eyes lit up when she opened it, revealing an antique marcasite and onyx brooch.

"Oh, sugar, you really shouldn't have."

"I saw how you admired it when we were shopping."

Mabel stared at it. "I didn't tell you at the time, but my mother had a brooch very much like this."

She ran her fingers over the piece of jewelry. "My father worked doing odd jobs for people on top of his regular job to save for it. She was so surprised when he gave it to her on her birthday."

She closed her eyes and shook her head. "Her mind wasn't clear when she got up in age. I never knew what happened to it."

She opened her eyes, now glistening with moisture. She cleared her throat. Then she leaned over and kissed Kendall's cheek. "Thank you, dear."

Mabel gestured toward the half-unwrapped box. "Now open yours."

Kendall finished removing the paper and lifted the lid. She looked at Mabel and then again at the contents of the box. Then she held up a lacy black shawl with long fringe.

"It's beautiful, Miss Mabel. Thank you."

"I'm a little embarrassed after you gave me this lovely brooch." She sighed. "It's not new."

Kendall smiled. "Then we're even. The brooch isn't new either."

Mabel smiled. "I never thought of it that way. I crocheted that shawl years ago. It's been packed away. It's more suitable for a young woman like you." She pointed to the tray. "Help yourself before it gets cold."

In between nibbling cookies and washing them down with hot chocolate, Mabel reminisced about past Christmases. It reminded Kendall of a time when she had known happy Christmases. They had never been the same after her father died. As an adult she understood that her father's death was bound to cause some changes. She also understood that the joy he had worked so hard to arrange did not have to end so completely after his death.

She had looked forward to recapturing the joy with her own family when she married Scott. For a while she had fooled herself into believing that he shared her feelings. When the whole truth was revealed, happy Christmases were the least of her worries.

Mabel's voice broke into what had turned into unpleasant memories. "Here I am rambling on about the past. You must be bored to tears."

Kendall smiled and shook her head. "You could never bore me, Miss Mabel." She glanced at her watch. "I think I should be going, though." She stood up. After putting their empty mugs back on the tray, she lifted it from the table. "I'll help you clean up."

"You don't have to do that, honey."

"I don't mind." She started toward the kitchen.

When they had finished putting everything in order, Mabel walked her to the door. Kendall donned her coat and turned to face her.

"I love my shawl." She swallowed and cleared her

throat. "I can't really explain how much your friendship means to me."

"I'm glad. You've become very dear to me, Kendall."

The two women hugged. "Merry Christmas," Kendall murmured.

"Merry Christmas to you, sugar."

CHAPTER 7

Kendall arrived at Valerie's house shortly after one-thirty the next day. When Gary greeted her at the door, she remembered Ben's confession.

"Merry Christmas, Kendall. Valerie's in the kitchen."

He ushered her into the living room, where an older couple was already seated on the sofa. "I don't think you've met my parents."

Valerie entered while he was performing the introductions. They greeted each other with hugs. "I was just checking on the ham. Can I get you a drink? Gary made a wonderful hot punch."

Kendall looked askance at him. "Gary made the punch?"

He puffed out his chest and nodded. "That's right, and it's delicious, if I do say so myself."

She smiled. "How can I resist after those testimonials?"

Later that afternoon, Valerie and Kendall had

their first opportunity at a private conversation. Kendall had insisted on helping clear the table.

"Have you talked to Francine lately?" Kendall asked.

Valerie frowned. "Why?"

Kendall shrugged. "I saw her in passing at work and she barely spoke."

"You didn't happen to tell her your opinion of Darren, did you?"

"No, I didn't think she'd appreciate my meddling in her personal life."

Valerie sighed. "Too bad I wasn't that smart. It's probably my fault that she's not speaking to you."

Kendall raised an eyebrow. "What did you say to her?"

"It's not like I told her about the business with Mrs. Ferguson. She's the owner of the Sterling property. I never said anything bad about him." She shook her head. "I talked to Francine earlier this month. When she started going on about how she thought she'd finally found the man of her dreams, I suggested she might want to slow down. Guess what she said?"

"Mind your own business?"

Valerie frowned.

Kendall held up her hands. "Hey, I'm only guessing at what she might have said."

"I'd have understood her telling me that." Valerie shook her head. "No, she told me that Darren had warned her about me. He told her that I had stolen one of his clients."

"So you never told her what really happened with the Sterling account?"

"No, her attitude made it clear that there was no

point in trying to explain." Valerie shook her head. "I didn't want to get into a childish verbal tug-of-war as to who said and did what."

Kendall shrugged. "You did the right thing. He's probably already convinced her of his side of the story. I hate to see her get hurt, but I guess she'll have to find out what he's really like the hard way. Especially if she's convinced she's in love with him."

Valerie's eyes narrowed. She looked at her friend. Kendall's attention was focused on her task. Was that what had happened to her? Kendall had mentioned that she'd been married to a sleaze. Thinking of Kendall's unhappy marriage brought to mind the possibility of a new relationship.

"I forgot to ask you, how was the party?"

"The party?"

"The one you were planning for Ben."

"It was fine. Everyone seemed to have a good time."

She was being too close-mouthed to suit her friend. "Did you have a good time, too?"

Kendall looked up then. "That's not why I was there."

Valerie rolled her eyes.

"Yes, Valerie, I had a good time."

"Are you going to see him again?"

Kendall shook her head. "Didn't you learn your lesson with Francine?"

Valerie pouted. "That's not fair. It's not like I'm telling you what to do. I just asked a question."

"All right. You'll find out eventually anyway. Yes, I'm going to see him again. He invited me out for New Year's Eve."

"New Year's Eve, huh? That's romantic."

You have no idea. "Maybe."

Valerie grinned. She tilted her head to the side. "Girlfriend, I have a feeling there's a lot you're not telling me."

Her grin disappeared. She placed her hand on Kendall's arm. "From the little you've said about your marriage, I have a feeling that it's time you had a break. I hope this works out for you."

"Thanks, Valerie. I'm not sure myself where this relationship is headed. Unlike Francine, I'm taking my time." Those intentions would be put to the test in the next few weeks.

As she packed her bag for her overnight visit, Kendall had second thoughts. She had fought her physical attraction to Ben from the beginning, convinced that he would never be interested in her.

That's not quite true, Kendall. You're first meeting was clouded by your belief that he had cheated Mabel. Then he broke your date abruptly. Then he showed his distaste for your treatment of your mother.

She sighed. Now that those obstacles had been eliminated, she had little defense against her own feelings. The desire, and especially the tenderness, she had seen in his expression answered any doubts about his interest in her.

She finished packing and went to scour her closet for an appropriate outfit. She pulled out several dresses, shook her head at each one, and returned it to the closet.

Finally, she settled on a cream-colored dress in a lightweight wool fabric. Its mock-wrap bodice gave way to a full gored skirt that fell in soft folds. She clasped a gold chain around her neck, its teardrop-pearl pendant lying just above the cleavage revealed by the V-neck of the dress. After clipping on the matching pearl earrings, she slipped her feet into low-heeled beige pumps.

Her luggage in one hand and her purse in the other, she made her way downstairs. After setting her suitcase beside the hall table, she went to the kitchen. Maybe a drink of water would help calm her nerves.

She had just placed the empty glass in the dishwasher when the doorbell rang. She took a deep breath and went to answer it. This time, she verified that her visitor was indeed Ben.

She opened the door. The deep breath and the glass of water did not still the butterflies that had been let loose in her stomach. When he leaned over and placed a kiss at the corner of her mouth, she was reminded of her vow to proceed slowly in this relationship. That might be even harder than she anticipated.

"You look beautiful. Are you ready to go?"

She nodded and turned to open the closet door. He helped her on with her coat and gestured toward the bag near the table.

"Is that what you're taking?"

"Yes."

He picked up the bag and waited while she set the alarm. A few minutes later they were settled in the car.

They had only traveled a few blocks when Kendall turned toward him, eyebrow raised. "It just occurred to me. I could have driven myself since both trips will be made during the day."

"Hmm, I hadn't thought about that. I like this

arrangement better, though." He glanced her way. "It makes it feel more like we're going out for dinner."

"Are you disappointed that I said I don't like going out on New Year's Eve?"

He grinned. "Are you kidding? This is much better than spending the evening with a noisy crowd of people."

Within half an hour they arrived at his home. The brick driveway was perfect for the colonial-style house.

"Is this one of your renovations?"

He nodded. "It wasn't in bad shape when I bought it. The first thing I did was modernize the kitchen and bathrooms. Then I built an addition and knocked out a few walls to combine some of the rooms." He pushed a button and the garage door opened. "And of course, things like this convenience."

A few minutes later, he ushered her through a short hallway into the family room. "This is part of the addition. I guess some people would wonder why I didn't just build a new house."

She scanned the room. "You'd never know that it's not part of the original house."

The dark red walls of the family room they had entered provided a warm backdrop for the tan chenille L-shaped sofa. The matching large square ottoman also served as a coffee table.

The long side of the sofa faced a brick fireplace topped by a mahogany mantel that was draped in a swag of evergreens in deference to the season. A

large spruce tree sat in the corner behind the
short end of the sofa. Floor-to-ceiling bookcases
flanked the fireplace as well as the French doors.

Two wingback chairs in a muted geometric tapestry print, separated by a square mahogany chest,
sat near the door Kendall and Ben had entered
from the garage. French doors on the other side of
the room were dressed in valances and Roman
shades that echoed the tapestry print.

Beneath the large ottoman, an area rug in the
same red, gold, and green as the tapestry print broke
up the expanse of beige carpeting. A brass urn lamp
atop a square mahogany chest in the space between
the chair and the sofa cast a warm glow over the
room.

Her survey was interrupted by Ben's statement.
"Let me have your coat. Then I'll show you more
of the house and the guest room where you'll be
sleeping."

The living room and dining room were fur-
nished in a more formal, yet comfortable, style.
Kendall had noticed a breakfast room behind the
sofa for casual dining.

He led her up the stairs and entered the first door
to the right. The first piece of furniture she saw when
he flipped a switch was a bronze metal wrapped
style bed against cream shadow-striped walls and
covered with a floral quilt and pillow shams. The
double-layered bed skirt featured a cream-lace
skirt over dusty rose. This same combination was
carried over to the round table cover with a cream-
lace square topper.

The dusty-rose damask chaise in the far corner
held a throw pillow embroidered in a floral pat-
tern similar to the quilt. They were accompanied

by other pillows in cream and pale green. A large Aubusson rug and runner covered most of the hardwood floor, repeating the various shades of rose and green on a cream background.

The room had the desired effect. The tension eased from Kendall's body. "This is beautiful, Ben. Did you do this yourself?"

He shook his head. "I can't really take the credit for this room. I put my mother in charge of it. She helped a lot with the living room and dining room, too."

He set her bag on the rose damask upholstered bench at the foot of the bed. "The bathroom is across the hall. You can hang up your clothes in the closet," he said, indicating the door a few feet from the chaise.

"Thanks."

"Come on down when you're ready."

When Kendall entered the family room for the second time, Ben was lighting a fire in the fireplace. He glanced up at her and smiled.

She took a seat on the sofa and glanced at the tree. "Your tree is beautiful. It's real, isn't it?"

He nodded. "Some of the artificial ones look great. I can't bring myself to give up the real thing, though."

"Like the fireplace?" She watched him coax the small flame into a roaring fire. "I'm glad you installed a gas version in my house."

He stood up. "I decided that would be a better selling point. Most people don't want to be bothered with the real thing. I have two others that are gas, one in the living room and one in the master bedroom. Taking care of one wood burner is enough."

Kendall's mind focused on the most interesting part of that statement, the fireplace in the master bedroom. His tour had not satisfied her dangerous curiosity about his bedroom.

Was it the fire he had built in the fireplace or her imagination that sent the heat flowing through her veins? If her imagination could cause this reaction, what would the real thing do?

"What can I get you to drink? I have wine, sodas, and either orange or cranberry grape juice. If you prefer, I can make coffee or tea."

The last thing she needed at the moment was a hot drink. "Cranberry grape juice sounds good."

She watched as he passed through the archway behind the sofa into the breakfast room and then to the kitchen. Then her attention was captured by the lamp atop the mahogany credenza behind the sofa. The base of the lamp was fashioned from a stack of books and topped with a beige linen shade.

While he was in the kitchen, she wandered first to the bookcases, noting the wide variety of reading material. Then she walked over to the tree to take a closer look. Among the fancy expensive-looking ornaments were several that were obviously made by a child.

She gently touched the chain made of construction paper. Then she sighed and turned away from the tree. She was resettled on the sofa when he returned a few minutes later.

"I was admiring some of the unusual ornaments on the tree."

"Like the reminders of my childhood? I couldn't

believe my mother saved them all these years. She gave them to me a few years ago, insisting that I should hang them on my own tree."

Why did she feel such a sense of relief in knowing that they had not been created by a child of his that he had neglected to mention? That would have been completely out of character for the man she had seen at the party. Even in that setting, she had glimpsed a closeness to his family that she envied.

He placed the large wooden tray on the coffee table. In addition to two filled glasses and two empty plates, it contained cheese and crackers and vegetables and dip. He sat down beside her.

Kendall grinned. Then she raised an eyebrow. "Is this dinner?" she asked, lifting her glass from the tray.

Ben chuckled. "Are you insinuating that I don't know how to cook?"

Her eyes widened. "Of course not, I just asked a question."

He nodded. "Right. In answer to your question, this isn't dinner." He glanced at his watch. "I planned to have dinner about seven. I thought I'd better feed you before then."

She stared at him. He was serious. Before she had time to dwell on that statement, he reached out and ran his finger down the side of her cheek.

"You really should smile more often. You have a beautiful smile."

She looked down into her glass. "I never realized that they were so rare until you mentioned it before." She shrugged. "I guess I had kind of misplaced my sense of humor in the last few years."

He leaned over and placed a brief kiss on her mouth. He raised his head and murmured, "I'm glad you found it."

They gazed into each other's eyes for a long moment. Ben was the first to recover. He pointed to the tray.

"Help yourself."

Kendall followed his suggestion. Maybe if she concentrated on the food, she could ignore the thumping in her chest.

"How was your Christmas?" he asked.

"Fine. You remember that I told you I was having dinner with Valerie and her family?"

"I remember."

She sipped her drink. "What about you? Did your mother cook dinner?"

"No, we had dinner at my sister's house. Her kids never want to leave their gifts, so she's elected to cook."

Kendall raised an eyebrow. "How does she feel about it?"

He grinned. "I shouldn't have put it that way. It's not as bad as it sounds. She loves to cook, and she prefers being at home on Christmas Day, too."

They talked for quite a while before Ben looked at his watch. "I'd better start dinner."

"Is there anything I can do to help?"

"Sure, you can keep me company."

She followed him to the kitchen and took the seat he indicated at the counter. "What are we having?"

"London broil." He took a dish from the refrigerator. "It's been marinating since this morning."

She watched as he transferred the meat to another shallow dish. "Do you have ketchup?"

He looked up sharply and narrowed his eyes. "I hope that's another example of your recovered sense of humor."

She grinned and held up her hand. "Yes, I'm joking."

He heaved an exaggerated sigh. "Good. Since you're my guest, I'd feel obliged to accommodate you if you were serious."

She tilted her head to the side. "Do you mean that you'd spoil your careful preparations if I insisted?"

He set the pan in the oven and joined her at the counter, taking a seat on the stool next to her. Placing his elbow on the counter, he caressed her cheek with his other hand.

"You wouldn't even have to insist. If you say that's what you want, that's what you'll have."

Kendall wished she had carried her cold drink into the kitchen with her. It might not help the flush spreading up her neck, but it could ease her parched mouth. She lowered her lids slightly, breaking the contact with his intent gaze. How long had it been since anyone had cared about what she wanted?

Ben leaned toward her and kissed her cheek. Then he stood up, breaking the spell that had held them in its grasp.

During dinner, Ben told her more about his family. Given the candlelight and her already tense nerves, Kendall was grateful for ordinary topics of conversation.

"I noticed you have quite a collection of books," she said.

He glanced toward the bookcases. "Believe it or

not, that's not even half of the total. I have a few in my bedroom and more in my office upstairs."

"Have you read all of them?"

He shook his head. "I keep telling myself that I'll get through them eventually. The problem is that I keep buying more."

"You have quite a variety. Do you have any particular preference?"

"Not really. I admit that I have an affinity for history and some biographies. I'll try almost anything once. I've been known to put a book down for good if it hasn't grabbed my interest in the first chapter. That's probably more a sign of poor writing than anything else. What about you?"

"I like a good mystery, but nothing too gory. I've read some science fiction and a few novels that don't really fit any specific genre."

He grinned. "What, no romance?"

She shrugged. "I've been known to read a romance novel every now and then."

The truth was that she loved curling up with a good romance novel. It was a perfect escape from her personal experiences. Maybe that was why she had omitted it from her list. It might offer a clue to information she was not ready to divulge.

"I have the same problem as you, though," she added. "It's one of the reasons I appreciate the built-in bookcases in my house. I haven't had much time to read anything, but I continue to add to the list."

"I don't wonder that you have little time to read. Working a full-time job and then planning all of those parties must be exhausting."

"I've already started cutting back on the parties. Now that I have the house I'd been saving for, I plan to spend more time enjoying it."

Ben smiled. If he had his way, much of her free time would be spent in his company.

From the topic of books, their conversation turned naturally to movies and television. They learned that they both enjoyed a good comedy. Ben raised an eyebrow when she admitted an affinity for fast-paced thrillers.

"Why do you look skeptical? Just because men don't like romantic movies doesn't mean that a woman can't appreciate action movies."

"Who says I don't like romantic movies?" He grinned. "I just happen to prefer the real thing."

When they returned to the living room after dinner, the fire was dying. He added more logs and coaxed the flames back to life. As they continued talking, she answered his questions about her friendship with Valerie. Then she told him of some of her more interesting party assignments.

He noticed that she volunteered little about her own childhood. He was undaunted.

"Where did you get the name Kendall?"

She smiled. "From my parents, where else?"

He rolled his eyes.

She laughed.

He never imagined laughter that would indeed be music to his ears. Was it the infectious quality of the sound, or was it the fact that it signaled a change in her, that warmed his heart?

"It was my grandmother's maiden name," she explained, "my father's mother. He had settled on that name if he had a son. When I was born, my grandmother convinced him that the name would suit a daughter as well as a son."

"He wanted a son?"

She shrugged. "I think, on some level, most men

want a son." She shook her head. "Don't misunderstand, though. He never made me feel that he was disappointed that I wasn't a boy." She smiled. "In fact, he was the one who encouraged me when I wanted to take ballet lessons. I'm sure he knew I'd never be a professional dancer, but he supported me anyway."

Ballet lessons were one explanation for the gracefulness of her movements. "How long did you take lessons?"

"I started when I was about five. I never tried the toe dancing, though. My father thought that was too dangerous for a child. I stopped when I was ten, about two years after he died."

"Why did you stop?"

"I guess I just lost interest," she lied, turning away from his probing gaze.

Ben was not buying that explanation. The way her eyes lit up when she talked about her father, he thought she would have continued her lessons out of devotion to his memory. The love in her voice when she spoke of her father was quite a contrast to what he had observed with her mother.

Fearing that any further discussion of her family might eventually lead to the topic of her relationship with her mother, he asked no more questions. This was not the time for any topic that might lead to another disagreement or, even worse, resurrect pain.

He picked up the remote control and pushed a button, raising a wooden panel in one of the bookcases and revealing a television set. He turned it on, muting the sound. He pushed another button and soft music emanated from hidden speakers.

"The television will let us know when the new year arrives. We can do without the noise." He stood up and held out his hand. "Dance with me?"

He took her hand and led her to a small empty space at the side of the sofa. His arms encircled her waist, pulling her close. Her spicy perfume wafted up to tease his nostrils. Her breasts brushed against his chest with each movement. She fit so perfectly in his arms.

With her hands splayed across his back, she rested her head against his chest. They moved together easily, not really needing music. His cologne teased her nostrils. The muscles of his back flexed against the palms of her hands with each movement.

They danced for a while until he decided that dancing was not enough. He led her back to the sofa. No sooner were they seated than she was in his arms again. Their lips met in a kiss that came as naturally as breathing.

His mouth slanted across hers. She willingly parted her lips, inviting his questing tongue to taste the honey he craved.

She raised her arms to caress the nape of his neck. Her tongue followed his lead.

He pulled her closer, crushing her soft breasts against his chest. The temptation was too great. His hand stroked her back and then slid the zipper down. He slipped his hand inside the neckline to claim one breast.

She gasped when his thumb stroked the tip. It hardened immediately. Heat radiated from the point of contact and down her body. She clutched his shoulders.

His lips left hers to leave a trail of moist kisses

down her neck and along her collarbone. After he pushed aside the lace covering her breast, his tongue replaced his thumb.

She automatically leaned back, allowing him better access. Giving herself over to the wonderful sensations, she moaned softly.

While his tongue was occupied laving and teasing first one breast and then the other, his hand moved to her thigh. His fingers moved slowly up her nylon-clad limb bringing the hem of her dress with them.

Liquid heat flowed through her veins, pooling at last in the lower regions of her body. She trembled beneath his touch. When his fingers reached the place where the heat was concentrated, she tensed. She was not ready for this.

He sensed the change in her. His hand stilled.

"I can't do this, Ben. I'm not ready for this."

With his help, she put her clothes back in order. She waited for some sign of disgust or anger. There was none. He enfolded her in his arms and kissed her forehead.

"It's okay, sweetheart." He looked at the silent television. "I think we missed the big moment, though."

She looked up. "The big moment?"

He nodded toward the television. "I think we're already about ten minutes into the new year. I can't think of a better way to celebrate it, though." He grinned. "I take that back. There is one way I can think of that would be better."

"I'm sorry. I shouldn't have let it go that far."

"I told you, it's okay. We both got carried away." He placed a brief kissed on her lips. "Happy New Year."

"Happy New Year."

* * *

Kendall awoke late the next morning to the smell of coffee and bacon. She smiled, sat up, and stretched. After a quick shower, she dressed and followed the enticing aromas to the kitchen.

Ben looked up from his task when she entered. The royal-blue A-line skirt skimmed the curves of her hips. The soft cowl-necked top hid the evidence of the passion they had shared the previous night.

As disappointed as he was, he had not been surprised when she called a halt to their activity before it reached the obvious conclusion. Part of him had known that it was too early in their relationship for that step. When he made love to her it would be because they both wanted it, and were ready for it.

"Good morning. Did you sleep well?"

She smiled. "I slept fine. Why didn't you wake me earlier?"

"I thought you'd appreciate sleeping in. Are you in a hurry to get home?"

"No, it's not a problem. I'm in no hurry."

He took a mug from the cabinet. "Help yourself to coffee."

She walked over to the counter. "Do I smell bacon?"

"It's in the oven. Do you like French toast?"

She nodded. "Yes, I like French toast." She leaned against the counter, sipping her coffee. "I hope you're not going to all of this trouble for me."

"It's no trouble."

"I'm not in a hurry to get home, but there is a friend I want to visit today. I need to call her first."

"Valerie?"

She shook her head. "No, an elderly lady from church. You've met her, Mabel Jenkins. She told me that you had come to her rescue when she had a problem with another contractor."

He smiled and nodded. "I remember Mrs. Jenkins." His smile faded. "She was one of Sam Farley's customers. When she called me, she was at her wit's end. She wasn't one to take his shady dealings lying down, but short of taking him to court, she didn't know what to do."

"And she couldn't afford to take him to court."

"No, but I could, on her behalf. I had a hunch it wouldn't have to go that far. I was right. All I had to do was threaten to take him to court and spread the word about what he had done."

Kendall smiled. He told the story so matter-of-factly. He had no idea what a big difference he had made in Mabel's life and peace of mind. From what his mother had said, Mabel Jenkins was only one of many he had helped.

"If Mrs. Jenkins is planning to be at home, why don't we stop there before I take you home."

"Are you sure you don't mind?"

"Not at all. I have no other plans. I wouldn't mind seeing Mrs. Jenkins again."

While they talked, he had finished making the French toast. Now he took the plate of bacon from the oven.

"Breakfast is ready. Have a seat."

Halfway through the meal, Ben made another suggestion. "I promised my mother I'd stop by today. How about coming with me after we visit Mrs. Jenkins."

Since she had already admitted that she had no other plans, Kendall had little choice. She had nothing against visiting his mother. The woman had been pleasant enough at the party, but what did she really think of Kendall? How would she feel about her son being involved with Kendall in more than a business relationship?

"Sure, that sounds fine."

When they arrived at Mabel's home, Kendall rang the bell. Mabel greeted them with a smile. "Happy New Year, Kendall." She looked beyond Kendall. "Mr. Whitaker, Kendall didn't tell me you were coming. What a nice surprise." She stepped aside to allow them to enter. "Come in and have a seat. Would you like a drink?"

"No, thank you."

Mabel looked first at one and then the other of her guests with a gleam in her eyes. "I didn't know you two knew each other."

"We met at one of the parties I arranged." She glanced at Ben. "Would you believe the house I bought was renovated by Ben?"

"You don't say." Mabel leaned toward Kendall and lowered her voice. "I guess I can't ask how you like it."

Kendall smiled. "I'm very happy with it. It's just what I was looking for, a new-old house, if that makes sense."

Mabel nodded. "I think it makes perfect sense. You wanted an old house without the problem of constant repairs."

"Exactly."

"I don't blame you. Both of you know about my problems with repairs." She smiled at Ben. "Thanks to you, I don't worry about that now."

"And don't forget that if you have any other problems," Ben said.

Mabel turned her attention back to Kendall. "I have to tell you that a few of the ladies at the senior center were admiring my brooch." She nodded slowly. "I think they were jealous."

Kendall smiled. "How was your Christmas?"

"I had a wonderful time." Mabel turned toward Ben. "I spent the day with my pastor's family. It's always a treat to watch children on Christmas."

A shadow seemed to pass over Kendall's face. She shook off the feeling. She would not let the past spoil this pleasant day.

They chatted for a while about their respective holidays. When Mabel later saw them to the door, she asked, "Where are you two headed?"

Kendall answered without thinking. "Ben was just taking me home." As soon as the words left her mouth, she wished she could recall them. She waited for the question that never came.

"I'm glad you stopped by. I suppose I'll see you in church tomorrow."

"I'll be there." Mabel hugged the older woman. "Take care of yourself."

When they were on the road again, Ben said, "I was waiting to see what you would tell her if she asked where we had been that I would be taking you home this early in the day."

"I should have known that wouldn't slip by you. If she had asked, I could have told her that we went out to breakfast."

Ben smiled. He wanted to believe that she had that response prepared in case she needed it in the future. He wanted to believe that she might need such a response in the future, that there would be another overnight visit when she would not be sleeping in his guest room.

* * *

Rosa hid her surprise when she opened the door to her son that afternoon. "Hi, honey," she said, giving him a hug. "Hello, Kendall. It's nice to see you again."

What Kendall had expected to be a short visit turned into having dinner with Ben's mother. She was sure Ben had not informed his mother that he was bringing a guest, but Rosa took it in stride.

Kendall could not help comparing Rosa with her own mother. Warmth and affection seemed to come naturally to Ben's mother. Kendall had felt it at the Christmas party. Rosa's gracious welcome eliminated any thoughts that she might disapprove of her relationship with Ben. She actually seemed happy to see them together.

When they arrived at Kendall's house, Ben waited while she turned off the alarm and followed her into the foyer. He set her bag on the floor and helped her off with her coat. She hung it in the closet and turned to face Ben.

"I enjoyed yesterday, and today. Your mother's a very sweet person."

"Yes, she is. She likes you, too."

He took her in his arms. "Should I make plans for next weekend? Dinner? Dancing? A movie?"

"Any of those would be fine."

"Good." He paused. "Kendall, after last night, I'm sure I don't have to tell you how I feel about you. There's one little detail that I need to make clear, though."

She wrinkled her forehead. "What?"

He hesitated. "I'm not sure how to say this, so I

guess I'll just say it straight out. Some men think it's okay to do whatever it takes to get women into their beds. I'm not one of those men. As much as I want you, having you in my bed won't mean anything if you're not ready for it. You mean too much to me for that."

He raised an eyebrow. "I hope that saying this doesn't mean that I'm killing my chances."

Kendall bit her lip. What could she say?

He smiled. "I'll take your silence to mean that I shouldn't give up hope." He pulled her closer. "On that note, I'd better leave." He lowered his head to claim her lips in a kiss that only hinted at the passion expressed in the one that had heralded the new year.

A moment later, Kendall closed the door behind him and leaned against it. She let out a long sigh.

CHAPTER 8

On Tuesday evening, Kendall was loading the dishwasher when the telephone rang. She had developed the habit of waiting for the answering machine to identify the caller. Several people had called her old-fashioned for not upgrading to voice mail or Caller ID. This suited her purposes much better.

"Hi, Valerie. How was your trip?"

"Great, the skiing was great."

"No broken bones?"

Valerie laughed. "Not even a sprain, thank you very much. How was your New Year's date?"

"It was fine. I had a good time."

"Where did you go?"

Kendall should have seen that question coming. She amazed herself with her quick thinking. "A small private party. It was better than one of those noisy hotel affairs."

"Well, I'm glad you had a good time."

The two chatted for a while before Valerie remembered another bit of news. "I almost forgot to tell you. Sheila Donovan called me today to thank me for my help with the Sterling mansion. It's been declared a historic landmark."

"That's great. Have you had any bites from possible buyers for the rest of the property?"

"Not yet. I'll give George Mueller another call this week and see if he's changed his mind about buying the land."

"Good luck."

"Thanks, I'll let you know what happens."

On Friday, Ben was waiting for her when she arrived home from work, suggesting an impromptu dinner. As he put it, after a long week at work, dining out seemed preferable to slaving over a hot stove.

"You must be tired yourself. You had your office move this week, didn't you?"

He nodded.

"How did it go?"

"Thanks to Evelyn's great organizational skills and planning, everything went pretty smoothly. One of the stores was a day late delivering additional supplies, but no major problems."

After spending quiet a evening at Ben's home on Saturday, they visited an art museum on Sunday afternoon. As they were leaving the museum, they strolled past two middle-aged women engrossed in a reproduction of a frieze from the Kama Sutra. The women made no effort to whisper as they exchanged comments.

"Think we could get our husbands to do that, Faye?"

Faye chuckled and shook her head. "Gloria, even

if we could, I think Arthur might have a say in whether we could do it ourselves."

Gloria laughed. "You're right. Arthur seems to have a say in everything we do."

Ben grinned. He came to a stop and glanced at the two women.

Kendall halted beside him. "What's so funny? Do you know what they're talking about?"

He nodded. "I've heard my mother and aunts talk about Arthur enough. They're referring to the kind of arthritis my mother says is bound to come when you're over fifty."

Kendall looked up at him and smiled. "I guess that's one of those things that you have to keep a sense of humor about."

The two women glanced their way. "I bet they wouldn't have any trouble," one said to the other.

Her cheeks flushed, Kendall avoided Ben's gaze. She thought her embarrassment was complete until Gloria came closer as she passed them.

"Enjoy it while you can, honey."

Ben chuckled. He winked at the two women. Then he took Kendall by the hand and proceeded to the door.

When they were settled in the car, he turned toward her. "What do you say we stop for dinner?"

"I think I'd rather get take-out."

He turned the key in the ignition. "What would you like? Chinese? Italian? Or there's a little soul-food cafeteria not far from here."

"The soul-food place sounds good."

On Monday evening, Valerie called. In the course of their conversations since New Year's Day, she had learned that Kendall was seeing Ben on a regular basis. Although she had teased her about Ben, Valerie was concerned about the possibility of her friend being hurt again. She had only met Ben once, at the settlement. That encounter was not enough to form an opinion on his character and personality.

"Hey, girlfriend, how's it going?"

"Fine, Valerie. What have you been up to?"

"Not much other than working hard. I still don't have a buyer for the Sterling property. I told you the mansion's been declared a historic landmark, didn't I?"

"Yes, but that's more of a hindrance than a help, right?"

"I don't really know yet. Mueller still isn't interested. Ben might get some work out of it, though. Sheila's looking for someone to restore the mansion. She says it's in pretty good shape structurally, but it needs some work. I gave her Ben's name."

"That doesn't mean he'll get the job, though. She's probably getting estimates from more than one contractor."

"Probably. Well, if he doesn't get the job to renovate the mansion, you still might get the job for the Open House."

"Open House?"

"Once the mansion is completed, the society is planning to have an Open House. Sheila's hoping to have everything done by February for Black History Month to tie in with the Underground Railroad discovery."

"How do you know she's not planning to arrange it herself?"

"I don't. When she mentioned the Open House,

I told her about you. I hope you don't mind. You can always turn it down."

"I've cut back on the parties. I wouldn't mind taking on that assignment, though."

There was silence on the other end for a few seconds. Then Valerie asked, "How's it going with Ben?"

Kendall was glad she was not face-to-face with Valerie. She remembered the past weekend. The grin that brightened her face would have been a dead giveaway.

"It's going fine."

Even over the telephone, the happiness in her voice told Valerie much more than her words. This was a Kendall she had never known. She could only attribute it to her relationship with Ben. She prayed that the joy would always be there.

They chatted for a while longer before Valerie ended the call. She could not resist a parting comment.

"Maybe the four of us could go out to dinner one weekend?"

It was Kendall's turn to hesitate. Her relationship with Ben was still too new to share.

"Sure. I'll let you know."

At the time that she had her conversation with Valerie, they were unaware that Sheila had made her decision. Kendall received the news when she met Ben for dinner on Friday evening.

He greeted her with a kiss and an apology. "Sorry I'm late. I started a new job this week, and I was so interested in the architecture that the time got away from me."

"That's okay."

Almost immediately, the waiter approached to take their orders. Afterward, she turned the conversation back to his original statement.

"What's this job that's so interesting?"

"I don't know if you've heard anything about the Sterling mansion. It was recently declared a historic landmark."

"Valerie told me about it. She's handling the sale of the rest of the property. She said the director was looking for a contractor and that she had given her your name."

He nodded. "I had given her an estimate about a week ago. I was surprised to hear from her so soon."

"Valerie mentioned that Sheila was hoping to have an Open House in February. Do you think you'll finish it by then?"

He shrugged. "She told me her plan. I didn't make any promises, but I'll give it my best shot."

He sipped his water. "Aside from relatively minor repairs and renovations, it's in pretty good shape structurally. The most work will involve the plumbing and electrical system." He shook his head. "The electrical system hasn't been updated in years."

Kendall frowned. "From what Valerie told me about the concern of the owner's children, I'm surprised they hadn't seen to that."

"After Mrs. Ferguson moved into a senior citizen's apartment, they probably didn't think about repairs beyond what's visible."

"I guess unless a problem arises, people tend to take for granted things like plumbing and electricity."

"Unfortunately, that's true. Sheila mentioned

that there had been some relatives living there for a while. The Fergusons probably assumed that they would keep up with the repairs, or at least tell them if there was a problem."

"That makes sense, but evidently they were wrong. Of course, the repairs wouldn't have mattered if the original buyer had had his way. He had planned to demolish the mansion."

Ben nodded. "I heard. In fact, I had bid on the development project."

Her eyes widened. "You were going to work for Mueller?"

"Don't look at me like that. I withdrew even before I heard that the mansion was being researched as a possible historic landmark."

"Why?"

He rubbed his chin. "When I met with Mueller there was something about him that rubbed me the wrong way. I overheard him complaining about the Historical Society's efforts. I asked why he couldn't build his resort without destroying the mansion itself. There's plenty of land for what he has in mind."

"That's the same thing Valerie's been telling him. He refused to consider that possibility."

He nodded. "I know. He said it didn't fit in with the modern condos and clubhouse he wanted."

"With what you and Valerie have told me about him, Mueller sounds like a real prince."

"He's like a lot of people, greedy and determined to have his own way."

When Ben took her home, he followed her into the house. "I have an appointment tomorrow afternoon, but I'll be free in the evening. What would you like to do?"

"Nothing special. Instead of having dinner out, we can have dinner here. I'll cook."

Taking her in his arms, he nodded. "I like that idea. Do you want me to bring anything? Maybe dessert?"

She shook her head. "Nothing at all, just yourself."

He smiled. Then, after a much-too-brief kiss to satisfy Kendall, he was gone.

Kendall awoke the next morning with the germ of an idea. She recalled all of the passionate moments they had shared. All of them stopping short of that final step.

Ben had never given any sign of impatience with this situation. It was up to her to make decision as to when, or if, they would take that step.

She dressed, had breakfast, and went grocery shopping. She purchased the food she needed for dinner. If she followed through with the plan that was forming in her mind, she would also need more substantial food for breakfast than her usual fare.

She had never subscribed to the idea of being so carried away by passion that making love just happened. She believed that taking that step was a decision, or at least it should be.

Later that afternoon, with dinner well on its way, Kendall treated herself to a bubble bath. Submerged in the soothing foam, she closed her eyes and let her mind wander.

She squelched the guilty feelings. She was contemplating taking a very big step in her physical relationship with Ben. Yet she had shared very little with him about her background.

More than once, he had inadvertently come to her aid in a difficult situation with Scott. In spite of that, he had never questioned her about the reason for her divorce. His comment about the restraining order hinted that he assumed it involved abuse.

Her failed marriage was only part of the baggage she carried. To her mind, she had put all of those problems behind her. Was that a good reason to keep the information from him? Would he believe her if she told him the whole truth? Or would he think she was exaggerating, or worse, neurotic? She sighed.

She pushed those thoughts aside. She refused to ruin this evening with unpleasant speculations.

She finished her bath, donned her robe, and went downstairs. After placing the roast in the oven, she returned to her bedroom to dress.

Ben arrived shortly before six-thirty. The geometric-patterned sweater in shades of red and gold accentuated his broad shoulders. She greeted him with a brief kiss and waited while he hung his coat in the closet.

Hand in hand, they made their way to the living room. He had long ago abandoned any attempt to explain his feelings for her. He was falling in love with her. Could anyone really explain that phenomenon? As far as he was concerned, there was no need to explain it.

When they reached the living room, he sniffed the air. "Something smells delicious. What's for dinner?"

"Stuffed pork roast, fried apples, rice, and string beans."

He grinned. "I thought you said this evening wasn't going to be anything special."

She bit her lip. *If you only knew. I certainly hope it will turn out to be very special.*

"Stuffed pork roast and fried apples. You don't play around when you cook."

"I enjoy cooking when I have time to do it right. Believe me, though, this isn't a sample of my usual cooking."

The early part of the evening passed pleasantly, if uneventfully. The ordinary conversation disguised the undercurrent of emotions.

When they settled on the sofa after dinner, he pulled her gently into his arms. When their lips met, the desire bubbled to the surface. Their tongues tested and tasted, rediscovering the places they had explored so many times before.

He pulled her onto his lap and escalated his assault on her senses. Nuzzling her neck, he inhaled her sweet scent. Then he blazed a path of moist kisses down to the valley between her breasts.

The muscles of his chest flexed beneath her fingers. That was not enough. She slipped her hands beneath his sweater, caressing the smooth skin. The spicy scent of his cologne tantalized her as she gently nipped his earlobe before running her tongue along its rim.

His hand cupped her breast, fondling the soft globe. Then it slid beneath the fabric of her neckline. His thumb stroked the already rigid nipple. His mouth soon replaced his thumb, first teasing and then suckling hungrily.

She gasped. She managed to catch her breath long enough to whisper his name.

He paused reluctantly. Then he took a deep breath and waited for her to tell him she was calling a halt to their lovemaking. "Yes?"

"Do you remember those ladies at the museum?"

He raised his head, frowning. "What?"

She cleared her throat. "The ladies we saw at the museum, do you remember what they said?"

"I'm not sure."

"They said for me to enjoy it while I can. I've decided to follow their suggestion."

He took a deep breath. "Are you saying what I think you're saying?"

She sighed. "I'm saying that if you'd like to spend the night, we don't need to make up the guest room." A flush spread upward from her neck. "I'm not very good at this seduction business."

"Sweetheart, if you're sure about this, you don't have to worry about seducing me."

"I'm sure." She eased herself from his embrace and stood up. In no time, she was leading him up the stairs to her bedroom.

She flipped the switch, and the small lamp on the table beside the bed bathed the room in a soft glow. She slipped her feet out of her shoes and went to turn down the bed. Afterward, with her back to him, she began to undress.

He removed his own clothes. Then he watched silently as she laid each article of her clothing on the chair in the corner. She was clad only in two pieces of blue lace when he approached her.

When she turned around, he was totally nude, standing less than two feet from her. She swallowed. She slowly took in the vision standing before her. His arousal was evident. The blush she had felt when she suggested making love was nothing compared to the heat that now suffused her face. When he reached out and ran his finger along her collarbone, the heat changed direction.

The temptation of his naked body overrode her shyness. When he moved closer, she stretched out her arms to run her hands over the smooth skin. Starting first at his shoulders, her fingers then moved to his chest, lingering in the mat of hair before moving lower. She smiled when the muscles of his abdomen tightened beneath her hands.

He caught his breath. "That's a wicked smile, sweetheart. Are you enjoying yourself?"

Her smile widened. "Immensely."

He smiled. "Good, because I think it's my turn now."

Her caresses continued as she followed him when he backed up a few steps. Then he sat down on the side of the bed, discreetly placing a small item on the bedside table.

With his hands at her waist, he urged her forward until she was standing between his legs. His arms encircled her torso, unhooking her bra and freeing her round full breasts from their lacy confinement. His hands covered the soft globes, gently kneading them. He leaned forward and captured one of them with his mouth, teasing the nipple into a hard peak. Then he gave the same attention to the other.

She clutched his shoulders. Her legs grazed his rigid shaft. Her knees weakened. Giving herself up to the sensations she had only imagined until now, she closed her eyes.

He moaned against her breast. Then his mouth left her breasts, placing soft warm kisses down her torso. He slipped his fingers beneath the waistband of her panties, easing them down over her hips. With little effort, they soon lay at her feet. He took a moment to enjoy the total picture.

"Beautiful."

His immediate arousal had hinted at the truth of his statement that he saw her as a beautiful, desirable woman. That one word and the emotion behind it confirmed his assertion.

She was given little time to dwell on these thoughts. With his arms around her, he leaned back on the bed. A moment later, he maneuvered their bodies and entangled legs to lie lengthwise on the bed with her atop him.

She gasped. His shaft pressed against her thighs, as if seeking entrance. It was hard to distinguish the thumping of his heart from that of her own. Her breath caught in her throat when his roaming hands slid down her back and settled on the curve of her buttocks. As he stroked and kneaded, she arched her back.

He immediately took advantage of her movement, taking one breast in his mouth to resume laving and suckling. His hands moved over the curve of her hips and down to her thighs, gently parting them. His fingers found her moist opening near his shaft.

She moaned loudly when he inserted first one, then two fingers. Her body shook with tremors as his fingers advanced and retreated. Just when she thought she could stand it no more, he reversed their positions and she was lying on her back.

Then he sat up on the side of the bed giving her time to catch her breath. Not that she wanted to catch her breath.

She was only vaguely aware of him opening the small packet he had placed on the table. A moment later, he lay beside her again.

His hand went immediately to the triangle of hair that covered the secret place he had begun to explore earlier. His fingers returned to the moist opening. This time his thumb stroked the rigid nub. Her body arched automatically as if seeking the source of pleasure.

While his hands worked their magic, his lips returned to her breasts. Inch by inch, he worked his way down her body, leaving a trail of moist kisses. When he reached the triangle of hair, his tongue outlined its perimeter.

"Ben, please."

"That's what I aim to do, baby."

He settled his body between her thighs. When her soft limbs entwined with his, his abdomen tensed. He claimed her lips again. She opened her mouth to his hungry explorations. When his swollen member pressed against the moist entrance, her body welcomed him and he pushed gently. Her legs moved higher on his thighs.

He needed no further prompting. He moaned into her mouth and drove deeper. When her body tensed, he stopped. She was so tight and hot and wet. He could not have imagined anything better than this.

She moved beneath him and the dance began. He advanced and retreated, slowly at first. His lips left hers to lave and suckle her breasts again, first one and then the other. Then he lifted his head to see her face.

She could hardly breathe. Her heart felt as if it would burst from her body. He felt so good inside her, so right. She moaned his name, pleading.

As his thrusts came faster, she met each one. Her legs encircled his waist, pulling him deep inside with each thrust. She linked her arms behind his neck, pulling him closer. Their lips met again.

When her body tensed, he retreated far enough for his fingers to reach the hard little nub that soon controlled her world. After a few strokes, her body was seized with shivers before it tensed. With one final thrust, he sent them both over the edge.

They lay there for a moment, unable to speak. Then she sighed. "I'm glad I took those ladies' advice. I was beginning to think that all the stories I heard were an exaggeration."

"Kendall?"

She opened her eyes. "Hmm?"

"Are you saying that this is the first time you've . . . ?"

She cut off the rest of his question. She had been so caught up in this new experience that she had given no thought to her comment.

"Yes." She closed her eyes again. "It shouldn't come as a surprise to you that Scott wasn't into pleasing anyone but himself."

He kissed her tenderly. "At the risk of being accused of being chauvinistic and selfish, I have to admit that I'm glad I was the first one to experience this with you."

"Chauvinistic maybe, but I'd hardly call you selfish."

He disengaged himself from her body and rolled to the side with her still enfolded in his arms. His hands continued to stroke her silky skin. It was a little incredible to him that she was lying here naked in his arms; incredible, but so right.

Her hand rested on his chest. The thumping of his heart matched the rhythm of her own. As their hearts returned to a slower beat, she closed her eyes and let contentment wash over her.

She had read about making love. She had heard other women talk about their wonderful experiences. After her own less than satisfying sexual encounters with Scott, she was almost ready to think that there was something wrong with her. Ben had done a thorough job of dispelling that concern.

The next morning, Kendall awoke still snuggled against Ben's warm body. She smiled and laid her hand on his chest. Her fingers played in the mat of hair before sliding down his torso. The muscles of his abdomen tightened in response to her questing fingers.

"You're asking for trouble."

She raised up on her elbow and grinned. "I wouldn't call it trouble."

He sighed. "I'm not prepared for a repeat of last night."

She ran her finger down the shaft that stiffened

beneath her touch. "That's not what it feels like to me."

He chuckled. "I wasn't referring to being physically prepared."

She rolled to the other side of the bed and opened the drawer of the nightstand, retrieving a small packet. She sat up and handed it to him. "Is this what you need?" She shrugged. "Since I hadn't informed you of my decision, I thought I'd better be prepared."

He nodded. "Why didn't you tell me about your decision before last night?"

She sighed. "I wasn't sure that I'd have the nerve to go through with it."

He took the packet from her. "You're not having regrets, are you?"

She rolled her eyes. "If I was having regrets, would I be giving that to you?"

She shrugged. "Of course, I understand that I may be expecting too much in spite of appearances. I don't want to put you on the spot." She shrieked when he pulled her on top of him.

"Is that a challenge?"

"Of course not. I just want you to know that I'm understanding about these things."

She kissed him. The bulge pressing against her thighs became even harder, contradicting her suggestion. She ended the kiss and raised her head.

He held up the small packet. "Since technically this belongs to you, I think you should put it on."

She giggled. "I don't think it will fit."

Her laughter was contagious. He chuckled and shook his head. He could hardly believe this was the same woman he had met a few months ago.

She knelt beside him. "I don't want to mislead you. I bought them, but I've never done this before. Are you sure you trust me?" She ran her finger down the silky skin of his rigid shaft. "After all, this is a very delicate instrument."

He grinned. "After last night, I think I know how much it means to you. I trust you to be very careful." He glanced at her and suggested, "It might be easier if you approach it from the front."

With some hesitation, she moved to straddle his legs. She licked her lips and took a deep breath. Then she took the packet from his hand. When she finished her task, she smiled and patted his member.

Leaning forward, she planted a kiss in the middle of his chest. Her tongue made a path through the mat of hair. When she placed her hand on his abdomen, his whole body tensed. She smiled.

"Let the games begin," she murmured.

He reached up to fondle her breasts with one hand. His other hand stroked up and down her back. Then his hands seemed to be everywhere, rediscovering the silky softness of her skin.

She gasped and clutched his shoulders when his fingers found the nub that soon became the center of her world once again. When her knees buckled, she stretched out on top of him.

Their lips met in a searing kiss. It was as if their appetites had only been whetted by the previous night's lovemaking. He urged her knees forward and entered her slowly, savoring each millimeter as he advanced.

She matched his rhythm as if they had been making love together for years. Just when she thought she could stand no more, his finger found the magic button that delivered her final reward. Her body contracted in spasms, evoking his own release as well as hers.

They lay in each other's arms, basking in the glow of sated passion. His hands roamed soothingly over her body. After a few minutes, he murmured, "You haven't fallen asleep on me, have you?"

"It would be your fault if I did." She raised her head slightly. "I made a point of buying food for a big breakfast, but I don't think I have the strength to cook it."

He chuckled. "Is that a hint that it's my turn to cook?"

"Hmmm, I hadn't thought of it that way. I think that's a great idea."

As they worked together preparing breakfast, her mind was on other matters. Twice during their conversation Ben had to repeat a comment before she answered.

After breakfast, they settled on the sofa. He could no longer refrain from questioning the dark mood that had descended on her.

"Kendall, something's bothering you. What is it?"

She glanced at him and then turned away from his probing gaze. She bit her lip. "This relationship has become serious, Ben, to me anyway. I'm not sure it's a good idea."

He frowned. Had he misread her signals? "I'm very serious about this relationship, too, Kendall. I don't understand what you're saying."

"I'm sure you know the concept of people bringing baggage to a relationship. You have no idea of the amount of baggage I'm carrying." She bit her lip. "I should have told you long before the relationship reached this point. It's unfair to involve you in my problems."

He reached over and took her hands in his. His thumb caressed her knuckles. "Honey, I've been involved for some time simply because of the way I feel about you." He placed one hand beneath her chin and lifted it until her gaze met his. "We all have baggage. I have baggage, too."

She shook her head. "It's not the same. Grief over losing a spouse is normal and understandable."

"There's more to it than that."

Kendall squelched the myriad of terrible scenarios that entered her mind. "What do you mean?"

He took a deep breath.

"Ben, if it's too painful, you don't have to discuss it."

He squeezed her hands. "I'm old enough to have learned how important communication is to a relationship. It's a mistake that a lot of men make. I don't want to make that mistake with you." He sighed. "I found out that my wife was having an affair before she died."

"Are you sure?" She immediately regretted her question. "I'm sorry, I shouldn't have asked that."

He shook his head. "It's all right. It's natural for you to wonder how I could be so sure. It was really quite unexpected and coincidental. I was checking out a job when I saw her leaving a hotel with a man. When they parted company, it was obvious that they were lovers."

He paused. "That memory is what flashed through my mind when I saw you with Gary. I felt very foolish about it later. It was nothing like what I had seen with Christine."

He rubbed his forehead. "I waited weeks for her to tell me about it. I wouldn't have been surprised if she'd asked for a divorce. Our relationship was already strained, partly because she had never been thrilled with my choice of careers. What I hadn't expected was the deceit."

He took a deep breath. "Instead of asking for a divorce, she came to me with the news that she'd been diagnosed with cancer."

"You never told her about your suspicions?"

"How could I? I knew the prognosis wasn't good, but I was shocked at how quickly she deteriorated. She fought the disease, but she had waited too long. She died less than six months later."

He released her hands and turned in his seat. His clasped hands dangled loosely between his knees. Gazing down at them, he continued.

"The worst part is that I felt like such a fraud accepting everyone's sympathy. I had already lost her before she died. The sadness I felt was more the fact that a young vital woman had had her life cut short. I felt, I guess sometimes I still feel, so guilty that I couldn't grieve as I should." He glanced at her. "Does that make any sense?"

She reached over and covered his clasped hands with one of her own. "Yes, it makes sense." She stroked his hand. "What doesn't make sense is for you to feel guilty. In spite of what you knew, you stayed with her and saw her through the illness. You didn't have to do that."

"I only did what anyone with a conscience and an ounce of compassion would have done." He turned toward her again. "Do you know that in all these years, you're the only person I've ever told the whole story." He shook his head. "So, you see, you're not the only one with baggage."

He caressed her cheek. "There's one thing you're forgetting about baggage."

She blinked. "What's that?"

"It's much easier to manage when you have someone to help carry it. I'd like to be the one to help you carry yours."

She looked down at her hands, which once again lay folded in her lap. She wanted to tell him. Would he believe her?

This time his hand reached out to cover hers. "Tell me about Scott."

She raised her head. The expression in his eyes was tenderness, not mere curiosity. It was time. He deserved to know the truth. She swallowed. Her voice was barely a whisper.

"He tried to kill me."

The anger he had felt before increased a hundredfold. Her statement explained that fleeting expression of fear that he had seen in one of her confrontations with Scott. What terrible conditions had she endured during that relationship? He squeezed her hand and she continued.

"We met in college. I was young and naive compared to most twenty-year-olds. I believed him when he told me I was the woman he'd been looking for." She grunted. "When I look back on it, I realize that he told the truth. He was looking for a meal ticket and I was it for years. In the three years that we were married, he had three jobs and only worked a total of about eighteen months."

"What was the problem?"

She shook her head. "According to him, it was

never his fault." She sighed. "When I got pregnant, the situation got worse. I was disgusted with myself for being so careless."

She could not bring herself to admit one of the reasons for her carelessness. After he hadn't touched her for months, she was convinced that Scott had no interest in making love to her.

"The pregnancy finally opened my eyes. I could raise a child better alone than with an irresponsible husband. I could support one child, but not two. He refused to leave, so I went to stay with a friend."

She cleared her throat. "A week later, I lost the baby."

That explained her refusal to plan children's parties. Her marriage also explained her aversion to planning weddings.

He squeezed her hand. "I'm sorry."

She took a deep breath. "The doctor assured me that losing the baby wasn't my fault. That helped a little."

She had painted a dismal picture of her marriage. None of it explained her first statement.

"You said he tried to kill you."

She nodded. "He attacked me one night about a month after I left him. He knew my friend, Erica, worked evenings. As it happened, she had called in sick that day. She heard me scream and immediately turned on the driveway lights. The lights scared him off and he ran to his car, but not before he stabbed me."

"You recognized him?"

She swallowed. "He made no effort to hide his identity. In the struggle, I scratched his face. It still might have been my word against his if Erica hadn't caught a glimpse of him. She also managed to read part of his license plate."

He took a deep breath. "What happened to him?"

"He was convicted of attempted murder and a few other charges. I'm not sure exactly how many years he served, but he went to prison." She bit her lip. "The police assumed his motive was the same as a lot of men whose wives leave them. You know. 'If I can't have you, nobody will.' Personally, I don't think that was it at all."

"Why not?"

"He didn't really care about me that much. Like I said, I was his meal ticket. What he wanted was my insurance. I think he expected that I hadn't thought to change the beneficiary since we had been separated barely a month." She shrugged. "His motive didn't matter."

"Is that when you moved here?"

She nodded. "After the trial. I deluded myself into thinking he wouldn't find me when he got out of prison if I left the state."

Ben watched her expression closely. There was more that she was not telling.

She looked down at their hands. "Now you understand what you'll be dealing with if you get involved with me." She shook her head. "I really believed it was all behind me, until he showed up on my doorstep."

He frowned. "Has he been here again?"

"Not since the last time you saw him. I guess he finally got the message."

He nodded slowly, looking for signs of fear. Her angry outburst seemed to have dispelled the fear. Maybe she thought it had also finally driven him away.

He moved closer, his arms encircling her shoulders. He kissed the side of her forehead. She was exhausted. Her narrative had taken an unexpected toll.

"I haven't heard anything to make me change my mind." He leaned back. With one hand, he tilted her chin up. "I'm a little concerned about you, though. Telling me this has been painful for you. That's the last thing I wanted."

She reached up and caressed his cheek. "It's actually been a relief. Like you and what happened with your wife, I've never discussed what happened except during the trial. I've never told anyone here the whole story, not even Valerie." She laid her head against his shoulder once again.

They lost track of time, drawing comfort from each other. He had offered to help carry her baggage. In truth, they were sharing each other's baggage. That was an even bigger step than the passion they had shared hours earlier.

CHAPTER 9

The following Friday, Ben came to pick up Kendall for a dinner date. A few minutes after his arrival, her mother called. When she heard her mother's voice on the machine, she was tempted not to pick it up. What would Ben think? She sighed and answered it.

"Hello, Mom. What's up?"

"I'm not sure. I went to the doctor's today."

"What's wrong?"

"It's probably nothing. I haven't been feeling well lately. He did some tests. I just thought since you didn't come home for Christmas, maybe you'd come this weekend."

"This weekend? What exactly is the problem?"

"I don't know. I won't know until I get the tests back."

"Well, let me know what the doctor says. I'm on my way out now. I'll call you tomorrow."

Ben listened to the conversation. Was this the

kind, gentle woman he had come to love? He had overheard another conversation with her mother. He had admitted that he might have been out of line with his comments then. This was different.

"Kendall, what was that about? Is your mother ill?"

She took a deep breath. "I don't know what my mother is trying to pull. She sounded fine and she wouldn't tell me much."

"What do you mean, you don't know what she's trying to pull? If she's sick . . . ?" He shook his head.

She went to get her coat. "Believe me, she's not sick. She was too vague when I asked for specifics. If she was really sick, she wouldn't hesitate to tell me. For some reason, she wants me to come to Philadelphia."

"She's your mother. If she wants to see you that badly, don't you think you should go? How can you just ignore her?"

She turned to face him. "You know nothing about my mother, or our relationship. Right now you think I'm the worst daughter in the world." She shook her head. "Fine, if that's what you think of me, so be it."

"Kendall, that's not true."

"Just go, Ben." She took her car keys from her bag.

"What are you doing?"

"I'm going to Philadelphia."

"Tonight?"

She stared at him. "Yes. That's what you wanted, isn't it?"

How had he let himself get into another argument about her mother? It had never occurred to him that he would get this reaction to his suggestion. She was not going to back down.

"Aren't you going to pack?"

"There's no need for that. I'll drive up there, find out that it's all a sham, and drive back home."

He shook his head. Even after overhearing her previous conversation with her mother, he was surprised at her attitude.

Her story about her marriage told him that she was strong and independent. Her actions with Mabel Jenkins told him that she could be gentle and patient. He now knew that she could also be stubborn.

"Kendall, you can't drive to Philadelphia and back alone in one evening."

"I'll be fine. The trip takes less than two hours."

"Each way, and it's after seven now."

She stared at him, teeth clenched. "I'll be fine."

He sighed. "Put your keys away. I'll drive you."

"No."

"Yes. I'm not going to argue with you about this, Kendall."

She dropped her keys back into her purse. "Fine."

A few minutes later, they were on their way. She had refused to pack any clothes. He stopped at a rest area along the way to eat. She refused that, too. The trip was made in silence until they reached the city. Then she gave him directions to her mother's house.

"Do you think you should call and let her know you're here?"

She glanced at her watch. The stop for dinner had delayed them. It was almost ten o'clock. She took her cell phone from her bag. Her mother answered on the second ring.

"Hi, Mom. I'm in the city. I'll be there in about half an hour." She clicked off the phone without waiting for a reply.

Ben glanced at her. How could she be so cold to her own mother?

She directed him to the alley behind the house where there was a short driveway. She let herself out of the car and started up the sidewalk to the door.

Her mother greeted her with an uncharacteristic smile. "I didn't expect you to come tonight." She started back toward the living room, leaving Kendall to close the door.

Ben entered as Kendall reached the living room. As he closed the door behind him, he heard Kendall's voice.

"I don't believe this. What's he doing here?"

He entered the living room as Jackie explained. "I invited him. You wouldn't even give him a chance. You wouldn't return his calls. You threw him out of your house."

Scott had risen from the sofa and was headed toward Kendall when Ben appeared in the doorway. He stopped abruptly.

"What's he doing here?"

"Who is this man?"

"He's the one who threw me out. I think she's living with him."

Kendall took a deep breath. Ignoring Scott, she looked at her mother. "I can't believe you'd sink this low, faking an illness to get me here. And for what?" She pointed at Scott. "For this?"

"I didn't fake an illness. I told you I had some tests done."

"Come off it, Mom. You implied that you were seriously ill. Why would you do this?" She glanced at Scott and then back at her mother. "How many times do I have to tell both of you that I'm not interested in anything he has to say."

"You won't even give him a chance."

"He tried to kill me!"

Jackie shook her head. "You know that's not true. You were upset. The man who attacked you resembled Scott, that's all."

Kendall took another deep breath. "You believe whatever you want." She grunted. "You know, I was mistaken. You *are* sick."

She put her hand on her hip. "Let me make this clear because I'm not going to have this conversation again. Scott, don't ever contact me again. Mother, if you insist on believing everything he tells you, that's your problem. I don't want to hear about it."

She pointed at Scott again. "If you think he's so wonderful, you marry him and let him sponge off you." Looking first at one and then the other, she nodded. "In fact, that's a very good idea. You deserve each other." With that statement, she turned and started toward the door.

Ben grabbed her hand. Then he put his arm around her shoulder. He stared at the two people who were undoubtedly responsible for most of the misery she had suffered.

"I have to say something."

Scott took a step forward. "This is none of your business."

"Wrong. I made the mistake of talking her into coming here. I owe her an apology for that. From what I've heard this evening, I'm not sure I can ever make it up to her."

He looked at Scott. "As for you, if I ever find out that you tried to contact Kendall again, I'll add my complaint to the police report. I'm sure you recall that I've had firsthand experience with your attitude toward her. Your attitude might even be considered threatening." His eyes narrowed. "On the other hand, maybe I won't bother with the police. Maybe I'll take care of you myself."

Scott took a step forward and sneered. "You can't threaten me. You're bluffing."

Ben raised an eyebrow. "You think so? Call it."

Scott clamped his lips together. He stepped back.

Ben turned toward Jackie. "This is your daughter and this man tried to kill her, after making her miserable for years. I don't know why you're so determined to take his side. I don't care."

He pulled Kendall close to his side. "I just have one more thing to say. I suggest you both listen carefully. Obviously, neither of you is concerned about her welfare. I am. I love Kendall. I'll do whatever is necessary to ensure her physical and emotional well-being, including protecting her from both of you." Still holding her close to him, he turned toward the door.

The return trip was made in silence. As they neared home, it occurred to Ben that Scott or Kendall's mother might call her that night. They impressed him as two people who would not give up easily. It was possible that his speech, rather than end their harassment, would goad them into retaliation against her for daring to involve him.

He glanced her way when they reached Baltimore. It came as no surprise that she was dozing. He made his decision. When he pulled into his garage, he called her name softly.

She stirred and opened her eyes. Scanning her surroundings, she frowned. "Where are we?"

"My house. I think you should spend the night here. Is that all right with you?"

Before falling asleep, she had considered the wisdom of unplugging her telephone. Although she had suspected that her mother's illness was a sham, it would never have occurred to her that her mother would actually arrange for Scott to be there when she arrived.

"Kendall, do you mind?"

"No, this is fine."

He ushered her into the house and helped her off with her coat. While he hung their coats, she went to the downstairs bathroom. When she entered the living room a few minutes later, he was standing beside the sofa.

"Why don't you sit down and relax. I'll fix something to eat."

She shook her head. "I'm not hungry."

"It's been a long day. You didn't have any dinner. You really should eat something."

She held her arms out at her sides. "Look at me, Ben. Do I look like I'll waste away by missing a meal?"

Without a word, he walked over to her and took her hands in his. He stared into her eyes for a few seconds. Then he lifted each hand in turn and kissed it.

"Don't do that. Don't you realize that your attitude is an insult to me?"

She looked away from him. He had called her beautiful more than once. Her question was almost like throwing those words back in his face.

"I didn't think of it that way. I'm s—"

He placed his finger over her lips. "Don't apologize. It's not necessary." His arms encircled her, pulling her close.

She closed her eyes and absorbed the comfort his embrace offered. "You're right. It's been a long day. I'm just tired."

He kissed the top of her head. "All right, honey, if you're sure you don't want anything to eat."

Taking her by the hand, he led her up the stairs. Bypassing the guest room, he ushered her into his bedroom. Between the exhaustion and the ideas running through her mind, she could hardly think straight.

He handed her a robe and showed her to a door near the far corner of the room. He opened the door and turned the switch. "This is the bathroom. You should find everything you need."

"Thanks."

When she emerged from the bathroom wearing the robe he had given her, he rose from the love seat. He held out his hand.

"I'll take that."

She placed her undergarments on the love seat and handed him her dress. While he went to hang it in the closet, she continued toward the bed. She snuggled into the covers, seeking comfort.

He closed the closet door and turned in time to see her yawning. He crossed the room and lay down beside her, enfolding her in his arms. Numerous questions ran through his mind. They would have to wait.

She sighed and nestled closer into his embrace. Within minutes, her soft even breathing told him that she was asleep.

He kissed her forehead. His hand absently caressed her back. Guilt assailed him. His suggestion was responsible for what she had been subjected to that evening.

His only saving grace was that he had insisted on driving her to Philadelphia. Facing those two alone would have been terrible enough. Driving back home alone after that confrontation could have been disastrous.

Kendall awoke the next morning alone in Ben's bed. The sound of the shower was evidence that he was not far away. She took the opportunity to examine the room she had barely noticed the previous night.

The king-size bed was covered in a luxurious midnight-blue velvet spread. The same shade of blue was picked up by the thin vertical stripes in the pale gold wallpaper. Behind her, the tall mahogany headboard was flanked by windows draped in scarves of a muted tapestry print of gold, blue, red, and green and covered with pale-gold Roman shades.

Gold-veined marble and mahogany encompassed and topped the fireplace that faced the bed. The love seat at the foot of the bed was covered in the same muted tapestry print as the window scarves. An assortment of large pillows were stacked on the floor near the fireplace.

She was still in the process of taking it all in when he appeared in the doorway leading from the bathroom wearing only a towel around his waist. She took a deep breath. She knew well what lay beneath the fluffy terry-cloth fabric.

He came toward her. "Good morning." He leaned over and kissed her cheek. "How do you feel?"

She bit her lip. "Do I dare say 'hungry'?"

He smiled. "In that case, you have ten minutes before I expect to see you in the kitchen to help make breakfast."

He headed back to the bathroom. The desire in

her eyes had not escaped his notice. Just before he reached the door, he grinned, unwrapped the towel, and threw it over his shoulder.

He re-emerged wearing another robe. Still smiling, he started toward the bedroom door.

"Ten minutes," he reminded her.

Fifteen minutes had elapsed when she joined him in the kitchen. She was wearing a luxurious silk robe she had found on a hook in the bathroom.

"I hope you don't mind the robe."

"Not at all, although I think you know what my preference would have been."

"It's a bit chilly for that."

He grinned. Handing her a mug of coffee, he glanced at the clock. "By the way, you're late."

She sipped her coffee. "Only because I took time to make the bed."

"You're excused."

"What do you want me to do?"

"Sit down and relax. I was only kidding about making you cook."

Neither of them mentioned the previous day's events until they had finished eating. Kendall was the first to speak.

Focusing her attention on her now-empty mug, she asked, "Did you mean what you said last night at my mother's house?"

She looked up when he made no immediate reply. He was standing beside her. Taking her hand, he urged her up from her seat and put his arms around her.

"Every word."

She looked up to meet his gaze. "I mean the part about . . ."

He nodded. "I know what you mean, sweetheart.

I meant exactly what I said." He kissed her tenderly. "I love you, Kendall. I think you love me, too." His thumb caressed her bottom lip. "That's not enough, though."

"What do you mean?" she murmured.

He sighed. "You have to trust me."

"I do trust you, Ben."

He loosed her from his embrace and took her hand, leading her from the kitchen to the sofa in the family room. He sat down, pulling her onto his lap.

"Why didn't you tell me about your mother?"

She bit her lip. "I was afraid of sounding neurotic."

"After what I saw and heard last night, you don't have to worry about that. Tell me now."

She sighed. "My mother. You saw my mother, my perfect size-six mother. She did look like she's gained some weight. She must be all of a size eight now." She shook her head. "I'm sure she'll do whatever it takes to keep from gaining any more weight. Heaven forbid that she should wear a double-digit size."

She clasped her hands together tightly. "Having a plus-size daughter threw her completely off balance. When my father was alive, he acted as a buffer between us so she tempered her comments. He and my grandmother, his mother, always made me feel special.

"Then they died, first my father and two years later, my grandmother. After that, my mother had full rein."

She looked up at him. "She didn't have as much control as she thought, though. She always packed my lunches for school, never allowing me to buy lunch in the cafeteria. Of course, she packed food like dry tuna fish and fresh fruit and vegetables.

"My friends in school felt sorry for me. They'd

share their lunches with me." She shrugged. "That was worse than if she had given me a normal lunch. I ended up with parts of lunches from four or five kids instead of one regular lunch. It drove my mother crazy. She couldn't understand why I was gaining weight."

"She never found out?"

She shook her head. "When I went away to college and started eating normal meals, I lost about thirty pounds. That thirty pounds wasn't enough for my mother, though. After a while, I accepted the fact that I'm just not meant to be petite."

He had the basic picture. There was one thing more. "You told me you met Scott in college. What was her reaction to that?"

She grunted. "When we started dating, her attitude was that I should be grateful that any man was willing to take a second look at me. When he proposed, I made the mistake of telling her that I wanted a big wedding." She swallowed. "She laughed. She said a woman my size had no business in a fancy white gown, that a tailored suit was more appropriate.

"No matter what Scott did, it wasn't his fault. He could do no wrong as far as she was concerned."

"What about when he tried to kill you?"

"You heard her last night. She refused to believe it. She said I had made a mistake, that he wasn't the one."

His eyes narrowed. "Yes, I heard and I could hardly believe my ears."

She had hesitated to tell him about her mother. After the previous night's fiasco, she had little choice. Once she started her narrative, she thought it might help to get it all out of her system after all this time. He'd said that she had no reason to fear that he would think her neurotic, but she wondered if she had made a mistake.

She nodded. "Now you know why I didn't want you to get involved in my problems."

He drew her close to him again. One hand caressed her hair while the other stroked her back. Then he leaned back to look her in the eye. He wiped away the tear that had escaped in spite of her effort to blink it back.

"Baby, please don't cry. I became involved when I started falling in love with you. Isn't that what people do when they're in love, help each other? Don't forget, it works both ways."

She nodded. "When I finally accepted the fact that I'll never please my mother, I thought the pain would go away. I guess it takes time for the pain to go away completely." She caressed his cheek. "You've helped more than you could know."

Grasping her hand, he turned his head slightly and kissed her palm. "That's the whole idea."

She frowned. "It may sound ridiculous, but as angry as she makes me, I can't help feeling a little sorry for her. As far back as I can remember, she's never had any friends."

That came as no surprise to him. If her mother had no friends, it was probably her own fault. She had driven her own daughter away. What had she done to her friends?

"Ben?"

"Hmmm?"

"Will I sound neurotic if I ask you why you love me?"

She had been living with her mother's demeaning attitude, and he could understand that there would be some remnants of insecurity. She needed to realize that her insecurity was not that unusual. He smiled.

"I could ask you the same question."

She snuggled closer into his embrace. "That's easy. You're strong and gentle. You're kind and intelligent. I'm comfortable with you. More than that, you make me feel special."

"You are special. You're all of those things you just named and more. It's hard to explain and I've decided not to try. Just being with you makes me feel good." Even before her betrayal, he had never felt this way about Christine.

She looked up into his eyes. "Strong?"

He nodded. "Maybe not physically, but you're strong. You've survived and succeeded in spite of what you've been through. Not only have you survived, it amazes me that you haven't become bitter and mean."

Kendall sighed. "I can thank my father and grandmother for most of that. Their love and acceptance are probably responsible for my resistance to anorexia or bulimia. I can't forget the friends who stuck by me, too. I think back now on the ones in elementary school who helped by giving me some control over my life." She looked up at him. "Or maybe I just like food too much to give it up and the idea of deliberating purging myself is more repulsive than being overweight."

He kissed her forehead. "Whatever the reason, I'm glad." He stroked her hip. "I like the way you feel in my arms." He nibbled her ear. "Maybe you need another demonstration to convince you."

A shiver passed through her. She caressed the nape of his neck. "If I say that I'm already convinced, does that mean I won't get another demonstration?"

His hand slid into the opening of her robe, fondling her soft full breast. "What do you think?"

His thumb stroked the tip while his tongue outlined the curve of her ear. Then he planted kisses in the crook of her neck, inhaling the sweet fragrance that pervaded her skin.

Her breath caught in her throat. Shivers ran up and down her spine. The scent of his cologne teased her nostrils. Her hands gripped his shoulders, the muscles flexing beneath her fingers.

He continued his trail of kisses until he reached her breast. Then his tongue traced circles around the tip before his mouth closed over the soft globe gently suckling the rigid nipple.

His fingers deftly loosed the belt of her robe, giving him access to her soft thighs. He ran his hands up the silky skin to the triangle of hair, where his fingers probed until he found the entrance. She was so hot and wet. His mouth left her breast to capture her lips in a kiss that increased the desire spreading through their bodies.

She moaned as his fingers advanced and retreated. Her legs parted in response to his explorations. Heat flowed through her veins. She welcomed his tongue as it mimicked the movement of his fingers. When his thumb stroked the magic nub, she trembled with spasms. Then the spasms gave way to ecstasy. A moment later, she collapsed in his arms.

He eased her back until she was lying down. A moment later he was settled between her thighs. He sighed when her hot wet sheath welcomed him. Her legs embraced him, drawing him deeper.

She would have been content to simply do her part to aid his fulfillment. Instead, as his thrusts increased, she was once again transported to a realm of incredible pleasure. Her body contracted around him, lifting him to those heights she had reached moments before.

He collapsed on top of her for a moment, before raising up to rest on his elbows. He kissed her neck.

She kissed his ear. "Did you plan this?" she whispered.

He grinned. "Not exactly. That little packet was in the pocket of my robe because I was hoping to convince you to come here after dinner last night."

She caressed his bottom lip with her thumb. "And I fell asleep and ruined your plans."

"You more than made up for it, baby."

CHAPTER 10

Kendall had been so wrapped up in her relationship with Ben that she had given no more thought to Valerie's information that Francine and Darren were dating. That is, until she encountered the two of them the following Monday.

As Kendall entered their office building after lunch, Francine was getting out of Darren's car. The smiles on their faces faded when they saw Kendall.

Kendall shook her head and continued walking through the lobby. A few minutes later, Francine joined the group of people waiting for the elevator. Kendall received no reply to her greeting.

Later that afternoon, Kendall came face-to-face with Francine again. This time, Kendall gave her no chance to ignore her.

"Do you have a problem with something I've said or done, Francine? You barely speak and I get the feeling that you've been avoiding me."

"I haven't been avoiding you. I just didn't want

to get into an argument with you. Darren told me what Valerie did and I know you'll take her side."

Kendall shook her head. "I don't know what Darren told you. Whatever it is, that's between the three of you."

"Well, maybe you don't know what your friend is really like. She's competitive to the point of stealing commissions. The Sterling property was Darren's account until she stole it from him."

Kendall bit her lip. She could not resist correcting Francine's statement.

"She didn't steal the account. Mr. Briggs reassigned it to her."

"After she told him all sorts of lies about Darren. Mrs. Ferguson knew what she was doing. She just changed her mind and blamed it on Darren."

Kendall held up her hand. "Francine, I'm sorry I said anything. I'm not going to get into a long discussion about who did or said what. You choose to believe Darren." She shrugged. "That's your right."

Francine grunted. "Valerie doesn't seem to think so. She said I should stop seeing him."

Kendall raised an eyebrow.

Francine pursed her lips. "Well, maybe not those words exactly, but the message was clear. Girlfriend thinks that because she has Gary, she can give me advice on my love life. I bet she does the same thing with you."

Her smirk told Kendall that she was not likely to change her attitude. "She doesn't mean any harm, Francine. Besides, you can always ignore the advice without getting angry about it."

"Maybe, but I can't ignore what she did to Darren."

"That's too bad. I hate to see your friendship ruined by this disagreement."

Francine shrugged. "That's up to her."

Kendall shook her head. "No, it's up to both of you." She sighed. "I'm not taking anyone's side. I'd still like to be your friend, Francine, but I won't be put in the middle of this situation."

After that exchange, they went their separate ways. Kendall thought about her own experience with Valerie's well-meaning advice. Would she feel the same if Valerie had voiced a dislike for Ben? Would she ignore her friend's advice and follow her own instincts? Probably.

She hoped, for Francine's sake, that she and Valerie were wrong in their assessment of Darren. Maybe he was different when he was with Francine. Maybe Francine would be a good influence on him. She posed this possibility to Valerie when she called on Friday evening.

"What's up, girlfriend?" Valerie asked. "Are you busy?"

"Just putting a few things together for the banquet tomorrow."

"I forgot that you're working this weekend. I was calling to see if you and Ben wanted to go out to dinner with us tomorrow."

"Sorry, Ben will probably be working weekends for a while. He started work on the Sterling mansion a couple of weeks ago."

"How's it going?"

"He said the house is in pretty good shape basically. The plumbing and electrical system need a lot of work. It's hard to tell how long it'll take to finish it."

"Has Sheila called you about the Open House?"

"No, maybe she decided to hire someone else or do it herself."

"That's possible. I guess she could get help from the Historical Society volunteers."

"If she decides to hire me, I hope she doesn't wait until the last minute. I'm free next month, but I still need time to arrange the catering."

They chatted for a few more minutes before Kendall recalled her conversation with Francine. "I talked to Francine earlier this week. I think it's hopeless trying to convince that Darren has any bad points."

"At least she's speaking to you."

"Is it possible that he's not as bad as we think? Maybe he's changed. She might have had a good influence on him."

Valerie sighed. "I wish I could believe that. His attitude at work is even worse than before. What did she tell you?" She immediately backed off from that question. "Never mind. I won't ask you to carry tales back and forth."

Kendall hesitated. "It's not a matter of carrying tales. He's blaming you for his loss of the Sterling sale."

"That doesn't surprise me. I'm just concerned that she's buying his story and that she'll be devastated when she learns the truth."

"There's not much we can do about it, Valerie. She'll have to find out for herself what he's really like."

"I hope she finds out before she gets too deeply involved."

Kendall made no reply to that. "If not, she won't be the first woman to face disappointment in a relationship."

There was no doubt that Kendall knew about such things firsthand. "Well, I'd better let you go and finish your work," said Valerie.

"I'll check with Ben. If you have no plans for the next few weeks, maybe we can get together one Saturday."

"That sounds good. We don't have any specific plans."

When Kendall returned home from her banquet the following night, she had a message from Sheila. She wrote down the number and went upstairs to prepare for bed. She had just turned down the bed when the telephone rang. She picked up the receiver and smiled when she heard Ben's voice.

"Hi, sweetheart. How was the banquet?"

"Fine. How was your day?"

"Good. We've almost finished the plumbing."

"I had a message from Sheila. I think she wants me to plan the Open House. I won't be able to talk to her until Monday."

"I wouldn't think that a job like that would involve as much work as some of your other jobs."

"That's what I'm counting on. If nothing else, it should involve little in the way of decorations. She might not even need a professional caterer. There are other options that would be less expensive and not too much work. I won't know until I talk to her to find out just what she has in mind." She yawned.

Ben chuckled. "You sound exhausted. I'll let you go to bed. I just wanted to say good night and I love you."

"Good night. I love you, too."

* * *

The following Saturday, Ben came by after work. He had worked the previous Sunday and every day and evening since then. Kendall greeted him with a hug and a kiss. Then her hand caressed his cheek.

"You look tired," she said.

Placing his hand over hers, he turned his head slightly and kissed the palm. Then his arms encircled her waist.

"I've missed you," he murmured before his lips claimed hers in a more satisfying kiss than the one that had greeted him.

She linked her hands behind his neck, parting her lips to welcome his questing tongue. Her fingers stroked the nape of his neck. When he finally lifted his head, breaking the kiss, she lowered her arms and wrapped them around his waist.

"I've missed you, too."

The rest of the evening was spent making up for lost time. It was as if they had been apart for weeks instead of days. Making love was their appetizer before dinner and their dessert afterward.

During breakfast the next day, Ben brought her up to date on the progress of the Sterling mansion. She told him about her conversation with Sheila.

"If the renovations are finished in time, will you be able to plan the Open House? Do you have any other parties next month?"

"I'm free for the next two months. Remember, I told you that I had started cutting back on the parties after I bought the house."

"I remember." He shook his head. "So here you

are with free weekends and I'm the one working six or seven days a week."

"That's not entirely true. I'm not really free next weekend. I have to go to Chicago on Sunday. I won't be back until Wednesday."

"Chicago?"

She nodded. "A conference for my job."

He frowned. "That means you'll be away on Valentine's Day."

"I know." It was ironic that she had finally found a man who gave Valentine's Day special meaning and she would be more than a thousand miles away from him.

He reached across the table and clasped her hand. "We'll just have to have a special celebration when you get back home."

She smiled. "That sounds interesting. What did you have in mind?"

"Whatever you like. If you don't have any suggestions, I'll think of something." He lifted her hand and kissed it. "Now, what would you like to do today?"

She shrugged. "Nothing special. After the week you just had, you deserve a rest. Maybe we can just relax and watch television or rent a movie."

They settled on a suspense movie. Neither cared that they had seen the movie already. All that mattered was that they were together.

Once Ben began the renovations on the Sterling mansion, no one gave any thought to the man who had wanted the property for development. They would never have believed his determination.

Red-faced, George Mueller paced his office. "I want that property."

"The property's still up for sale, Mr. Mueller. Even without the mansion, it's still a large piece of property."

Mueller stopped abruptly and slammed his fist down on the desk. "Whoever heard of a modern resort with an outdated house smack dab in the middle of it."

"The mansion's not really in the middle of it. There's already a fence around it. You could put up a higher fence around the resort and no one would even notice the mansion."

The veins in Mueller's neck bulged. "You telling me my business? You sound like that woman. She's been trying to sell me that crap. She's the one responsible for keeping me from tearing it down."

His eyes narrowed. "If you want to make any money on this deal, you better get rid of the house."

"How?"

Mueller sat down in the chair behind his desk. He leaned back.

"That's your problem. When you figure it out, we can do business."

Mueller's visitor took the hint. The conversation was over.

On the Friday evening before her trip, Kendall awaited Ben's arrival for dinner. Instead, she received a telephone call.

"Hi, baby. I'm at the hospital."

Her breath caught in her throat. Immediately after her initial reaction, she realized he must be all right since he made the call.

"What's wrong? Are you okay?"

"I'm fine. Joe's been injured. Part of the second

floor of the mansion collapsed. He was lucky that there was a sofa beneath him when he fell."

She could not help latching onto one sentence. "The floor caved in? I thought you said it was structurally sound." She regretted her question immediately.

There was a pause before he answered. "I thought it was."

She was uncertain if he was keeping some bit of information from her or if he was embarrassed by being wrong in his assessment. The tone of his voice was definitely not normal.

"I'm sorry. I didn't mean that the way it sounded."

"I know. It's okay. Don't worry about it." He sighed. "I'm a little puzzled myself."

"Is Joe all right?"

"He'll be fine. They took X rays. Nothing's broken, just a few bruises and scrapes."

He paused. She heard voices in the background. Then he was back on the line.

"Honey, I have to go. I think Joe's ready to leave."

"Are you taking him home?"

"No, he insists he can drive. I'll take him to pick up his car and then follow him home. He'll probably insist that that's not necessary either, but I'll feel better if I see him safely home."

"Do you know what time you'll be here?"

"Probably not for at least another hour."

"Okay, I'll see you later."

Although he had assured her that he was uninjured, Kendall breathed a sigh of relief when he arrived. He was still wearing jeans and a sweatshirt sprinkled with plaster.

She hugged him tightly. That and her kiss told him that she had not been as unconcerned as she sounded on the telephone. Soon the white dust dotted her caftan.

When she broke the kiss, he stepped back and shook his head. "I should have gone home first and changed clothes."

"No, you shouldn't have." She glanced at the bag he had set on the floor when he entered. "Aren't your clothes in there?"

He nodded.

She shrugged. "Then going home first would have been a waste of time."

He smiled and kissed the tip of her nose. "If you say so." He started toward the stairs, and then turned back to face her. "I'm going to take a shower. Would you care to join me?"

"I have to warm your dinner." She tilted her head to the side. "I took a shower when I got home from work. Do you think I need another one?"

He closed the short distance between them and took her in his arms. "Dinner can wait." His hand petted the curve of her derriere. He grinned. "The shower that I had in mind isn't just for getting clean."

He loosed her from his embrace and took a step back, holding out his hand. She placed her hand in his and together they ascended the stairs.

They left a trail of clothes on her bedroom floor. When they reached the bathroom, she handed him the small packet she had taken from her caftan pocket.

"If this is leading where I think it's leading, you'll need this."

He grinned. "I thought 'Be Prepared' was only the Boy Scouts' motto."

She shrugged. "You've taught me to live by that motto when you're around."

He chuckled and set the packet on the side of the tub. Lifting the shower spray from its holder, he stepped into the tub behind her. Before long, they were lathering each other's bodies.

"Turn around, please," she requested softly. When he complied, she splayed her hands across his back. Reveling in the sensation of his muscles flexing beneath her fingers, she worked her way down to his taut buttocks and gently squeezed. Still not satisfied, she slipped her hand between his thighs. She smiled when her explorations evoked his sharp intake of breath.

Then she moved to stand in front of him once again. This time, she started by drawing soapy circles on his chest before moving lower.

He called up his reserves of self-control as she stroked his member. Finally, he could stand it no longer. He stilled her hands.

After rinsing himself and her, he dropped to his knees. His hands squeezed the round cheeks of her buttocks as he blazed a trail of kisses across her torso and abdomen. He paused only long enough to unfurl the contents of the packet onto his rigid member.

She clutched his shoulders and moaned when he resumed his sweet torture, his fingers entering her slippery sheath. Her legs parted, allowing him complete access to the rigid nub. Her knees weakened. He lowered her onto his shaft. As he leaned back on his haunches, her legs encircled his waist.

They moved together, slowly at first. Their lips met eagerly. His thrusts increased in intensity as his mouth left hers to taste and tease each breast in turn.

She trembled in his arms when he raised slightly on his haunches. Her breathing and pulse rate increased with each thrust.

"Please, Ben, oh, please."

"Soon, baby, very soon."

He tightened his arms around her, drawing her closer. That movement was all she needed. Her body shuddered with a series of spasms before she cried out his name. With a final thrust, he found his own release.

With her legs still around his waist, he eased his body into a sitting position. His hands continued to stroke her silky skin as soft tremors shook her.

She loosened the grip she had on his waist, stretching her legs out behind him. Splaying her hands across his back, she gently nipped his earlobe.

"Is this one of those positions those ladies warned us about?" she whispered.

They were still joined together, too tired and content to move. He chuckled. His breath caught in his throat when her body tightened in response to his laughter.

"I don't know, but I think we should take their advice and enjoy it while we can." He kissed her lightly and eased their bodies apart. "I can't imagine why, but suddenly I'm starved."

A few minutes later, she headed downstairs, leaving him to gather the clothing strewn across the floor. When he joined her, clad in his robe, she was placing several dishes of Chinese food in the microwave oven.

He helped himself to water from the refrigerator and took a seat at the small table. "I'm going to have to call Sheila tomorrow and give her the bad news. With this setback, I don't think we'll finish the job this month."

"We should all just be grateful that Joe wasn't seriously injured."

He nodded. "I still don't know how I overlooked the rotted flooring. I'll check it more thoroughly in the morning."

She set a plate and utensils on the table in front of him. "Do you want anything else to drink?"

"No, thanks." He smiled. "I'm just basking in all this service."

"Don't get accustomed to it." She leaned over and kissed his cheek. "I'm just glad to see that you're all right."

The timer went off and she removed the containers from the oven. She set them on the table and took a seat across from him.

"You're not eating?" he asked.

She shook her head. "I've been nibbling from the containers since you called. I'm sure I've had an entire meal by now. I'm not hungry." She smiled. "I guess our little exercise was more strenuous for you than for me."

"Hmm, I'll have to remember that. Next time I'll let you do the work."

"Next time, huh? When would that be?"

He looked up at the clock on the wall. "Maybe a few hours."

She shook her head. "I plan to be asleep in a few hours."

He shrugged. "Oh, well, I guess I'll have to wait."

As it turned out, his first estimate had been correct. He was awakened before dawn by the caress of her hand. Soon she was straddling his hips. Their renewed passion soon carried them to the rapture they always shared so completely.

While Ben was at the Sterling mansion the next day, Kendall packed for her trip. She was due at the airport by one o'clock the next day. She wanted no last-minute packing to interfere with their evening together.

After he left the mansion, Ben visited his mother. Although he called his mother at least twice a week, he could not assuage a sense of guilt. His last visit had been more than two weeks earlier and brief.

That concern was minor compared to the problem he had discovered in his examination at the mansion. Something had eaten away a section of the floorboards. He was certain that the rot had not been there at his first inspection. The problem was being able to prove it.

He considered the possibility of termites. The mansion had been treated for termites years ago. As a precaution, Sheila had also had the building inspected by an exterminator. Ben had enough experience himself to recognize termite damage. What he saw had nothing to do with insects.

He had taken a piece of the rotted board. He had no idea what he would do with it. If he took it to the police to be tested and they found nothing unusual, he would look and feel like a paranoid fool.

His only other option was to be more careful. Sheila had limited access to the code for the alarm system because the house still contained a few valuable antiques. As far as he knew, aside from

Mrs. Ferguson, he and Sheila were the only ones with the code. It was the best they could do short of hiring a full-time security guard. Mrs. Ferguson had seen no need for that, and the society could not afford such an expense.

It crossed his mind that Kendall was bound to ask what he had discovered. If he shared his suspicions with her, she would worry. He had no choice but to let her believe that he had erred in his original assessment of the mansion's condition.

He was reminded of this decision when his mother raised the topic of his latest assignment. "How's the work coming on the mansion?"

As he planned to do with Kendall, he saw no need to worry her about his concerns. "We've run into some unexpected problems. It's nothing we can't fix, but it means that we probably won't be able to finish the work this month."

"That's too bad, but it seemed to me that it was a lot to expect with such short notice."

Rosa was more concerned with personal matters. Other than the visit he and Kendall had paid on New Year's Day, she had had no opportunity to see them together. Since then, he had missed two of his weekly visits. When he'd called, she'd brushed aside his apology, explaining to him that she had never felt those visits were necessary. This change and her observations of Ben and Kendall on New Year's Day were enough to suggest to Rosa that theirs was more than a casual relationship.

"How's Kendall?"

He chuckled. "Kendall's fine, Mom." He nodded

slowly. "And to answer the other question that's on your mind, I think she's the one."

"So, what's the problem?"

"You don't seem surprised by my statement."

"I've seen and heard enough to have guessed what was happening between you two. You don't seem heartbroken, so I have to believe that she shares your feelings. So again, what's the problem?"

"It's not really a problem. She survived a really bad marriage. I hope it's just a matter of being patient. I don't want to rush her."

He grunted. "Her marriage was only one of her problems," he went on. "You were right about her mother. I met her. She's a real piece of work."

"From what you told me about the conversation you overheard, at least Kendall's found a way to cope with her."

He recalled Kendall's speech to her mother at their last encounter and their conversation the following day. He nodded. "She's still hurt, but yes, she's learned to cope."

He smiled. "Enough about me. What have you been up to lately?"

"I'm thinking of taking a cruise." That was enough to send her off on a tangent. She spent the next half hour telling him about her planned trip with her friend Delia.

Ben was prepared for Kendall's questions when he arrived at her house early that afternoon. He let her believe that he had overlooked a few rotted floorboards.

"Do you have any idea how long it will take to repair the damage?"

He shook his head. "Not yet. I called Sheila and told her that I'd let her know next week. She was disappointed in having to delay the Open House, but she agreed that it's best not to rush the repairs."

Before she had time to ask more questions, he changed the subject. "What time to you have to be at the airport?"

"One o'clock. My flight leaves at three."

"We can have lunch at the airport after you check in. How does that sound?"

"Sounds good, if it doesn't take two hours for me to check in."

"We can go earlier if you like. Maybe we can beat the crowd if we get there by noon."

"Sounds good, as long as everyone else doesn't have the same idea."

"Let's hope not. We'll give it a shot."

After sharing lunch at the airport the next day, Ben and Kendall said their good-byes at the security gate. "I'll pick you up on Wednesday. Don't work too hard."

She smiled. "That should be my line to you."

He watched as she walked toward the gate. For one fleeting moment, he was tempted to call her back. Now that she had come into his life, he could not imagine life without her.

CHAPTER 11

While Kendall was overseeing her conference and Ben was working hard to repair the damage at the Sterling mansion, George Mueller was entertaining a visitor. Well, maybe calling it entertaining was stretching the definition.

Mueller shook his head in disgust. "I can't believe that you thought a few rotting boards would stop them."

"I didn't know what else to do. I thought they would conclude that the house was too damaged for it to be safe and that it would be condemned."

"Haven't you learned that you can't wait for them to condemn the building themselves? You have to get rid of it completely. Fix it so that there's nothing left to be repaired. Like a bomb, or a fire."

His visitor's eyes widened. "A bomb? You can't be serious."

"I'm very serious. This isn't a game. Either you want the money or you don't."

"I don't know anything about bombs."

Mueller shook his head again. "There must be a hundred books out there that can teach you how to make a bomb. If not, I'm sure you can find what you need on the Internet."

The man bit his lip. He had never counted on this. Getting into the house the first time and causing damage was one thing. Planting a bomb was a different matter. He would have to make sure that he was far enough away before it went off. He wanted the money Mueller had promised him. He needed that money.

Mueller interrupted his musings. "Time is running out. I'm tired of waiting. If I change my mind, you'll lose. If I have to, I can build my development somewhere else and still make a bundle of money."

His visitor had no idea that Mueller was bluffing. The developer had been looking for another piece of land with no luck. Nothing suited his plans like that acreage.

"It's up to you."

Kendall awoke to bad news on Wednesday. The snowstorm the previous day had delayed all flights. In spite of this, the airline insisted that her flight was scheduled to leave only three hours late.

Soon after she arrived at the airport, another storm hit. As a result of the second storm, no flights would be taking off that day.

She retrieved her cell phone from her handbag to call Ben. She had called earlier to inform him of the late arrival. There was no need to interrupt him at work again. She would leave a message on his home telephone.

She dialed the number and was greeted by a woman's voice. "May I speak to Ben?"

There was an obvious testiness in the voice. "You have the wrong number." Before she could ask any more questions, she heard a click.

Kendall turned off the cell phone and stared at it. She tried not to jump to conclusions. Why was a woman answering his phone? Who was she? The voice sounded too young to be his mother. Maybe it was his sister, but why was she there? And why did she hang up so abruptly? She shook her head.

Twenty-four hours later, her flight finally took off. It was late on Thursday when her plane landed. At least she did not have to worry about going to work the next day. When she called Mr. Briggs to tell him of the delay, he had insisted that since the next day was Friday, there was no need for her to come in to the office.

As she stood in the baggage-claim area, she was surprised to see Ben walk through the door. "What are you doing here?" she asked after he greeted her with a hug and a kiss. "How did you know when my flight would get in?"

"After your call, I figured I'd better check with the airline before coming out here, especially after hearing about the second storm. Why didn't you call back?"

She said nothing of her call to his home. "I didn't want to bother you at work again and I wasn't sure exactly when the flight would take off."

She spied her bag just as she finished her explanation. Thankful for the diversion, she started toward it.

Ben reached it first and lifted it from the conveyor belt. Placing his other hand beneath her elbow, he steered her toward the door.

When they arrived at her house, he carried her bag up to her bedroom. "Are you hungry?"

"A little. I'm more interested in a nice hot shower."

"Soup and a sandwich okay?"

"That's fine."

He left her to her shower and unpacking. Something was wrong. Other than to tell him that the conference had gone well, she had been silent during the ride from the airport. He'd chalked it up to exhaustion, at first. Now he was not so sure.

When Kendall exited the bathroom after her shower, he was sitting on the side of the bed. "I thought you were fixing something to eat," she said.

"I did." He walked over to her. Taking both of her hands in his, he backed up. Then he sat back down on the bed and pulled her down onto his thigh.

"What's wrong?" he asked. "I know you must be exhausted, but that's not the real problem. What is it?"

They had come too far in their relationship to beat around the bush. "You asked why I didn't call a second time. I did call, but I called your house, not the cell phone."

"You didn't leave a message?"

"I didn't get a chance. A woman answered the phone and abruptly hung up after telling me that I had the wrong number."

"And you didn't call back?"

"What would have been the point? Who was she?"

He shook his head. "Honey, I have no idea. You must have dialed the wrong number."

That explanation seemed too easy. She squirmed as if she was trying to stand up. His arms tightened around her waist.

"I dialed the number on the back of the card you gave me months ago. Did you change your number?"

He took a deep breath. "No, I haven't changed the number. Where's the card?"

He loosed his hold on her. She retrieved the card from her day planner and read the number on the back.

He frowned. "That's not the right number. It's two-eight, not two-nine."

She held out the card. "Are you telling me that last number is an eight?"

He nodded and looked more closely at the card. "I plead guilty to having terrible handwriting. I guess the lower loop on the eight would be in question."

She looked closely at the card again. She could just glimpse what could be construed as a loop instead of a straight line. She walked over to the telephone beside the bed, picked up the receiver, and dialed what he insisted was the correct number. This time she heard his voice.

He came up behind her and enfolded her in his arms. He kissed the top of her head.

She sighed. "I'm sorry. I guess you don't have a monopoly on jumping to conclusions."

He turned her around to face him. Placing his hand beneath her chin, he urged her to meet his gaze.

"Do you what's the really important part of this lesson?"

"What?"

"That you didn't sweep your suspicions under the rug, that you told me what you suspected."

"Mostly because you wouldn't let me ignore it."

He kissed her forehead and smiled. "Good, I'll have to remember that."

"That's not all of it, though." She took a deep breath and looked away from his gaze. "I remembered what you said about trust. I remembered all of the time we've spent together. Deep down, I didn't really believe that you would be that deceitful." She met his gaze. "Can we just say that I was tired and didn't quite know what I was doing?"

He chuckled and hugged her tightly. "Sweetheart, we can chalk it up to whatever you like as long you believe that I love you and that I would never do anything to hurt you."

"I do believe that. I love you, too."

He kissed her cheek. "Let's go see about your dinner, such as it is."

Ben sat across the table from her while she ate. Aside from her exhaustion, she appeared to be in pain.

"Are you okay? You look like you're hurting."

"I'm just stiff. Twenty-four hours sitting in airport chairs isn't really conducive to relaxing."

"We'll see what we can do about that after you've finished eating."

She raised an eyebrow.

He shook his head. "I know I seem to have a one-track mind when I'm with you, but that's not what I mean. What I have in mind is a relaxing massage."

"Oh."

Ben was true to his word. Kendall soon found herself stretched out on her bed while his hands gently kneaded and soothed her aching muscles. She closed her eyes and gladly submitted to his ministrations.

He continued to work his magic until her soft breathing suggested that she had fallen asleep. He called her name softly. There was no response. He pulled the covers up over her and tucked them in around her shoulders. After placing a kiss on her cheek, he turned out the light.

A few minutes later, he slid into bed beside her. She snuggled closer to him. He pulled her into his arms. A feeling of pure contentment washed over him and soon he, too, was sound asleep.

Kendall awoke late the next morning alone in bed. She listened for the sound of the shower. Then she spied the note on the pillow reminding her that Ben was at work. She left the bed and made her way to the kitchen.

Ben called shortly before lunch. "I hope I didn't wake you this morning when I left."

"I don't even remember your leaving. I did see your note, though."

"I promised you a belated Valentine's Day celebration, remember? Have you rested up enough for dinner and dancing tonight?"

She laughed. "Considering the fact that I've only been up for about an hour, I should be very well rested. Dinner and dancing sounds fine. What time?"

"I'm hoping to leave here by five. I'll pick you up at six-thirty. If I run into a problem, I'll call you."

* * *

Later that afternoon, Kendall prepared for her date. She clipped the tags from the dress she had purchased a few weeks earlier with just such an occasion as this in mind. It was red, not a subtle burgundy or claret, but definitely red. The silk fabric of the mock-wrap-style sheath was gathered at the side of the waist and accented with a circular rhinestone pin.

She clipped on pendant-style rhinestone earrings. After trying several necklaces, she shook her head. The cleavage exposed by the vee neckline needed no enhancement.

The doorbell rang as she slid her feet into silver strappy high heels. Picking up the matching clutch bag, she went to greet Ben.

She stared at him for a few seconds when she opened the door. She had long ago concluded that whoever said, "Clothes make the man," had been mistaken. Whether dressed in a sweatshirt and jeans or a tuxedo, he took her breath away. But then, she was prejudiced. She was in love with him.

He was having similar thoughts of his own. He still sometimes wondered at the good fortune that had brought her into his life. He smiled.

"May I come in?"

She stepped aside. "Sorry, I guess my mind was somewhere else."

As he entered, he took two boxes from behind his back. "These are for you."

The heart-shaped box contained the usual assortment of chocolates. She slid the ribbon from around the other box and lifted the lid to find what had to be at least two dozen roses.

Her eyes widened. "They're beautiful, Ben. You didn't have to do this. I thought our celebration was dinner and dancing." She started toward the kitchen. "Let me put these in water."

"You can't have Valentine's Day without chocolates and roses," he insisted, following her.

She pulled a vase from a cupboard and filled it with water. He waited while she arranged the roses and then set them on the table.

"They really are beautiful. What made you decide on two colors?"

He took her in his arms. "I know the red roses are for love. I think I heard somewhere that yellow roses are for friendship. You can't get a better combination than that."

"You're absolutely right." She linked her arms behind his neck, urging his head down. Their lips met in a kiss that promised an evening of pleasure and passion.

"We'd better get going or we'll lose our reservation and end up ordering pizza for dinner."

The evening, and the night, lived up to the promise of that kiss. The candlelight and dancing were only the beginning. His reason for questioning whether she had had a good night's rest became clear when they returned to his house.

After he lit the fire in the bedroom, he went into the bathroom. While he was gone, she quickly undressed. When he returned to the bedroom, she was clad only in two scraps of red lace.

She smiled. "Happy Valentine's Day. I feel a little guilty. You gave me chocolates and those beautiful flowers and all I gave you was a card." She sighed as she strolled toward him. "I guess I'll have to come up with something else for you."

He grinned. "I think you already have."

She started unbuttoning his shirt, shaking her head. "This is only the beginning."

She took her time undressing him. Her hands and lips teased every inch of skin that was exposed with each article of clothing that she removed. She ran her fingers across his shoulders and down his chest, threading them through the springy tendrils. Then her hand followed the trail of hair down his abdomen.

His body reacted to each touch. If he had been able to form a cohesive thought, he might have compared her actions and his reactions to a musician slowly tightening the strings of a violin. He co-operated for as long as he could stand the sweet torture.

He moaned when her hand encircled his member and then began sliding back and forth. "You're killing me, baby."

"I can't help myself. I love touching you." She smiled. "You'll survive. I promise." She leaned forward, inscribing circles on his chest with her tongue.

Then she allowed him a moment to catch his breath when she took him by the hand and led him to the bed. She retrieved the little packet from the bedside table. His respite was short-lived. She knelt in front of him and slowly unfurled the contents of the packet onto his rigid shaft. She patted his organ before letting her fingers play in the mat of hair surrounding her handiwork.

Then she stood up. First her thumbs and then her tongue lightly scraped his nipples. She closed her eyes and inhaled the tangy scent that infused his skin.

He had reached his limit. His hands encircled her body, unhooking the lacy fabric and freeing the full round breasts that seemed to beg for his touch. He obliged enthusiastically, fondling and kneading the soft globes. His thumbs grazed the nipples, smiling when they hardened immediately.

She moaned and clutched his shoulders. Her hands slid down his spine to stroke and squeeze his taut buttocks.

When her hands moved up to his waist, he eased her down onto the bed. Slipping his fingers into the waistband of her panties, he quickly disposed of the last barrier. Then he lay down beside her.

"Now it's my turn."

His fingers inscribed circles on her abdomen while he lowered his mouth to her bosom. He inhaled her sweet, intoxicating fragrance while he suckled each enticing breast. His hand moved lower, seeking the hot wet sheath.

She gasped. This magic he created with just a touch amazed her. Her body tightened around his probing fingers. Heat coursed through her veins and settled in that same spot. There was only one thought in her mind.

"Ben, I need you."

"I'm all yours, baby."

He settled between her thighs. His lips claimed hers, drinking in all of the sweetness that she offered.

Her legs immediately encircled his waist when he entered her. She clasped his buttocks and met each thrust eagerly. Her breath caught in her throat as her body shook with spasms.

His next thrust sent them both over the edge. When they were able to breathe again, they sighed in unison.

He lay there on top of her for a moment. Then he rolled onto his back, pulling her into the crook of his arm. He pulled the covers up over them, tucking them around her shoulders. He kissed her forehead.

"Happy Valentine's Day to you, too, sweetheart." Passion sated, they were asleep within minutes.

CHAPTER 12

On the Wednesday before her first meeting with Sheila, Kendall had dinner with Valerie. Both Ben and Gary were working late, and the two women decided it was time to catch up on each other's lives.

"I feel guilty for neglecting you," Kendall told her friend.

Valerie leaned forward and smiled. "You could make it up to me by telling me what's going on with you and Ben."

The smile that spread across Kendall's face was unlike any Valerie had seen in all their years of friendship. "He loves me, Valerie. He really loves me."

"I can't say that surprises me. If you remember, I told you there was something special in the way he looked at you as far back as the closing."

"Your observation was a little premature."

"Maybe. What about you?"

"Do you really have to ask?"

"No, but I wanted to hear you admit it."

She sighed. "Yes, I love him. I guess that's why I've been afraid to believe that he feels the same about me." She took a deep breath. "Saying it aloud is a little scary. You know what my track record is like."

Valerie rolled her eyes. "Are you still holding those blind dates against me?"

Kendall shook her head and smiled. "No, I've forgiven you for those."

Valerie tilted her head to the side. "You know, in a roundabout way, I can take credit for introducing you to Ben."

Kendall raised an eyebrow. "How did you come up with that?"

"His house."

"You're forgetting that I had met him before I bought his house."

Valerie waved that suggestion aside. "That doesn't count. I think meeting you at settlement and having that connection was just what he needed to start the ball rolling."

Kendall chose not to burst her friend's bubble by telling her about their first date. "If you say so."

Their lunch arrived, and they chatted about other topics. Before they parted company, they tentatively arranged for the four of them to have dinner on Saturday.

Kendall and Sheila's meeting took place on Saturday as planned. Ben had completed the renovations on Thursday. The Open House was scheduled to take place in two weeks, barring any other unexpected problems.

"I have the caterer's contract and I've arranged for extra chairs and a podium," Kendall said.

"Good. Mr. Jordan from the NAACP will speak on the mansion's connection to the Underground Railroad. Josh Ferguson, the owner's son, agreed to provide information on the general history of the estate." She glanced at her notes. "Although she actually still owns the property, I plan to make a presentation to Mrs. Ferguson for making the property available to us and to the public."

"Mrs. Ferguson is probably just as grateful to you. She was extremely upset at the possibility that the property would be destroyed."

Sheila nodded. "It just occurred to me that we should also recognize Valerie Hamilton since she's the one who started the process by giving my name to Mrs. Ferguson."

They discussed the details of the Open House for another half an hour. Then Kendall raised a question.

"Would it be possible for me to get into the mansion next week? I'd like to see the dining room for the caterer's setup."

"That shouldn't be a problem. I'm supposed to accompany Ben Whitaker to the mansion anyway. I told him that I wanted him to have a look at the gazebo and shed. I hadn't included them with the original renovations." She glanced at her calendar. "Is Saturday at one o'clock okay for you?"

"That's fine."

Sheila nodded. "I guess that's everything then. I'll see you next week."

*   *   *

That evening, Kendall dressed for dinner in a black silk crepe sheath. The fitted lace bodice extended just below the waist and had a boat neckline and long sleeves.

Ben was picking her up at six-thirty. They were scheduled to meet Gary and Valerie at the restaurant at seven.

She clasped the pearl-pendant necklace around her neck and clipped on the matching earrings. After slipping her feet into the black peau de soie pumps, she picked up her matching bag. Draping the shawl Mabel had given her over her arm, she went down stairs.

Ben arrived a few minutes later, greeting her with a gleam of admiration in his eyes and a warm kiss. "Have I told you lately how beautiful you are?"

She smiled. "I think so, but I don't mind if you repeat yourself."

He helped her on with her coat, his knuckles brushing against the nape of her neck. He smiled. He no longer had to wonder if the skin beneath the fabric was as soft and silky as that small area.

Valerie and Gary were already seated when they arrived at the restaurant. Ben reintroduced himself as he and Kendall joined them.

When they were seated, he turned to Valerie. "I understand I have you to thank for referring Sheila to me."

She shrugged. "All I did was give her your name. The decision to hire you was hers."

The evening passed pleasantly. Dinner was followed by dancing. Valerie's instincts had been proven correct. The looks that passed between

Kendall and Ben almost sizzled. It was more than that, though.

She was certain that the tenderness in Ben's expression when he looked at her was totally foreign to Kendall. She wondered if Kendall had ever before known the joy Valerie now saw in her eyes.

It was after eleven when they called it a night. The two couples parted company in the parking lot.

"Maybe we can do this again sometime," Valerie suggested.

"Sure," Ben agreed. "Now that I've finished the work on the Sterling mansion, my schedule should be more reasonable."

Kendall waved to the other couple as they drove out of the parking lot. Then she turned toward Ben.

"So, now what do you think of your suspicions that I was having an affair with Gary?"

Ben glanced at her, relieved to see the smile on her face.

"I should have known that would come back to haunt me."

Kendall laughed. "I couldn't resist reminding you of that."

"All right, I'm just glad you didn't mention it to either of them." He glanced at her again. "You didn't, did you?"

She shook her head. "I'm saving that threat for another time. It might come in handy to keep you in line."

He shook his head. "I'm not sure I'll survive your newfound sense of humor."

They had only driven a short distance when he turned to her. "Where to?"

"What?"

"Am I taking you home or are we going to my place?"

She frowned. "That question sounds like taking me home means that you'll drop me off and then leave. Am I missing something? Is this a brush-off?"

He frowned. "How could you think that?" He glanced at her. "We've been spending a lot of time together. I was afraid that you'd start to think that I'm taking you, and our relationship, for granted."

She placed her hand on his knee. "I'd never think that of you. You'd probably have just as much reason to accuse me of the same thing."

She paused. "In answer to your question, I think your place. It's a little chilly tonight. I like the idea of a nice roaring fire, and you didn't see fit to put a fireplace in my bedroom."

He raised an eyebrow. "I thought I'd been doing a pretty good job of building a fire in your bedroom, even without a fireplace."

She grinned and nudged him gently. "Like I said before, you have a one-track mind."

He chuckled. "When I'm near you, guilty as charged."

When they entered his bedroom later, she excused herself and started toward the bathroom. "I'll be right back."

In her absence, he turned down the covers on the bed and complied with her request of a fire. Then he undressed.

He was hanging his clothes in the closet when he heard the bathroom door open. A few seconds

LOVE IS NOT ENOUGH

later, he closed the door of the closet behind him.
His body tensed at the sight that greeted him.

Kendall reclined on the love seat at the foot of
the bed, wearing only the lacy shawl she had carried that evening. As he approached, she stood up.
Throwing one end of the shawl over her shoulder,
she draped the other end around her waist. Her
thighs, and the much more interesting area between them, peeked through the long fringe.

Her gaze traveled down his body, lingering at
the evidence of his arousal. She licked her lips and
advanced toward him. When only inches separated them, she unwound the shawl and dropped
it to the floor. Then she took a step forward and
slipped her arms around his neck.

"I wonder if Mabel Jenkins would approve. The
shawl was a Christmas gift from her."

"I get the impression that she's a pretty feisty lady.
Somehow, I think she'd approve wholeheartedly."
He wrapped his arms around her. "You do a pretty
good job of building a fire yourself."

His hands roamed over her warm naked flesh.
He breathed in her distinctive scent as he nuzzled
her neck while one hand moved to fondle her
breast. Their lips met in a slow leisurely kiss, a
tame portent of what was to come.

Her hands caressed his shoulders and then
moved to his waist and lower. She ended the kiss
only to satisfy another urge. Her tongue drew circles in the midst of the hairs on his chest while her
hand moved down his abdomen and then to the
rigid shaft. She stroked the member before her
hand closed over it, gently squeezing.

At first his breath caught in his throat, and then

he moaned. His heart thumped rapidly beneath her other hand.

She knelt in front of him, reaching back to retrieve the packet she had earlier placed on the love seat. "Pretty soon, I'll be an expert at this."

He submitted willingly to her preparations, and then to her further explorations, until he could stand it no longer. Then he raised her to her feet. His hand slid down her abdomen to the tempting curls at the juncture of her thighs as he lowered himself to his knees. He loved this woman more than he ever thought possible.

She clutched his shoulders. Was the heat coming from his hand or from her own body? She trembled. Her knees buckled.

With his hands at her waist, he lowered her to a sitting position on the love seat. His mouth replaced his hands, planting moist kisses from her neck to the silky triangle of hair. Gently parting her thighs, he explored the hot wet area. Then he spread her legs wider.

"Oh, baby, I'll never get enough of you. I'm a greedy man when it comes to you. I want it all."

The circular motion of his thumb along the rigid nub sent tremors through her body. She clung to his shoulders. She moaned as her body to moved to meet each advance of his finger into the hot wet sheath.

Still his thumb continued its magical movements. It was as if a rubber band inside her was being stretched to its limit. When his moist tongue replaced his thumb, it took her breath away. She vaguely remembered his earlier words that he wanted it all. Her whole body trembled. Caught up in the unbelievable sensations, she could only moan

his name over and over. Then her body was overcome with spasms.

Before the spasms ceased, he entered her swiftly
and deeply. She wrapped her legs tightly around his
waist. After a few quick thrusts, the rubber band
snapped. She cried out his name in release.

He claimed her lips, hungrily drinking the sweet
nectar she offered. Seconds later, his body stiffened
and he shared her rapture.

Her legs slid down to loosely encircle his thighs.
They clung to each other as the world slowly came
back into focus. She was the first to speak, her
voice barely a whisper. "I was wrong about needing
a fire in the fireplace to remove the chill."

He kissed the corner of her mouth. He let out a
long sigh. "This fire is much more satisfying, but it
cools too quickly."

"Since this was your idea, you're responsible for
finding a way to get us to the bed."

He chuckled. "I'll take care of it. Just give me a
few minutes to get my strength back."

She closed her eyes. "Whatever you say."

She was almost asleep curled up on the love seat
when, after a quick trip to the bathroom, he urged
her to her feet. Then he lifted her in his arms and
carried her to the bed. He lay down beside her,
pulled her into his arms, and they drifted off to
sleep.

CHAPTER 13

Before meeting with Sheila the following Saturday, Kendall and Ben visited Mabel Jenkins. Kendall had been concerned when the elderly lady was not in church the previous Sunday. She was even more concerned when she called and Mabel told her that she had been ill. She tried to convince Kendall that it was just a little cold. Kendall was relieved when the elderly lady greeted them at the door.

"Hi, Miss Mabel. I was worried about you, so Ben and I decided we'd stop by and check on you."

"That was sweet of you, sugar. As you see, I'm fine. I told you it was just a little cold." She led them into the living room.

"I know, but I wanted to see for myself. I hope you don't mind."

"Of course not, dear."

While they chatted, Mabel looked from one to the other of them and smiled. She had seen them together in church twice since their visit on New

Year's Day. It was easy to see that they cared a great deal for each other.

As with Valerie, Kendall had never talked with Mabel about her past. It had come out in their conversations that she was divorced, but she had offered nothing beyond that bare fact. Explanations were unnecessary. As much as she tried to hide it, Mabel had enough experience to recognize pain when she saw it.

In spite of the pain, there had been hints of a very different woman somewhere beneath the surface. She had seen gradual changes in Kendall in the past few years, the greatest of them in the past few months.

The radiant woman sitting in her living room had been hidden for too long. Mabel had no doubt that the young man sitting beside her was largely, if not totally, responsible for the glow that seemed to radiate from her.

After leaving Mabel Jenkins's house, Ben and Kendall stopped for lunch before driving to Sheila's office. Sheila was on the telephone when they arrived. She motioned them to have a seat.

Seeing them arrive together, she recalled Kendall stating that she knew Ben. It appeared that they were more than casual acquaintances.

After she hung up the phone, she sighed. "I'm sorry. I'm afraid I have to change the plans. I have some calls I have to make. I'll probably be tied up here for a while."

She looked at Ben. "You don't need me to check out the buildings. My plan was to examine them with you, but that's not really necessary. You can get back to me later."

Then she turned her attention to Kendall. "You know what I have in mind. You've arranged enough parties to determine what the caterer will need." She shrugged. "If you don't mind, why don't you two go ahead without me?"

Kendall glanced at Ben before she asked, "Are you sure?"

Sheila nodded.

The couple left the office after Ben promised to contact Sheila by the end of the following week. "I should have an estimate by then."

Kendall shook her head as they approached the Sterling mansion. "Why would anyone want to destroy this beautiful old house?"

"Like I said, greed does strange things to people. Mueller's convinced that his modern resort and condos will make so much money that a beautiful old house is just an obstacle to be removed. He's also convinced that the resort will make more money without the mansion on the property."

He stopped the car in the circular driveway at the front of the house. After he opened her door, Kendall stepped out of the car. She stood on the sidewalk admiring the building until he urged her toward the house.

When they entered the house, Kendall was again awed by the beautiful structure. The mahogany woodwork gleamed. The staircase across the wide foyer curved to the left, the banister forming a railing along the upstairs hall. The archway straight ahead led to the music room, where the brief program would take place.

Ben placed his hand beneath her elbow and led her toward the stairs. "Would you like the grand tour?"

"Of course."

Their tour ended in the kitchen. In addition to the original wood-burning stove, the Fergusons had added a gas version whose appearance replicated a model more suitable to an earlier period. Except for the stove, the room had not been modernized. Ben had replaced some of the cabinets, but the style had been maintained.

"There's a pantry through this door," he explained, walking to the other side of the room. "There's a dumbwaiter, too, behind those doors over there."

She tilted her head to the side and smiled. "A dumbwaiter could be a great convenience even in a modern house. Breakfast in bed without lugging a heavy tray up the stairs." She reached for the cupboard doorknob.

"Maybe I'll consider adding one to my house," he said. He opened his mouth to tell her about the summer kitchen, and was interrupted by her quaking voice.

"I think you'd better come here and see this," she said, holding the cupboard door open.

He started back across the room. "What is it? Did one of the workmen leave trash in there?"

She shook her head. She seemed rooted to the spot. "I don't think you can blame this on one of the workmen."

He frowned and opened the cupboard wider. A

ticking bomb greeted him. The timer indicated a little more than five minutes left. He took his keys from his pocket before gently lifting the bomb from its resting place.

Her eyes widened. "What . . . what are you doing?"

"I'm taking this out of here. I'll drive into the field across the road and leave it there."

She silently questioned the wisdom of that decision, but he seemed determined. "Fine," she said, starting toward the kitchen door. "Let's go."

He followed her, gingerly carrying the bomb. When they reached the foyer, he glanced at her. "You stay here."

"No way. You can't drive and carry that thing, too."

"I'll set it on the floor. You're staying here."

She stared at him for a second before gently taking the keys from his hand. "You're wasting time arguing, Ben." She opened the front door.

He shook his head and went through the door as she held it open. As quickly as he dared, he settled into the passenger seat of the car.

"Hand me that alarm remote on the dashboard," he instructed when she was seated behind the wheel.

As they neared the gates, he punched in the alarm code. The gates swung open as they approached them.

Eager to dispose of the bomb, she increased the car's speed as soon as they cleared the gates. She drove straight across the road and into the empty field before turning to the left, away from the house.

Ben made no comment on her driving. He was thankful for excellent shock absorbers. There were two minutes left on the timer when he told her to stop. Quickly depositing the bomb on the ground, he jumped back into the car.

There was no need to give her the "go" signal. He had barely closed the door before she accelerated, heading back to the road and then toward the mansion. They had just reached the gate when the explosion shattered the air and shook the ground.

She stopped the car abruptly. Still clutching the wheel, she closed her eyes.

He reached across the space between them and gently pried her fingers from the steering wheel. Then he pulled her into his arms. They sat there quietly for a few minutes, willing their hearts to settle into what was an almost normal beat. He kissed the side of her forehead.

"You're one stubborn lady."

She looked up at him. "It was obvious that what you intended to do wasn't a one-person operation."

He hugged her tighter. Then he took his cell phone from his jacket pocket. "I'd better call the police."

He dialed the emergency number. "I'm calling to report a bombing, but I'm not sure it's an emergency. We already disposed of the bomb."

"What do you mean, you disposed of it? Where are you, sir?"

"We're at the Sterling mansion. We moved the bomb to an open field before it exploded."

A few seconds of silence on the other end of the line followed this statement. "Are you in the house?"

"No, we're outside at the gate."

"Stay there. Don't go back into the house. I'm dispatching the bomb squad."

"The bomb already exploded."

"There may be other explosive devices in the building, sir. Hold on, please." A few seconds later, the voice continued. "The police are on their way. Wait for them in a safe area away from the building."

Ben hung up the telephone and looked at the mansion. The possibility of other bombs had not occurred to him.

"What did they say?"

He repeated the information from the dispatcher. Then he looked beyond her at the crater caused by the explosion. He tried not to think of the consequences had she not been curious about the dumbwaiter.

When the police arrived, the bomb squad took dogs into the house. While they conducted their examination, Sergeant Price questioned Kendall and Ben.

They told him what had led to the discovery of the bomb. He raised an eyebrow when they described how they had disposed of it, pointing to the spot in the field where it had exploded.

"That was very foolhardy. You should have called us and left the house immediately."

Neither of them replied. What could they say? He was right. Their action had been rash, especially in view of the dispatcher's suggestion that there might have been more than one bomb. In spite of this, Ben attempted to justify his decision.

"I knew we had more than five minutes to get rid of it."

Sergeant Price shook his head. He glanced at

Kendall. There was no need to frighten her by mentioning the instability of bombs in general, no matter what the timer showed.

"I'd like for both of you to come to the station and make a formal statement."

They looked at each other and back at Sergeant Price. "Now?"

"It's best while everything is fresh in your minds." He shrugged. "Maybe you'll remember something else, something out of place when you arrived or an unusual sound while you were in the house."

Ben suppressed the urge to voice his response to that statement. *You mean other than the ticking of a bomb?*

Neither appeared hopeful of being able to provide further information, but they agreed to accompany him. A few minutes later, the bomb squad exited the house after conducting a thorough examination of the house and grounds. They gave them the all-clear and started toward the field to examine the area where the bomb had exploded.

Sergeant Price waited while Ben locked the house and reset both the alarm on the door and the one for the gate. After the couple was settled in Ben's car, they followed him back to the station.

While their formal statements were being typed, Sergeant Price questioned them again. He scanned his notes. Ben had explained his connection to the mansion. Kendall told him the reason for her presence at the house that day. He focused his attention on his notes.

"Can either of you think of anyone who would want to harm you?"

Kendall's eyes widened. That thought had been lurking in the back of her mind. She would have preferred to leave it there. How could this be happening again? She had to be wrong.

Ben reached over and clasped her hand in his. "Kendall? I think you should tell him about Scott."

"Who's Scott?" asked Price.

She took a deep breath. "My ex-husband."

"What about him?"

She gave him a brief history, including the attempted murder. "I can't believe he's involved in this. It makes no sense. The other time he wanted the insurance money. What possible motive could he have now?"

Sergeant Price voiced Ben's immediate thought. "Revenge."

She swallowed. Her heart raced. Then she shook her head. "That's too farfetched. How would he know that I'd be there? How did he get into the house?"

Ben sighed. "She has a point, Sergeant. There are only three people who have keys and the code to the alarm system, myself, Sheila Donovan of the Historical Society, and of course the owner, Mrs. Ferguson. Even if someone tried to cut the line, the alarm would sound."

Then light dawned in his mind. "Sergeant Price, I'm not trying to tell you your job, but there's another possibility."

"What do you mean?"

He rubbed his chin. "I don't think either of us was the target. I think the target was the mansion itself."

He explained the disagreements involving the mansion and the property. "There might be a few people with a motive, but I think George Mueller would head the list. He wants that property in its entirety, and he's decided that the mansion is in the way of what he has planned. He'd probably go to any lengths to eliminate it."

Sergeant Price made a few notes. George Mueller's name rang a bell. If he remembered correctly, this would not be the first time Mueller was involved in a shady deal. He looked up from his notes.

"Can either of you think of anything else that might be helpful?"

They both shook their heads.

He handed them each a business card. "If you think of anything, give me a call." He rose from his chair. "Thank you both for coming down here." He looked at Ben. "You might want to change those alarm codes."

Ben nodded. "I've already thought about that."

When they were settled in his car, Ben took his cell phone from his pocket. "I'd better call Sheila and let her know what happened."

Kendall sat silently with her hands folded in her lap. Her body tensed as she listened to him recount the events of that afternoon.

When he finished his conversation, Ben became engrossed in his own thoughts. He had decided not to mention the rotted piece of flooring during their interview with Sergeant Price. Even if they determined that someone had tampered with it, the particle offered no clue as to who was responsible. His musings were interrupted by Kendall's voice.

"Ben, do you really think Scott will try to get revenge?"

He had seen that question coming. There was no need to tell her that that thought had also crossed his mind. He sighed.

"Sweetheart, I'm sorry Sergeant Price said that to you. After hearing Scott's history, it was natural that he would consider that possibility. Looking at it realistically, I can't see how he could have anything to do with the bomb."

He reached over and squeezed her hand. "To answer your question, no, I don't think Scott will try anything that might land him back in prison. He's smart enough to know that if anything happens to you, he'll be the first one blamed. I don't think you have to worry about him bothering you again, in any way."

She took a deep breath. What he said made sense. Scott never did anything unless it afforded him a tangible benefit. Revenge did not fit that bill.

"Thanks, I needed that."

"I really believe what I told Sergeant Price. I think someone is out to destroy the mansion. That makes more sense than a personal enemy. We happened to be in the wrong place at the wrong time."

"How did Sheila take the news?"

"After I assured her that we were fine, she said pretty much what Sergeant Price said. We should have let the police handle the bomb." He shrugged. "She did thank me for saving the mansion. She couldn't believe someone would go to those lengths."

She sighed. "You said it before, greed."

Neither of them had thought about dinner until they neared Ben's house. He glanced at Kendall.

"Would you like to stop for dinner?"

She shook her head. "Not really. Maybe we can just order in."

He nodded. With the afternoon they had had, it was no wonder she just wanted to get comfortable and relax.

Fifteen minutes later, they entered his house. He helped her off with her coat and turned to hang both of their garments in the closet. He closed the door and turned back to find her standing near the sofa, lost in thought.

He walked over to her and enfolded her in his arms. His hands caressed her back. He kissed the side of her forehead.

"It'll be all right, baby. The police are on the alert now and Sheila's calling the alarm company today to change the codes."

She rested her head against his chest. "I'm okay. It's just a delayed reaction. I'm exhausted."

He gestured toward the sofa. "Why don't you lie down? I'll see about dinner."

She took his advice. Within minutes, she was asleep.

After ordering dinner, he returned. Taking a quilt from the closet, he tucked it around her. He built a fire, and then sat down on the end of the sofa staring at the flames.

Until now, he had avoided considering the likely outcome of events if she and Sheila had gone to the mansion alone as they had originally planned. His concern was not the possibility of the destruction of the mansion. His concern was that he might have lost her.

He had closed his heart against love years ago. It had been easy. No woman had ever come close to touching that special place deep in his heart. He smiled. Without even trying, she not only touched that place, she filled the void that he had been un-aware existed.

When their dinner arrived, he set the contain-ers on the kitchen counter. Then he went to wake her. She stirred and looked up into his gentle, lov-ing eyes.

"I hated to disturb you, but dinner's here."

After dinner, they spent the evening relaxing. Just being together took on a whole new meaning.

Sergeant Price began his investigation by delving into previous reports concerning George Mueller. Most of the complaints were due to problems re-sulting from the use of inferior materials. The re-ports also revealed that Mueller was an expert at arranging his scams so that someone else was left holding the bag.

So who could he have conned into planting that bomb? The easiest person would be someone who also had something to gain by the sale of the prop-erty. Who else had lost out when Mueller's devel-opment project was put on hold? He jotted down likely possibilities.

First on the list was the contractor Mueller had hired to build his resort. Then there was the real-estate agent who'd lost a hefty commission when the sale was called off. The last person on the list was the owner.

Price frowned. Whitaker said the owner had tried to call off the sale because she wanted the mansion left intact. Aside from that, it was impossible to en-vision the elderly woman planting a bomb, or even hiring someone to do it. He crossed her name off the list.

There was a possibility that the person who planted the bomb had no direct connection to the development project. Mueller could have simply hired someone off the street. The problem with that idea came back to the most important element of the case. Who had access to the alarm codes?

They had determined that the alarm wires were still intact when the police arrived. As Whitaker had said, the alarm would have sounded if the wires were cut. Someone had to have obtained those codes from one of the three people Whitaker had named.

Sheila called Kendall on Friday evening to inform her of the steps that the police had taken to ensure safety for the Open House. "They'll take the dogs through the house and grounds early tomorrow morning. A few officers will remain there during the Open House, along with one of the dogs."

"What time do you want me there?"

"If you arrive in time to help set up the chairs and direct the caterer, that'll be fine."

"Okay, that's not a problem. Ben will be with me, so we'll have some extra muscle for rearranging the furniture."

Sheila laughed. "Good, extra muscle might come in handy. I'll see you tomorrow."

The Open House was scheduled to begin at noon. By eleven o'clock the music room was filled with rows of chairs. The caterer was in the process of setting up in the large dining room.

There were two police officers to keep an eye on the building and grounds. Another officer was in charge of the dog that sniffed each car after it was parked in the driveway.

The caterer's bags and boxes had been searched upon his arrival. Against Sheila's objections, each guest was asked to submit to a cursory examination of all bags.

Mrs. Ferguson arrived shortly before noon. Sheila greeted her in the foyer.

"I'm so glad you could come."

"I wouldn't miss this. Thank you for helping to preserve this old house." She turned slightly to the side. "This is my son, Joshua, his wife, Camille, and my grandson, Mark."

Sheila motioned to Ben as he came through the archway from the music room. "Mrs. Ferguson, this is Ben Whitaker, the contractor responsible for the renovations."

Mrs. Ferguson held out her hand in greeting. Instead of simply shaking his hand, she clasped it in both of hers. Her eyes misted over.

"Thank you for making this old house even more beautiful than I remember it as a child."

"You're welcome. I enjoyed restoring it. It is a beautiful old house."

She glanced toward the door. "I never thought the house was valuable enough to warrant all of this security, though. Most of the antique furnishings have been removed."

Sheila thought fast. "You know, you can't be too careful with all of the vandalism these days."

Mrs. Ferguson nodded. "I had some cousins living here for a while and I didn't have to worry about that." She looked around again. "You do beautiful work, Mr. Whitaker. I've had some work done over the years, but it was nothing like this."

"Thank you. I'm glad you're pleased with it."

She turned to her son. "I'd like to see the upstairs."

Joshua shook Ben's hand. "I have to second my mother's appreciation. As she said, we've had some minor work done before. I guess I made the mistake of thinking that the cousins who were living here for a while would at least take care of the basic maintenance. Until we put the property up for sale, I hadn't realized the extent of the repairs needed. Thanks again."

He turned to his mother. "All right, let's take the grand tour."

The family crossed the foyer. With her son on one side and her grandson on the other, Mrs. Ferguson slowly made her way up the stairs.

"It's a shame her other son couldn't be here," Sheila said.

"Why not?"

She wrinkled her forehead. "Actually, I'm not sure if he couldn't be here or if he simply chose not to participate. She didn't offer an explanation and, of course, it wasn't my place to ask questions. There was something in her voice that made me think that she wasn't pleased about his not being here."

"She doesn't seem upset by his absence now."

"No, she doesn't. Maybe I was wrong."

Sheila glanced toward the music room. "I'd better make sure everything is running smoothly. Excuse me."

Ben turned his attention to Kendall, who was also busy ensuring that there were no problems. She mingled with the guests, directing them to one of the volunteers to answer questions concerning the mansion.

At one o'clock Sheila made an announcement that the program was about to begin. She instructed the volunteers to pass the word to the visitors on the second floor. Mr. Jordan had arrived shortly after twelve-thirty. Mrs. Ferguson and her family were already seated in the music room. Kendall and Ben watched the proceedings from the back of the room.

Sheila began by mentioning Valerie's part in referring Mrs. Ferguson to the Historical Society, although she made no mention of the battle between the owner and George Mueller. After Sheila's opening statement, Joshua Ferguson was the first to speak.

He read first from the notes he had made from papers they had discovered in the mansion. Then he shared some of the information he had gleaned from his mother's memory of stories she had heard from her parents and grandparents.

He thanked Sheila for her help in seeing that the structure was preserved. Kendall glanced at Ben and smiled when Joshua delivered his final statement.

"Finally, I want to thank Ben Whitaker, who's responsible for returning this old house to its former glory."

After Joshua Ferguson took his seat, Sheila introduced Mr. Jordan, who discussed the mansion's role in the Underground Railroad. He told of the discovery of hidden passages and artifacts that had led to this conclusion.

"There are houses that are well known for the number of slaves who were channeled through them on the path to freedom. Others, like this structure, aren't as well known, but are no less important." Finally, he thanked Mrs. Ferguson for making the house available to all of the descendants who had been aided by its existence.

Sheila then took to the podium to wind up the afternoon's program. "I'd like to add my appreciation to Ben Whitaker for the beautiful job of restoration."

Then she gestured to Mrs. Ferguson, who approached the podium. Sheila held up a plaque.

"You've already seen the plaque that's been installed outside with a short history of the house. This is just a small token of appreciation from the Society for making this house available to us and for your generous contribution to aid in maintaining it."

Mrs. Ferguson was then helped to her seat once again. As her final official act, Sheila read off a list of other organizations and private citizens who had donated funds to the Society specifically for the upkeep of the mansion.

By three o'clock the guests had departed and the caterer was packing up. Kendall helped Sheila and the volunteers fold the chairs and restore the music room to order. The rental company was scheduled to pick up the items at five o'clock.

"I'll stay and wait for the rental company, Kendall. A couple of the volunteers are staying, too, so you and Ben can leave."

"Are you sure?"

She nodded. "Thanks for your help." She looked at Ben. "And thank you again for your work."

"You're welcome. Keep me in mind for any future projects. I love this kind of work."

Sheila smiled. "After today, you might get more than you bargained for. Don't forget that I'm still waiting for the estimate on the outbuildings."

"I haven't forgotten. I'll get back to you as soon as I can." He glanced at Kendall and then turned again to Sheila. "If you're sure you won't need us anymore, we'll get going."

CHAPTER 14

On the Friday after the Open House, Ben went to see Sergeant Price. Ben had heard nothing regarding the investigation. He expected the police to be reluctant to share information with him. He had to be tactful in his approach. He was surprised when he was shown into Sergeant Price's office with no hesitation.

"Have a seat, Mr. Whitaker. I can't say that I'm surprised to see you." He leaned back in his chair. "What can I do for you?"

"If you're not surprised to see me, you must know that I'm here to find out if you've made any progress in the investigation of the bombing."

Sergeant Price hesitated, sizing up the man sitting across from him. Finally, he decided that his visitor might be able to provide valuable information. He sat up and opened the folder on his desk.

"As you suggested, it appears that Mueller might be behind it. You were also right about there being several other people with a motive to eliminate the mansion. All of them lead back to Mueller's plans for development."

Ben nodded. "I assume that you have the contractor listed as one of the suspects?"

Sergeant Price's eyes narrowed. "You know who that is, don't you?"

"Sam Farley?"

Price nodded. "We've looked into his background and his current financial problems. I believe he was your partner at one time. Is that why you didn't mention him in our previous discussion?"

Ben shrugged. "I knew that you'd find out for yourself. I don't want to believe that he'd go to those lengths."

"We don't know that he did. For now, he's just a suspect."

Ben looked down at his hands. "Who else do you suspect?"

"The real-estate agent lost a big commission when Mueller pulled out of the sale. If the mansion is eliminated, he'll be back in the running to purchase the property."

Ben sighed. That thought had already occurred to him. He had pushed it to the back of his mind. The sergeant appeared to be unaware that the real-estate agent in question was not a "he," but a "she." That "she" also happened to be Kendall's friend.

"Is that it?"

"We haven't ruled out the possibility that Mueller simply hired someone to do the job."

"But how would he get the code?"

"That's a question that I have for you and Ms. Donovan. How well did you guard those codes and the key?"

"I can't speak for Sheila, but when I think back

on it, I wasn't as careful as I should have been. It may be like closing the barn door after the horse is loose, but I've since remedied that carelessness."

He stood up. "Thanks for seeing me, Sergeant Price, and for sharing your information."

"We need all the help we can get, Mr. Whitaker. Maybe this conversation will spark some memory or additional piece of information. If nothing else, extra caution should prevent any further problems."

While Ben was having his discussion with Sergeant Price, George Mueller was reading the riot act to a visitor of his own. "You have to be the most inept excuse for a criminal that I've ever seen."

His visitor blanched at being referred to as a criminal. To his mind, he was only trying to get what he felt was owed to him, what he had been cheated of.

"You were the one who suggested the bomb," the visitor said. "How could I know it would be found? How could I know anyone would even be in the house?"

"That's what I mean about being inept."

"What do you suggest now?"

Mueller shook his head. "I'm through making suggestions. You can't seem to do anything right. Maybe I'd better hire someone to take care of it."

Mueller's visitor drew himself up to his full height. He still held a card up his sleeve. "And how do you propose he get into the house?"

"You can take care of that."

"And who's going to pay this person you plan to hire?"

"It'll come out of your cut, of course."

"No way. I'll take care of it." He turned without another word and strode out the door.

Mueller watched his departure with a smirk on his face. If his visitor failed to succeed with whatever plan he devised, Mueller would take matters into his own hands.

On Saturday afternoon, Valerie received a call from Sheila Donovan. "What can I do for you, Sheila?"

"Actually, I'm trying to contact Darren Leedom."

"Darren? I didn't know he was he handling a contract for you. He's not in right now."

"Oh, maybe he's on his way. He's one of our volunteers here. He was supposed to come by today to help with some mailings."

Valerie frowned. "Maybe he forgot. I think he's out with a client. I'll leave him a message."

"Thanks."

Valerie sat staring at the telephone for a while. Sheila Donovan evidently knew nothing of Darren's involvement with the Sterling mansion. When did he volunteer to work for the Historical Society? And why?

Her client arrived at that moment. Speculations concerning Darren's activities were pushed to the back of her mind.

Kendall had been on cloud nine for months. A discussion with Ben would soon bring her down to earth. They had planned to spend a quiet evening at her house on Saturday. They were having coffee and dessert on the living room sofa when she raised the question that had been on her mind for more than a week.

"Have you heard anything from Sergeant Price? I was tempted to call him to see if he had any more information." She glanced at him. "I decided I didn't want to get my feelings hurt. I didn't think he'd appreciate my meddling."

"I don't think he'd have had a problem telling you what little he knows. As a matter of fact, I talked to him yesterday. He was very open about the investigation. They have a few suspects, but it seems they've made no real progress."

"Did he give you any idea who they suspect?"

He hesitated.

"Ben? What did he tell you?"

"Aside from Mueller himself, they have their sights on the contractor and the real-estate agent."

Her mouth dropped open. "The real-estate agent? You mean Valerie? I hope you told them that they were being ridiculous."

"They're only in the investigative stages, and she did have a motive, Kendall. I can't very well tell the police how to conduct their investigation."

Her eyes widened. "You can't be serious. How could you consider the possibility that Valerie would actually plant a bomb, or have anything to do with such a thing."

"I didn't say I believed it, Kendall."

She grunted. "You haven't said that you think it's totally out of the question either."

"Kendall . . ."

She gave him no chance to explain his position. "There is someone else who had a motive—you. It would be the perfect setup for you. Mueller hires you to build his resort. When that falls through, you're conveniently hired to renovate the mansion. Of course, that's not nearly as much money as the resort contract. In the end, you make out like a bandit from both projects. After all, you didn't even have to figure out how to get into the mansion."

"That makes no sense. You're forgetting that I was in the mansion with you. Even if I hadn't been there, do you honestly think I'd let you be put in that danger?" He shook his head. "How could you even think that I'd be involved with something like that?"

"If you can believe it of Valerie, why couldn't I believe it of you?"

"It's not the same thing and you know it."

"Maybe not, but it tells me what you think of my judgment of people." She stood up. "I think you'd better go, Ben."

"I can't believe this. Are you actually breaking up with me?"

"I didn't say that. I just think that maybe we need some time apart."

He stared at her for a moment. Then he turned to leave. "If that's the way you want it. Call me when you're thinking clearly again."

She heard the door close behind him, but made no move to reset the alarm. She sank down onto the sofa and buried her head in her hands. Why had she said those awful things to him? She knew he had nothing to do with the bomb. She also knew that Valerie had nothing to do with it. Why couldn't he see that?

Ben sat in his car going over their argument in his mind. Her statement about questioning her judgment had not escaped him. She had completely twisted his words.

He knew too little about Valerie, and her husband, to convincingly defend them. That did not mean that he believed they were guilty. Why couldn't she see that?

Kendall sought serenity in church the next day. As always, it calmed her nerves. She felt a twinge of guilt for the strong words she had thrown at Ben.

After church, she drove to the mall. Her guest bedroom and bath still needed work. Maybe a few hours of shopping would lift her spirits. When she returned home, the remainder of her evening was spent watching television.

On Monday evening, Kendall received an interesting call from Valerie. Her friend started the conversation with a question that Kendall should have expected.

"The Open House was nice, but what was with all the security?"

Kendall hesitated a few seconds. Then she told her about finding the bomb and Ben's decision to dispose of it.

"What were you two thinking?"

"That's basically the same question that the police asked." She sighed. "What can I tell you? The timer had five minutes left and it seemed like a good idea at the time."

"Who would do such a thing? And why?"

"The general idea is that Mueller is behind it. He wants the mansion out of the way."

"How could he have gotten into the mansion? Was there a break-in?"

"They didn't find any evidence of a break-in. They think the person somehow got the alarm code and the key to the house."

Valerie remembered Sheila's telephone call and the fact that Darren had been extremely upset with the problems surrounding the sale of the Sterling property. She relayed this information to Kendall.

"I don't know how long ago he started volunteering, or why. It just seemed a little strange, not at all how I envision Darren spending his free time."

"Maybe you should call Sergeant Price and tell him about Sheila's call. He's interested in anyone who has access to the mansion. Even if Sheila never gave him the key or the alarm code, I imagine it wouldn't be that difficult for him to get them somehow."

"I guess you're right."

Kendall gave her Sergeant Price's number. The two chatted for a few more minutes about more pleasant subjects before hanging up.

Sergeant Price hung up the telephone the next morning and then opened the file on the Sterling mansion case. He was not ready to cross Ms. Hamilton off his list of suspects, but he did add another name.

The story she'd told him was intriguing. Mr. Leedom had a definite motive of revenge, to say nothing of the money he could be expected to receive for his help. It was very possible that he was in league with Mueller. With the information Ms.

Hamilton had provided, Price now knew that his new suspect also had opportunity and indirect access to the alarm code and the key to the house. Leedom had just moved to the top of his suspect list.

The day after his telephone call from Valerie, Sergeant Price had an interview with Sheila Donovan. As with Whitaker, she admitted to a certain amount of laxity in security until after the bombing attempt.

"I'll need a list of employees and volunteers," he said. "Any of them could have obtained the alarm code and a duplicate key."

She turned to the computer and a few minutes later, the printer dispensed the requested list. Price scanned the names. Sure enough, there was Darren Leedom on the list.

"Does this date next to the name indicate when they joined the Society?"

"That's right."

He picked out Darren's name on the list. He had conveniently offered his services as a volunteer three weeks before the bomb was planted.

"Will there be anything else, Sergeant?"

He folded the list and slipped it into an inside coat pocket. "No, this is all for now, Ms. Donovan. Thank you for your help." He stood up.

"I should be the one thanking you," she said, rising from her chair to show him out. "I hope that list will help."

He started toward the door, and then turned back to face her. "There is one more thing, Ms. Donovan. I understand that there's one more person who has complete access to the mansion."

"That's right, the owner, Mrs. Ferguson."

"She should be alerted as to what's happened."

Sheila frowned. "Is that really necessary? She's elderly and rather frail. I was careful not to mention the bomb when she questioned the security measures at the Open House."

He shrugged. "All the more reason to question her own safeguards. She might not be as careful as you and Mr. Whitaker. It'll make our job easier if we can be assured that access to the mansion will be safeguarded from now on."

"Maybe I can warn her son and give him that responsibility."

He nodded and left her office.

After Sergeant Price departed, Sheila looked up Joshua Ferguson's telephone number. After a few rings, she was connected to his voice mail. She left her name and number, but did not tell him the reason for her call.

Joshua Ferguson returned her call just as she was preparing to leave her office on Friday. He explained that he had been out of town on vacation.

"Is there a problem at the mansion?" he asked.

She took a deep breath. "Not at the moment, but the police felt that you should be put on the alert."

"The police?"

"Yes, there's an investigation under way. I may owe you an apology for not being totally honest with you before now. The story I told your mother at the Open House was to keep her from worrying. The truth is that someone had planted a bomb in the mansion the week before the Open House."

"A bomb?" He ran his hand through his hair. "This is too much. Why would someone try to destroy the mansion?"

"I think you know the answer to that question. It appears that Mr. Mueller doesn't give up easily when he wants something. I have to qualify that by saying that the police haven't been able to prove his involvement."

She told him about Sergeant Price's visit. "He suggested that those of us with access to the mansion should have more careful safeguards."

Joshua sighed. "And of course, my mother and I fall into that category."

"Yes. I don't know if she's passed on a key and the code to anyone other than you. You might want to check with her. Afterward, if you feel that the alarm code needs to be changed, I'll take care of it."

"I'll do that. Thank you, Ms. Donovan."

He hung up the telephone and stared at it. There was one other person who very likely had access to the mansion, his brother, Philip.

He shook his head. Philip was greedy. He had been angry when their mother had had the mansion declared a historic landmark, inadvertently stopping the sale of the property.

Would Philip actually try to destroy the house that he knew meant so much to his mother? Joshua was always amazed, and disgusted, by people who felt that they were entitled to an inheritance. His brother was one of those people. Even so, Joshua could not believe that his own brother would go to those lengths.

Their mother had been more than generous with both of her sons, but maybe that was not enough

for Philip. Joshua did not want to think that his
mother had made a mistake by telling Philip that
he would receive a third of the money that she expected to realize from the property sale.

When Joshua visited his mother the next day, he
learned that she had given Philip access to the
mansion months earlier. She had then given him
the new code, supposedly so that he could verify that
the house had been put in order after the Open
House.

Now what? Was Joshua expected to call the police and tell them that there was a possibility his
own brother was involved in trying to destroy the
mansion?

He had to talk to Philip. He owed him that much
before sending the police to interrogate him.

A week had passed since Kendall's argument
with Ben, and still she had not called him. Anger
at his suggestion arose again when she saw Valerie
in church the next day. The two chatted for a few
minutes after the service before deciding to continue their conversation over lunch.

After they were seated and had placed their orders, Valerie could not contain her curiosity. "Do
you know if the police have learned any more about
the bomb at the mansion? They must have some
suspects in mind."

"As far as I know, they're investigating anyone
who has a connection to Mueller. One of their suspects is the contractor who lost a big job when
Mueller put the resort development on hold."

Valerie's eyes narrowed. "Why do I have the feeling that you're not telling me everything? Is he their only suspect?"

Kendall cleared her throat. "Funny you should ask. They're also considering the real-estate agent who lost a big commission when the sale of the property fell through."

It took a few seconds for that statement to sink in. Her mouth dropped open. She pointed to herself.

"Me? The police suspect me of planting a bomb?"

"I don't think they seriously suspect you. They're only thinking of the people who might have had a motive."

Valerie shook her head. "Well, I guess it's only a matter of time before they question me."

"Did you call Sergeant Price about Darren?"

Valerie nodded. "I gave him all of the information. I have no idea if he's seriously considering him as a suspect." She frowned. "Maybe I'm suspicious because I don't like him. Maybe his reasons for joining the Society are legitimate and I'm just prejudiced."

"It doesn't matter what you think about him personally. The police need to know about his connection to the Society. They can sort it out for themselves."

As soon as the words left her mouth, Kendall realized that the opposite was also true. If you happened to be biased in a person's favor, the police still had to be the ones to determine the truth.

She had argued with Ben because he refused to defend her friend. His attitude had been no different than the advice she gave Valerie. It was up to the police to investigate and learn the truth.

She had accused Ben of questioning her judgment of people. She had questioned that judgment herself after her break with Scott. Maybe underneath the anger and accusation was that old insecurity. Their food arrived and conversation ceased for a moment.

Valerie was convinced that something else was on her friend's mind.

"Kendall? What else is bothering you? You're not just worried about my being on a list of suspects."

She sighed. Then she told her friend of her disagreement with Ben.

"Kendall, I appreciate your defending me, but I don't understand why you'd be angry with him. From what you've said, it's not like he accused me. He doesn't know Gary and me. You said yourself that it's up to the police to sort out the truth."

"I know. I thought about that afterward. I was just so angry that he would even entertain the possibility that you would be involved in something like planting a bomb. It's ludicrous."

Valerie smiled. "Well, it's nice to know that I have such a loyal friend, but I hope you won't let it ruin your relationship with Ben."

"No, I won't. I'll apologize, eventually."

Valerie did not have long to wait for Sergeant Price to contact her. The interview was surprisingly brief.

Until she was questioned, it had not occurred to her that she had an alibi. She had been in her office all day on Friday. She had spent the greater part of that Saturday, when the bomb was discovered, escorting a client to various properties.

Sergeant Price had crossed Valerie off his list when he interviewed Sam Farley and Darren Leedom in turn. Both men struck him as likely cohorts for Mueller. They each had a motive.

Sam Farley might have easier access to the makings of a bomb. Leedom came out ahead in the consideration of access to the mansion.

Joshua Ferguson contacted his brother on Wednesday. Philip appeared shocked at the news that someone would try to destroy the mansion. When Joshua mentioned the necessity of safeguarding the key and access to the mansion, Philip agreed.

On the Friday after her lunch with Valerie, Kendall prepared to visit Mabel Jenkins. In the past few months, she had become accustomed to spending her weekends with Ben. She now tried to convince herself that this break was good. Maybe she had been in danger of becoming too dependent upon him to fill her free time.

Whether the break was good or bad did not alter the fact that she owed him an apology. Saying the words would be easy. Waiting for his reaction to that apology would be the real test. What if he decided that their relationship was not worth the aggravation and hurt of her accusations?

His offense had been merely reluctance to blindly trust *her* friend. She, on the other hand, had accused him of committing a crime. Did he love her enough to forgive her for that?

She hung her business suit in the closet and donned a sweater and slacks. Taking her charm bracelet from her jewelry box, she prepared to clasp it onto her wrist. She frowned. One of the charms was missing. The last time she had worn it was at the Open House. She would start her search there.

She bit her lip. Ben had access to the mansion. That thought raised the possibility that she might have lost it in his car. If she called him for help, she would have to be ready to make her apology. There would be no more putting it off. She could enlist Sheila's help in searching the mansion first. She would do that the next day. At the moment, Mabel Jenkins was awaiting her arrival.

The next day, Kendall called Sheila. "I'm missing a charm from my bracelet. I think it may have come off at the Open House."

"I'm sorry. Are you sure that's where you lost it?"

"Not really, but I've checked everywhere in my house and the Open House was the last time I wore it. I'd like to check the mansion, if you don't mind."

"Sure, no problem. The cleaners have been through it. They didn't report finding anything. I hope they didn't vacuum it up."

"I know it's a long shot, but I'd like to have a look."

Having seen Kendall with Ben, Sheila wondered briefly why she hadn't called him to take her to the mansion. She set that thought aside. It was none of her business.

"Sure, Kendall. You can come by and get the key and the code. I'll be here until four."

CHAPTER 15

Scarcely a week had passed after their argument when Ben questioned his statement to Kendall that it was up to her to call him to iron out their differences. How many times had he picked up the telephone and started dialing her number? Each time, he'd recalled those words.

On Saturday, he decided he was ready to eat those words if necessary. He gave in to the temptation that had plagued him for two weeks. He dialed Kendall's number. There was no answer. He could call her cell phone number, but he preferred to catch her at home. He needed to see her.

He had been so busy since the Open House that he had forgotten his promise to examine the outbuildings and gazebo on the Sterling property. Today was the first opportunity to follow up on that promise.

* * *

Kendall picked up the key from Sheila's office and wrote the code on a slip of paper. "Thanks, Sheila. I'll return the key before four o'clock."

As she was leaving Sheila's office, she encountered Darren entering the door. He ignored her greeting and brushed past her.

Until that moment, it had not occurred to her that returning to the mansion could be dangerous. At least she could count on Darren being at the Historical Society and not at the mansion. She had no way of knowing that he was only there to pick up a few brochures.

After stopping for gas, she headed for the mansion. As she approached the house, she noticed a car parked in the driveway directly in front of the stairs. She pulled up behind it and stepped out of her van.

She ascended the stairs, looking around for the owner of the other car. She opened the door, pausing when a man came around the corner of the porch. He seemed slightly familiar.

He stopped abruptly when he saw her. "Who are you? What are you doing here?"

"I was going to ask you the same question. I'm Kendall Chase. I think I may have lost something here a few weeks ago. I came to look for it."

Momentarily forgetting her earlier question, she sniffed at the odor coming from the open door. She pushed it further and started to enter. "What's that smell?"

The last thing she remembered was a terrible pain in the back of her head. Then her whole world went black.

*   *   *

When Kendall's world slowly came back into focus, her first sensation was the pain in the back of her head. The second was the stench surrounding her. It was much stronger now. In spite of the fog in her brain, she recognized the smell as gasoline. The man was planning to burn down the mansion, with her in it.

She pushed herself to her knees and then managed to stand, if somewhat unsteadily. She was in the music room. Straight ahead, but what seemed at the moment to be miles away, the door stood open.

She smelled no smoke, which probably meant that he had not lit a match to the fluid yet. She had to assume that he was not far away. Looking around for a weapon, she spied the poker beside the fireplace. She snatched it up and slowly made her way to the door. For good measure, she picked up a large vase near the entrance.

The man was just outside the door with his back toward her. He descended two steps before she reached him. He turned and she swung the poker, hitting him in the chest, but not hard enough. He straightened up.

Before he could completely catch his breath, she raised the vase with both hands and brought it crashing down on his head. That finally stopped him. He tumbled down the remaining stairs and lay still.

Holding onto the railing, she took two steps and slumped down onto the stairs. Folding her arms across her knees, she rested her forehead on them. She prayed for the throbbing in her head to subside. Her whole body trembled from her racing heart, like a car that was unaccustomed to the speed at which it was being driven.

A few minutes later, she looked up when she heard a car approaching. When she recognized the truck and the man behind the wheel, her eyes filled with tears. She wanted to run to him, to feel his arms around her. Exhausted, head throbbing, she could only sit and stare.

Ben frowned when he noticed two figures as he drove through the gates of the Sterling mansion. As he drew closer, he recognized Kendall seated on the stairs and a strange man lying on the ground.

He stepped out of the car. Giving the stranger a cursory glance, he approached Kendall. His eyes narrowed when he spotted the gasoline can. He sat down on the step beside her. Within seconds, she was in his arms. He kissed her forehead and gently stroked her back until the trembling stopped.

The figure on the ground stirred. He opened his eyes and looked up at the couple. He moved as if to stand.

Ben stared at him. "I'm not sure exactly what happened here. Until I find out, I think you'd better stay right where you are." He turned his attention back to Kendall when she spoke.

"He tried to burn it down."

Ben nodded. "I guessed that much. Are you all right?"

She gingerly touched the back of her head. "Except for feeling like my head might explode, I think so. He hit me."

"I'd better call the police, but first I'll take care of our friend."

After taking a rope from the back of the truck,

he returned to where the stranger lay. After tying his hands behind him, Ben jerked him to a standing position. He fished in the man's pocket and pulled out a driver's license.

He pulled his cell phone from his pocket and dialed Sergeant Price's number. He was informed that Sergeant Price was off duty.

After identifying himself, he added, "I'm at the Sterling mansion. A man just tried to torch it. You might want to send someone to pick him up and I think Sergeant Price would want to know about it."

"We'll send a car. I'll contact Sergeant Price."

He looked at Kendall. "Send an ambulance, too. There's a woman here who was injured in his attempt."

Kendall frowned when he hung up the telephone. "I don't need an ambulance. All I need is some aspirin and rest."

"Why don't we let the paramedics decide that. You could have a concussion."

She closed her eyes. "Who is he? He looks a little familiar."

Ben sighed. "That's because he bears a resemblance to his brother. He's Philip Ferguson."

Her eyes widened. "Ferguson? He tried to destroy his mother's house?"

Before thinking, she shook her head. Wincing, she touched the tender spot again. "I guess he's the one who was in league with Mueller."

"It would seem so. Proving that Mueller was behind it might not be that easy."

She closed her eyes in an attempt to stop the fresh tears that threatened to spill out. She swallowed.

"Why do people keep trying to kill me?"

He touched her cheek. Then he wiped away one of the tears that had escaped. "It's probably no consolation, but this time it wasn't personal."

In spite of the pain, she was determined to get the words out. With what had just occurred, she might never have had the chance.

"I'm sorry, Ben. I didn't mean what I said about you and Mueller."

"I know. It's not important now."

"You forgive me?"

He leaned forward and kissed her forehead. "Of course I forgive you. I love you, Kendall. What good is love without forgiveness?"

Fifteen minutes later, he raised his head at the sound of sirens. Then the ambulance came through the gate that he had opened a few minutes earlier.

The police took Philip Ferguson into custody. Sergeant Price questioned Ben as Kendall was being examined by the paramedic. He shook his head.

"Can I tell you something in confidence, Whitaker?"

Ben shrugged. "Sure, what is it?"

"I blew it. I was more concerned with whether or not the Fergusons were safeguarding the key and the alarm code. I never seriously considered them as suspects."

He shook his head again. "After what Ms. Donovan told me, I hate to think what this will do to the old lady."

Ben nodded. "It may not be as bad as you think. Most parents know what their children are capable of doing. They may not admit it, but they know."

"I hope you're right. I wouldn't like for this to come as a total shock to her."

The paramedic approached Ben. "I don't see any

signs of concussion. I've suggested that she go to the hospital for X rays and to have the doctor check her out. She's not happy with that idea."

"I'll talk to her." He walked over to where she sat on the gurney the paramedics had removed from the ambulance.

"They tell me that you're refusing to go to the hospital."

"I'm fine. He said there's no concussion."

He raised an eyebrow. "He also said you should have X rays and that you should be examined by a doctor."

"You don't understand. I have a thing about hospitals."

"Kendall, it's not likely that they'll keep you. They just want to make sure that it's not serious."

"What about my car?"

"That's no excuse. I'll see that your car gets to your house. If nothing else, I'm sure I can get someone to bring me back here to pick it up."

She sighed. "All right. I'll go."

"I'll follow the ambulance." He kissed her cheek. "I'll see you at the hospital."

While he waited for the doctor to complete his examination, Ben realized that Sheila Donovan was unaware of the afternoon's events. He called her office.

"Hi, Sheila, it's Ben Whitaker. I'm not sure where to begin." He told her the reason he had gone to the mansion and about Philip Ferguson's attempt to set fire to the house.

"Philip Ferguson? I can't believe it. I just talked to his brother earlier this week." Another thought occurred to her. "Kendall went out there today. Where is she? Is she all right?"

He assured her that she would be fine. "I'm at the hospital waiting for her now. Ferguson hit her over the head. She's having X rays taken."

There was no immediate response to his statement. "Please excuse me, Ben. I'm still trying to get a handle on all of this. I can't imagine what it'll do to Mrs. Ferguson."

He repeated what he had said to Sergeant Price. "I'd better go now, Sheila. I expect Kendall will be ready to leave soon."

After driving her home, Ben had called Jim to take him to pick up her car. When he returned with take-out from their favorite soul-food restaurant, she had changed into her pajamas and robe. By nine o'clock that evening, she was sound asleep.

The next morning, Kendall awoke to the sound of running water. She raised her head and then immediately lowered it. She took a deep breath and waited for the throbbing to subside. Then she raised her head again, more slowly, and sat up. Closing her eyes against the pain, she eased her legs over the side of the bed. She took a deep breath.

At that moment, Ben entered from the bathroom. "What are you doing?"

"Contemplating the best way to navigate the space between here and that door without having my head fall off."

He stifled a smile and shook his head. After crossing the room, he helped her to stand. His arm encircled her waist as he walked her to the door.

When she exited the bathroom, he was dressed. With his assistance, she returned to the bed.

"Did you take something for your headache?" he asked as he helped her into bed.

"Yes."

"Just lie back and let it do its work. I'll bring your breakfast up to you."

By the time he arrived with a tray, the pain had diminished. Fluffing the pillows behind her, he helped her sit up. He placed the tray across her lap.

"You should eat before it gets cold. I'll get the coffee."

After breakfast, Ben took the tray to return it to the kitchen. Kendall showered and donned a robe. Then she went downstairs.

Ben looked up from his task of loading the dishwasher when she entered the kitchen. "Feeling better?"

"Much better. My head doesn't hurt much anymore."

"Good. Maybe you should take it easy for a couple of days, though."

"I don't plan to do anything more strenuous today than lying on the couch and watching television. I'll see how I feel tomorrow."

Later, as Kendall lay with her head in his lap, Ben raised a question about the previous day's events. "What were you doing at the mansion?"

Until that moment, all thoughts of her missing charm had been pushed to the back of her mind. She told him of the mission that had taken her to the mansion. She closed her eyes.

"I need to go back there and look again. My father gave me that bracelet on my eighth birthday, six months before he died."

He stroked her hair. "We'll go back in a few days."

She opened her eyes. "Did you call Sheila? I forgot that I had her key to the mansion."

"She didn't mention it when I talked to her. She probably had more than one copy. After I told her what had happened, I'm sure the key wasn't her biggest concern."

She frowned. "She mentioned the cleaners when I told her about the charm. I'd better give her a call. If they haven't already vacuumed it up, she can ask them to look out for it." She knit her brows. "Why were *you* there?"

He explained the reason for his visit. "I'm beginning to wonder if I'll ever complete that estimate for Sheila." He shook his head. "There's a good chance that I'll have more work to do in the mansion, thanks to Philip Ferguson."

"What do you mean? He didn't have time to set the fire."

"No, but the gasoline may have damaged the wood. Sheila was hoping to get a cleaning crew out there immediately. I told her I'd go out there next week and examine the damage."

They were silent for a moment. Then Kendall spoke. "Ben, I know you said you forgive me, but I still feel terrible about what I said to you."

He leaned over and kissed her tenderly. "It doesn't matter now, sweetheart. Let it go." He grinned. "If you insist, when you're feeling better, you can make it up to me."

Ben convinced Kendall to take the next day off from work. Sheila called that afternoon to assure herself that Kendall was all right. She also assured her that she would alert the cleaners to look for the charm.

Afterward, Kendall called Valerie and filled her in. "The irony is that if I hadn't gone to the mansion yesterday, I don't think anyone would have suspected Philip Ferguson. I feel sorry for his mother. The things some people will do for money . . ."

"I know." Valerie paused. Kendall had almost been killed and she was sitting there feeling sorry for her would-be murderer's mother. At least it was all over now.

"I just thought of something," Kendall said. "I saw Darren entering the Historical Society when I went to pick up the key. Since he's been cleared of any involvement with the attempts to destroy the mansion, I guess he really was just trying to help."

Valerie grunted. "No way, girlfriend. He was using the files to get leads on properties that were being considered as possible landmarks. I guess he thought that if a property was turned down, he might be able to talk the owner into selling."

"I don't understand. Just because a property isn't declared a historic landmark doesn't mean the owner is interested in selling."

"That's true, but sometimes the owner is having trouble maintaining the property. They're hoping that if it's declared a historic property, they'll be able to obtain funds for repairs." She paused. "You're right. It's a very strange way to go about getting properties to sell."

"How did you find out about it?"

"Once again, one of the owners called to complain about Darren's tactics. This time she called Sheila, who in turn called Mr. Briggs." She took a deep breath. "Darren will be lucky at this point if he doesn't lose his job."

"Well, he brought it on himself. I can't believe he didn't learn his lesson with Mrs. Ferguson." She paused. "I guess as Ben said about Philip, it's just another example of what greed does to people."

"Speaking of Ben, does this mean that you've ironed out your differences with Ben?"

"Yes, Valerie. With all that happened, our disagreement was suddenly put into proper perspective."

"I think that's a lesson we should all take to heart."

They chatted for a few more minutes. Valerie made no mention of the status of the Sterling property sale. Selling her property was probably the last thing on Mrs. Ferguson's mind at the moment.

Ben arrived early that evening. He greeted her with a kiss that hinted at the passion she remembered. "Do you have any idea how long these past weeks have seemed?"

"I have a very good idea. I missed you, and I had no one to blame but myself."

"How are you feeling today?" he asked as they headed toward the living room.

"I'm fine. I fixed dinner. Are you hungry?"

He grinned. "It depends on what you're offering."

She smiled. "I suggest we start with the roast chicken in the oven. I have a feeling we'll need some nourishment if we're going to satisfy your other hunger."

Later that evening, having satisfied both hungers, she lay snuggled next to him. "This is much better," she murmured before succumbing to sleep.

The next few days followed their usual routine. Kendall returned to work on Tuesday. Sergeant Price had taken her statement on Monday, but offered no information of his own until Ben spoke with him on Friday. Kendall and Ben had settled on the sofa after dinner when Ben filled her in.

"Philip admitted that Mueller put him up to destroying the mansion. According to Price, Mueller is quite adept at leaving someone else holding the bag. He slipped up with Philip, though."

"How?"

"Evidently, Mueller's reputation preceded him. After their first meeting, Philip taped their conversations. It was probably more as insurance that Mueller would pay him. The money he'd get from his mother after the sale of the property wasn't enough for greedy Philip."

"I want to go back to the mansion tomorrow and look for the charm."

He pulled her closer. He retrieved a small box from his pocket and handed it to her. "I already did that. I went back to the mansion alone and looked for your charm. I searched my car, too," he explained while she opened it. He sighed. "I couldn't find it."

She had told him that the missing charm was a pair of ballet slippers. For her, it represented her father's unconditional support of her efforts. For him, it represented the physical grace that came so naturally to her.

She lifted the charm from the bed of cotton. Tears filled her eyes.

"Don't cry, sweetheart. I'm sorry. I didn't mean to assume that I could replace what your father gave you. I just thought that at least this could complete the bracelet."

She touched his arm and shook her head. "Don't apologize." She swallowed and wiped away the tears. "You didn't do anything wrong." She cleared her throat. "I can't believe you went to the trouble to do this. It's wonderful. Now the bracelet has even more meaning for me." She kissed his cheek.

He took a deep breath. "You don't know how glad I am to hear you say that." He lifted her hand from its resting place in her lap. "I have something very important to discuss."

She looked up at him. "What is it?"

"I know how much you love this house. Is there any chance I can convince you to give it up?"

She frowned. "Give it up? Why would I give it up?"

He shrugged. "It doesn't make much sense for a husband and wife to have separate houses."

Her eyes widened. Her heart thumped. "Husband and wife?"

He nodded. "I guess I should have started by asking another question. Will you marry me?"

"You want to marry me?"

"I love you, Kendall. Do you remember when I told you that love isn't enough? I want to share my life with you, completely. I want your face to be the first that I see in the morning and the last that I see at night. I want to know that when I walk in the door at the end of the day, you'll be here."

She swallowed. Her eyes misted. "I like the sound of that. Under the circumstances, I think I could learn to love your house as much as I love this one."

He smiled. "Is that a yes?"

"Yes, yes, yes." Her hand caressed his cheek. "I love you so much."

He kissed the palm of her hand. "It still amazes me how everything just fell into place when you came into my life. Now, I can't imagine my life without you. I don't want to imagine my life without you."

Their lips met in a kiss that promised forever. When the kiss ended, she rested her cheek against his chest listening to the pounding heart that echoed her own.

"Ben, can we have a big wedding?"

"Sweetheart, we can have whatever kind of wedding you want as long as it doesn't mean that I'll have to wait another six months to hear you say, 'I do.' "

CHAPTER 16

When she began making her wedding plans, Kendall naturally considered Valerie, who immediately agreed to be her matron of honor. Laura had agreed to be an attendant.

She then thought of the friend she had left behind. She was unsure of Erica. Although she had kept in touch, their contacts had mostly been limited to e-mails and greeting cards on holidays. The last time she had seen her friend face-to-face was at Erica's wedding six months before Kendall left Pennsylvania.

This request called for a telephone call. She dialed the number, half expecting to hear a voice-mail message.

She took a deep breath when she heard her friend's voice. "Hi, Erica, it's Kendall."

"Kendall, it's so good to hear your voice. E-mail just isn't the same. It's been too long. How are you?"

"I'm fine, Erica. I guess I owe you an apology. I

should have called before now. You're right. E-mail isn't the same. I feel especially guilty since I'm calling to ask a favor."

"You don't have to feel guilty. I'm just glad to know that you're doing okay. What's the favor?"

"I'm getting married. I want you to be in my wedding."

"You're getting married? That's wonderful." *I think.*

Kendall heard the question in her voice. "It is wonderful, Erica. He's wonderful."

"In that case, I wouldn't miss it. I'd love to be in your wedding."

After Kendall gave her the particulars, the two women chatted for almost an hour. The joy in her friend's voice assuaged any doubts Erica had.

After that telephone call, Kendall faced a dilemma. The only person remaining to be asked was Francine. The relationship between her and Valerie was still strained. As far as Kendall knew, the two had not spoken in months.

Three weeks after Ben proposed, Kendall's anticipated conversation with Francine took a different turn. Francine approached her desk late one morning.

"Do you have any plans for lunch, Kendall?"

She hid her surprise at this overture. She shook her head. "Nothing special. I hadn't really thought about it."

"Do you want to go out? I need to talk to you, but not here."

"Sure, give me a buzz when you're ready and I'll meet you at the elevator."

* * *

An hour later, the two women were seated in a nearby cafe awaiting their orders. Francine folded her hands and rested them on the edge of the table. She focused her attention on them and took a deep breath.

"I owe you and Valerie apologies. Valerie never really made any accusations against Darren, but I think she had doubts about his ethics." She grunted. "That should have been my first clue. He certainly had no problem with bad-mouthing her."

"Is that what made you question his ethics?"

Her eyes stayed focused on her hands. "Not entirely. I started having serious doubts when I overheard him talking to a buyer. I couldn't understand why he was working so hard to convince her not to have her own inspector take a look at the property."

Although she had heard a lot about Darren's underhanded tactics, Kendall took the role of devil's advocate. "It's not really necessary for a buyer to go to that expense. The real-estate company pays for an inspection themselves."

"I know, but that's usually just to report any major problems, to be sure it's livable. There could be some minor problems the inspector wouldn't think needed to be mentioned. If a buyer is paying a private inspector, he'd probably be more likely to look out for potential costly repairs."

Kendall agreed. "I suppose that's possible."

Francine raised her head, meeting Kendall's gaze. "It gave me a bad feeling."

"Did you ask him about it?"

She grunted again. Then she took another deep breath. "Oh, yes, I asked him. His answer was that selling real estate requires persuasion." She bit her lip. "I asked him specifically why he didn't want the client to hire her own inspector. He didn't bother to deny that was what he was trying to prevent. That's when I knew he wasn't on the up-and-up. His only answer was that I knew nothing about the real-estate business."

Kendall could imagine that such an attitude would be taken as an insult. Was that what was really bothering her friend? When Francine continued, it became clear that being insulted was not the problem.

Conversation stopped for a few minutes when the waiter returned with their orders. They turned their attention to their food. Then Francine continued the conversation between bites.

"I gave it a lot of thought later. It wasn't so much what he said. It was his condescending attitude." She wrinkled her forehead. "It made me think about other situations that I had overlooked. I began to see them in a different light."

"Like what?"

She shrugged. "Little things, like the way he talks to waiters and waitresses. His generally superior attitude toward certain people." She shook her head. "I don't know. What I've said probably sounds strange and vague. All I can say is that when I put everything together, it left me with the feeling that he's a very devious person." She sighed. "I'd never be able to trust him. If you can't trust a person, the relationship doesn't stand a chance."

Ben's own words echoed in Kendall's mind. She shook her head. "I don't know what to say, Francine. I'm sorry it didn't work out for you. I was hoping that we were wrong, that Darren was different with you."

"He was. I guess that's what fooled me at first."

The conversation turned to more pleasant topics as they finished their meal. When the waiter brought the check, Francine commented, "Thanks for hearing me out, Kendall. Are we still friends?"

Kendall smiled as they stood up to leave. "I never stopped being your friend, Francine."

She frowned. How could she broach her happy news after what she had just heard?

"What's wrong, Kendall?"

Kendall sighed. "I was going to come to talk to you later. I have a request, but after what you've told me, I wish I'd had better timing."

"I don't understand. What did you want to ask me?"

"I wanted to ask you to be in my wedding."

For the first time, Francine noticed the diamond on her friend's finger. "You're getting married?"

Francine hugged her. "I can't believe I've been going on and on about my problems and never even noticed the ring. Who is he? When did all this happen? Why didn't I know about this?" She held up her hands. "Never mind. I guess I didn't know because I haven't been exactly friendly in the past few months."

She hugged Kendall again. "I'm happy for you, Kendall. I'd love to be in your wedding. When do I get to meet the groom?"

"I'm not sure. If you're not busy Saturday, I was thinking about having you and Valerie over for lunch."

Francine's smile faded. "Valerie . . . I'd almost

forgotten. I think I owe her an even bigger apology than you." She touched Kendall's arm. "I didn't tell you this looking for sympathy. Maybe subconsciously Valerie's suggestion sunk in. I'm glad I hadn't become more deeply involved before the truth came out. I'm slowly putting it behind me."

Kendall shrugged. "Maybe Saturday would be the perfect time for you and Valerie to iron things out."

"I'll be there. At least I'll have a few days to prepare myself, and my speech."

On Friday evening, Kendall told Ben about her luncheon plans. "Does that mean you're kicking me out tomorrow after breakfast?"

She smiled. "No, I'm not kicking you out until my guests arrive." She snuggled up to him and kissed his chin. "I have to show you off to Francine first."

He chuckled. "Show me off?"

She frowned. "Actually, I shouldn't have put it that way. It sounds like I'm flaunting my good fortune. That's a little tactless since she just came out of a bad relationship."

He kissed her forehead. "It's our good fortune. Don't even think about feeling guilty. We've both paid our dues."

"I feel bad for what she's going through, but I don't feel guilty. I did promise Francine that she'd meet you tomorrow."

After the introductions the next day, Ben said his good-byes to Kendall's friends. "What time am I allowed to return?" he asked, grinning.

Kendall smiled and shook her head. "You make

it sound like I'm banishing you to some horrible exile."

Ignoring the guests, he took her in his arms. "Being away from you is a horrible exile."

Before she could respond, he claimed her lips in a kiss that made her friends smile in appreciation. When he broke the kiss, heat suffused her neck and face. Almost breathless, she murmured, "You did that on purpose."

He chuckled. "I deserved a prize for my cooperation. Besides, I needed that to hold me for a few hours." He kissed the tip of her nose. "I'll pick up dinner on my way back." A moment later, he was gone.

Kendall rejoined her friends after seeing him to the door. They were still grinning.

Francine cleared her throat. "So that's Ben. Girlfriend, I'd say that you picked a winner this time."

Valerie shook her head. "From what I saw, he was the one who did the picking. Girlfriend was almost ready to brush him off."

Francine raised an eyebrow. "That's even better."

"All right, you two. That's enough. Give me a break."

"Okay, we'll save the rest of it for the shower."

"Shower?"

"Of course, you don't think we'd let you get married without giving you a shower, do you?"

"I don't need a shower. Between the two of us, we don't need any household items."

Francine and Valerie looked at each other and grinned. "Who said anything about household items. There are other kinds of showers, you know."

* * *

A few weeks before her wedding, Kendall discovered exactly what her friends had in mind. In addition to boxes of sensuous lingerie, there were candles and flavored massage oils. As if the gifts were not embarrassing enough, the women had invited Ben's mother and Mabel Jenkins.

Valerie nudged Francine. "Whoever said black people don't blush told a lie."

Kendall heard, and gave them both a pointed stare. "I'll get you two for this. I don't know how, but I will."

A few minutes later, Valerie and Francine excused themselves to get the refreshments. Kendall insisted on helping. While they were gone, Rosa scanned the array of gifts. She turned to Mabel.

"From what I've seen, I don't think they really need any of these items."

"You're right, Rosa. It's been a while since I've seen the kind of looks that pass between those two." She smiled. "It does my heart good."

Rosa nodded. "Mine, too."

Although Ben had seemed content with his life before meeting Kendall, there was no comparison to what Rosa saw in him now. He practically beamed whenever Kendall was in the same room.

As for Kendall, Rosa had no idea what her life had been. All she knew was that the young woman was a perfect example of what people said about the glow that comes with being in love.

CHAPTER 17

A week after the shower, Kendall entered her pastor's study with her portfolio under her arm. Ben had raised an eyebrow when they finally set the date for their marriage. She'd convinced him that a wedding in the heat of August was not a good idea. He'd smiled and sighed when she reminded him that she had stayed within his request of six months.

Mrs. Franklin, her pastor's wife, greeted her. "Hello, Kendall, the big day is fast approaching. We need to finalize your plans for the music and schedule a rehearsal."

After they had completed that part of the discussion, Mrs. Franklin looked through her notebook. "I'd like to go over some of the other information. You're having four adult attendants and two junior bridesmaids, is that correct?"

"That's right, three friends of mine and my fiancé's sister. His nieces are the junior bridesmaids."

Mrs. Franklin turned a page. "What about your mother? Will she be there?"

"To tell you the truth, I don't know. I sent her an invitation. I haven't had a response, but I really don't expect her to be there."

Mrs. Franklin wondered at the fact that Kendall had sent her mother an invitation rather than seeing her face-to-face. She ignored that, and addressed Kendall's last statement.

"You don't expect your mother to be at your wedding? Does she disapprove of Ben?" She shook her head. "I'm sorry, I should know better than to pry. If you'd rather not talk about it, I undertand."

Kendall shrugged. "There's not really much to tell. I don't know if my mother approves or disapproves of Ben. The truth is that she disapproves of my having a big wedding."

Mrs. Franklin nodded. "Because you're divorced?"

Kendall sighed. "No, ma'am. My mother doesn't approve of my having a big wedding and wearing a long gown because of my size."

She frowned. "Because of your size? What does that have to do with it?"

"To most people, nothing. It's a long story, Mrs. Franklin. It's not important, not anymore."

Two weeks after that meeting, Kendall stood in the study of the church waiting for the signal from Mrs. Franklin that it was time to start her walk down the aisle.

She smiled at Valerie and Francine, thankful that their friendship had survived their differences. Her two friends approached to give her some last-minute touches. Kendall was unaware of the scene taking place in the church vestibule.

Mrs. Franklin frowned and sighed when she noticed the woman entering the church. She was dressed in a long ivory beaded gown.

Ben and his mother noticed her, too. Rosa turned to her son. "I know I may be old-fashioned in my thinking, but I consider it very poor taste for a guest to wear white to a wedding. Do you know who she is?"

He clenched his jaws and nodded. "Yes, I know who she is. She's Kendall's mother. If I had told you the whole story about her, you'd understand her choice of color." He touched his mother's arm. "I'll be right back."

He headed Mrs. Franklin off before she reached Jackie. "Excuse me, Mrs. Franklin, I have a very large favor to ask."

"Certainly, Ben, what is it?"

"That woman who just arrived is Kendall's mother. I don't want her to see Kendall before the ceremony. That probably sounds like a strange request, and I can't explain now. Will you do it?"

She nodded. "I don't know the whole story, Ben. I've heard enough to agree with you, though." Jackie approached one of the ushers, who pointed toward the study. "I'd better head her off."

She stopped Kendall's mother as she crossed the foyer. "May I help you?"

"That's all right. I'm Kendall's mother. The young man over there already informed me where I can find her."

"I'm sorry. I don't think that's a good idea."

Jackie raised an eyebrow. "What do you mean, that's not a good idea? I told you, I'm her mother."

Ben watched the exchange. Then he took a deep breath and joined the two women. "Hello, Mrs. Chase. Is there a problem?"

"This woman is telling me that I shouldn't see my daughter. I'm the one who should be in there helping her prepare and making sure everything is all right."

"I think you and I both know that the last thing Kendall needs right now is to have you in there finding fault and picking her apart. You'll have plenty of time to talk to her after the ceremony."

Jackie pursed her lips. She stared at him and then at Mrs. Franklin for a moment. Then she stalked off.

"I'll have one of the ushers show her to her seat. You'd better take your place. It's almost time to begin."

He nodded. He rejoined his mother for a moment, and then went to take his place at the front of the church.

A few minutes later, Jean Franklin went to give the cue to the rest of the wedding party. Before doing that, she took Kendall aside.

"I feel that I should warn you. Your mother is here." She paused. "You should also know that she's wearing a long ivory beaded gown." She smiled and touched her shoulder. "In spite of that, she can't compete with you. You're absolutely beautiful. I guess love does that to a person."

She turned to the others. "It's time to line up, ladies."

Kendall hugged her friends as they exited the room. She took a deep breath and followed, lingering out of sight as they marched down they aisle.

When her turn came, Kendall started down the

aisle. She took her first few steps looking straight ahead at Reverend Franklin. Then she glanced to his side and met Ben's steady, loving gaze. She smiled.

Ben's gaze never left the vision approaching. The bodice of the silk ivory-colored gown had a square neckline and long sleeves encrusted with beads and embroidery. The embroidery and beading continued more sparsely down the A-line skirt.

Her hair was swept up on top of her head and crowned with a matching beaded circlet. Attached to this was a shoulder-length embroidered veil. She carried a bouquet of yellow roses and baby's breath.

Kendall had seen Ben dressed in a tuxedo only once before this day. Had he looked as handsome then as he did now? The light in his eyes when he smiled at her chased away any small doubts that she might have had.

After the ceremony, Kendall faced her mother. She only had to listen to Jackie's complaints for a brief moment before she was whisked away to take photographs. Afterward, Ben quickly ushered Kendall out of the church, to be showered by the waiting crowd and then settled into the limousine.

Ben managed to shield his bride from her mother during the early part of the reception. But he could not follow her to the ladies' room. It was the opportunity Jackie had waited for.

A few minutes later, Kendall came face-to-face with her mother. Jackie wore her usual frown. "Why did you tell your friends to keep me away from you?"

"I didn't. Quite frankly, I'm surprised that you bothered to come. I didn't think you'd care to see me make a fool of myself, as you put it, by wearing a long white gown. Although, technically, it wasn't white, it was ivory."

Jackie shook her head. "Why do you hate me? All I've ever tried to do is to help you."

Kendall closed her eyes and shook her head. "I guess you would see it that way. At least, that's what you'd tell yourself. That's why you belittled me as a child and made me feel that I was unworthy of love because of my size."

"You don't understand. I was only trying to find a way to help you lose weight."

"I might be able to buy that excuse for what you did to me when I was a child, but later . . . Why couldn't you just accept me?"

"I've seen what being overweight can do to a person's self-esteem. You don't remember, but we had a teenage neighbor who committed suicide because she was so unhappy with her weight. I watched how humiliated she was over being teased about her weight. If she ever tried to lose weight, she wasn't successful. She became more and more depressed over it. Finally, I guess she couldn't stand it anymore."

Kendall listened to her mother's explanation. She actually believed what she was saying. She shook her head.

"You really don't get it, do you? You're right, I don't remember, but I'm sure she didn't commit suicide because she was overweight. She committed suicide because of the teasing and humiliation, because no one would accept her for who she was."

Jackie's eyes widened. She took a step back, shaking her head. "No, that's not true."

"Believe whatever you like, Mother. I don't have the time or the inclination to stand here trying to convince you. This is my wedding day. There's a man out there who loves me and who thinks I'm beautiful, just as I am. I will not let you ruin this day for me."

Before her mother could respond, Valerie and Erica came through the door. Erica was very familiar with Jackie. She had watched her in disbelief during Scott's trial.

Erica had been glad when her friend had moved away. She had hoped that the distance would help heal the damage that Scott and Kendall's own mother had done. The Kendall Erica had seen today was not the same naive, frightened woman who had escaped the manipulations of her husband and mother.

Valerie and Erica took a close look at their friend. Whatever had happened between her and her mother, Kendall was fine now. Valerie was the one who spoke.

"Your husband asked me to tell you that he misses you. He said if you take much longer, he's coming in after you."

Kendall smiled. "I was just leaving."

When she returned to the table, Ben was sitting alone, drumming his fingers on the table. His attention was focused on the other side of the room. She approached from his blind side, leaned over, and kissed his cheek. Smiling, he turned to face her.

He pulled her chair out and she sat down. He took her hand in his and kissed the palm. "Did I tell you how beautiful you were coming down that aisle today?"

She leaned forward and placed a kiss on his cheek. "Yes, you did. It was written all over your face."

Jackie had returned to her seat soon after Kendall deserted her. She watched the couple now. The look in Ben's eyes was one that she had never seen in Scott's expression when he looked at Kendall. She never expected that any man could look at her daughter with such love. What did he see in her that she had missed all these years? Could she really be mistaken in her ideas?

She was wary when Ben approached her a few minutes later. She was shocked when he held out his hand.

"May I have this dance?"

As they moved in rhythm to the music, she could not resist questioning him. "After all the harsh words you've directed at me, I'm surprised you'd want to get this close to me."

"You know that my harsh words were in the interest of protecting Kendall. I told you that was my intention when I came to your house."

"Do you think I deliberately set out to hurt my own daughter?"

He shook his head. "No, I don't believe that. What I believe isn't really important, though." He paused. "Mrs. Chase, contrary to what you believe, Kendall doesn't hate you. I don't think Kendall has it in her to hate anyone."

"That's hard to believe when she hasn't returned any of my calls. Did she tell you that Scott moved to California?"

"No. Did you tell her that?"

She nodded. "I left her a message about a month ago. She never called me back."

"Maybe because she had no interest in discussing Scott's decision, or anything else concerning him."

Jackie ignored that comment. "I'm surprised she even sent me an invitation."

Ben bit back the response that was on the tip of his tongue. She was obviously unwilling to take any responsibility for the strained relationship. Maybe in time it would improve. At least, they were speaking to each other again.

Whatever had happened in their relationship, now that Scott was out of the picture, he would not interfere. Kendall could decide for herself the best way to handle her mother.

When the DJ called for the bride and groom to cut the cake, it signaled that the evening would soon come to an end. Before long he was calling for the single women to gather at the edge of the floor. The bride was ready to toss the bouquet.

The evening seemed to go quickly after that. Soon the bride and groom were bidding good-bye to their friends and relatives. They would spend the night at the hotel before leaving the next afternoon for a honeymoon cruise through the Caribbean.

When they entered their hotel room, Kendall turned to face Ben. She smiled and looped her arms around his neck. "I heard you were threatening to storm the ladies' room earlier this evening."

His arms encircled her waist. "I saw your mother go in right after you. All of my rescue instincts kicked in." He kissed her forehead. "When you returned, I realized that my rescue was unnecessary."

"You don't ever have to worry about rescuing

me from my mother. I think you can take partial credit for that."

He shook his head. "No, I won't take credit for that. You did it all by yourself."

He kissed her again, more thoroughly. Then his thumb caressed her bottom lip. "I keep asking myself what I ever did to deserve you. How many people go through life never finding the right person?"

"Let's make sure we never forget that we're two of the fortunate ones."

"I'll remind you of that fifty years from now."

Dear Readers,

I hope you enjoyed reading Kendall's story. I refer to it as hers because the idea for it began with her.

If you've read my other novels, you know that none of my heroines would be described as slim or petite. As in my first novel, *Step by Step*, I decided it was time for another heroine who is specifically full-figured.

This story illustrates some of the problems encountered by full-figured women. Although the story is fiction, there are real men who find full-figured women beautiful and desirable. Isn't that what romance is about? Everyone deserves a little romance.

My other novels are *Step by Step*, *Secrets*, *False Impressions*, *Secrets of the Heart*, *Everything to Gain* and *One Heartbeat at a Time*.

Thanks again to all of you who have written to me. I appreciate your feedback as well as your support. You may contact me at Marilyn Tyner P.O. Box 219 Yardley, PA 19067, e-mail to mtynerl@juno.com, or see my Web site—www.geocities.com/marilyntyner/.

More Sizzling Romance From
Gwynne Forster

__Obsession	1-58314-092-1	$5.99US/$7.99CAN
__Fools Rush In	1-58314-435-8	$6.99US/$9.99CAN
__Ecstasy	1-58314-177-4	$5.99US/$7.99CAN
__Swept Away	1-58314-098-0	$5.99US/$7.99CAN
__Beyond Desire	1-58314-201-0	$5.99US/$7.99CAN
__Secret Desire	1-58314-124-3	$5.99US/$7.99CAN
__Against All Odds	1-58314-247-9	$5.99US/$7.99CAN
__Sealed With a Kiss	1-58314-313-0	$5.99US/$7.99CAN
__Scarlet Woman	1-58314-192-8	$5.99US/$7.99CAN
__Once in a Lifetime	1-58314-193-6	$6.99US/$9.99CAN
__Flying High	1-58314-427-7	$6.99US/$9.99CAN

Available Wherever Books Are Sold!

Visit our website at **www.BET.com**.

SIGGLING ROMANCE BY
ROCHELLE ALERS

Put a Little Romance in Your Life With
Bettye Griffin

__At Long Last Love $4.99US/$6.50CAN
    0-7860-0610-2

__Closer Than Close $6.99US/$9.99CAN
    1-58314-276-2

__From This Day Forward $6.99US/$9.99CAN
    1-58314-275-4

__Love Affair $5.99US/$7.99CAN
    1-58314-138-3

__A Love of Her Own $4.99US/$6.99CAN
    1-58314-053-0

__Prelude to a Kiss $5.99US/$7.99CAN
    1-58314-139-1

Available Wherever Books Are Sold!

Visit our website at **www.BET.com.**

More Sizzling Romance From
Francine Craft

Available Wherever Books Are Sold!

Visit our website at **www.BET.com**.